DRAGON AND
HERDSMAN

BOOKS BY TIMOTHY ZAHN

A TOM DOHERTY ASSOCIATES BOOK | NEW YORK

STARSCAPE

DRAGON AND HERDSMAN

THE FOURTH DRAGONBACK ADVENTURE

TIMOTHY ZAHN

DRAGON AND HERDSMAN: THE FOURTH DRAGONBACK ADVENTURE

A Starscape Book
Published by Tom Doherty Associates, LLC
175 Fifth Avenue
New York, NY 10010

www.starscapebooks.com

Library of Congress Cataloging-in-Publication Data

Zahn, Timothy.
    Dragon and herdsman : the fourth Dragonback adventure / Timothy Zahn.—1st ed.
        p. cm.
    "A Tom Doherty Associates book."
    ISBN-13: 978-0-765-31417-8
    ISBN-10: 0-765-31417-7
    1. Adventure and adventurers—Fiction. 2. Dragons—Fiction. 3. Mercenary troops—Fiction. 4. Soldiers—Fiction. 5. Orphans—Fiction. 6. Science fiction. I. Title.

    PZ7.Z2515 Dh 2005
    [Fic]—dc22

                                                                                        2006042237

First Edition: June 2006

Printed in the United States of America

0 9 8 7 6 5 4 3 2 1

For Jack and Marna—
For their help in the care and feeding
of our own personal herd

DRAGON AND HERDSMAN

A light breeze was blowing softly through the streets of Avrans City on the world of Bigelow, making the cold night air feel that much colder. Huddled in a darkened doorway, Jack Morgan shifted restlessly in his sleep, pressing himself a little deeper back against the ancient stonework here at the edge of the city's Old Town.

Draycos, pressed in two-dimensional form against the boy's back, arms, and legs, felt yet another shiver ripple through the skin beneath him. Reflexively, he lifted himself slightly away from the skin, turning part of himself three-dimensional. That would at least create a thin insulating layer to protect Jack from the worst of the cold.

"Uh-uh," Jack murmured.

So he wasn't asleep after all. "Sorry," Draycos murmured back as he lowered himself flat again. He was a poet-warrior of the K'da, and part of his job was to protect his host as best he could. It bothered him terribly that he hadn't been able to lift a claw to ease Jack's discomfort these past few nights.

But as usual in these matters, Jack was right. If he was going to play the part of a homeless street kid, he had to play the part completely. Huddled against the night in the shadow of a mercenary recruitment center, they couldn't take the chance that someone with sharp eyes would notice something odd. And a fourteen-year-old boy sleeping all warm and peaceful in thin shirt and slacks would definitely be odd.

Shifting his position on Jack's skin, Draycos peered out through the open shirt collar toward the recruitment center, a one-story white building across the street and two doors down. If the pattern of the past six nights was repeated, two men wearing the uniforms of the Malison Ring mercenaries would arrive soon to get the center ready for the morning's activities.

Three nights ago, Jack had begun shambling over to them as they arrived, trying to beg some spare change. The men had, naturally, told him to get lost. Last night one of them had added to the script by aiming a kick at Jack's rear that had nearly connected.

Tonight, the script was going to change completely.

Draycos shifted his gaze back down the street, marveling yet again at the delicious irony the universe had played. For the past three months, ever since this unlikely partnership had been thrust upon them, he had been trying to teach Jack the way of the K'da warrior. The way of honor, and service, and trust.

It hadn't been easy. Jack had been raised by his uncle Virgil since the age of three to be a thief and con man, taught to care only about himself. The concept that there were standards of right and wrong that didn't change with mood or situation was completely new to him. But Draycos had kept at it, showing in both word and deed that a true warrior tried always to do what was right, whether it gained him anything or not.

Down deep, Draycos knew Jack had a good heart. But eleven years of habit were hard to break.

Making it that much harder was the presence and influence of Uncle Virge, the shadow personality that Uncle Virgil had left imprinted on the *Essenay*'s computer before he died a year ago. Uncle Virge had the same me-first philosophy as the real Uncle Virgil, and he'd been fighting Draycos's efforts every step of the way.

And then, even as Jack began making his first genuine progress in the K'da way of thought, the universe had handed them a gift. In the midst of Jack's ordeal as a slave on the planet Brum-a-dum, a small and nearly forgotten act of mercy had unexpectedly paid off. It had paid off big.

Now, at last, they had all the pieces of the puzzle. It was members of the Malison Ring mercenary group who had intercepted and destroyed Draycos's advance team of K'da and their symbiotic hosts, the Shontine. They were working with the assistance and financial support of the powerful Brummgan Chookoock family, with the whole conspiracy under the direction of the renegade Arthur Neverlin, once second-in-command of the megacorporation Braxton Universis.

And lurking behind them all were the Valahgua, the deadly enemies whom the K'da and Shontine had left their homes to escape in the first place.

Neverlin wanted to destroy Cornelius Braxton and take over Braxton Universis. The Malison Ring and Chookoock family presumably wanted a share of the plunder from the approaching refugee ships.

All of them wanted the K'da and Shontine dead. And unless Draycos and Jack could find out where the refugee fleet was supposed to rendezvous with the now-destroyed advance team, the Valahgua and their allies were going to get their wish.

In the distance down the street, a pair of headlights winked into view. "Here we go," Jack said. "Uncle Virge?"

"Ready at this end, Jack lad," the computerized voice replied from the comm clip fastened out of sight beneath the boy's shirt collar. Uncle Virge didn't sound exactly happy, but he sounded much less frustrated than he had for most of the past three months. He hadn't liked Jack signing up to be a soldier with the Whinyard's Edge mercenary group. He'd absolutely hated the boy's brief taste of slavery.

This time, Jack was only going to have to be a thief. For him, that would be like a walk in the park.

"Draycos?" Jack asked.

Again, the K'da shifted around on Jack's skin, slithering down his right leg. He touched the two items stuffed into the boy's sock, confirmed they were ready to grab and throw. "Set," he said.

"When I tap my toe," Jack reminded him, getting a little unsteadily to his feet. Maneuvering himself to where he could peek out from beneath the right-leg cuff of Jack's slacks, Draycos saw the approaching car come to a halt in front of the Malison Ring office. Still moving like someone weak from hunger, Jack headed across the street.

The two men saw him coming, of course. "Oh, great," Draycos heard one of them mutter.

"Spare coins, mister?" Jack asked as he reached them.

"Listen, kid—"

Inside his low boot, Jack tapped his toe.

Lifting one front paw slightly from Jack's ankle, Draycos plucked the money clip from its hiding place inside Jack's sock. He flicked it outward from beneath the cuff, sending it to land in the grass beside the mercenary office door.

"—if you don't get out of my sight in the next *two seconds*—"

"Holy—" Jack broke off in a strangled gasp and started to duck around behind the men.

He didn't get far. He'd barely made it around one man's side when there was the sound of a hand on cloth and the boy was jerked to an abrupt halt. "Hey, hey, hey," the mercenary growled. "Where do you think *you're* going?"

"Hey, Chips," the other man said. "Look."

"I saw it first!" Jack snarled, and from the movement of his arms Draycos could tell he was beating his fists weakly against his captor's shoulder. "Get away. I saw it first."

"How much is in there?" Chips asked, ignoring both Jack's protests and his attack as he dragged the boy over to where the other man was examining the money clip.

"Gotta be at least three hundred," the other said. "Make that *four* hundred."

"It's *mine*," Jack insisted. "Come on—I saw it first."

"Don't be ridiculous," Chips said severely. "Four hundred auzes? Somebody's gotta be missing this."

"It's got an ID plate," the other man said. "Shouldn't be any trouble to get it back to its proper owner."

Draycos felt a surge of disgust. There was no ID on the money clip, which meant the mercenaries had no intention of giving the lost money to anyone. A quiet fifty-fifty split, and they would go about their business with no feeling other than satisfaction over their unexpected bonus.

"But I saw it first," Jack repeated plaintively. Shifting his stance, he moved his right leg right beside the door and tapped his toe.

Again lifting his front paw from Jack's skin, Draycos plucked the small button-shaped sensor from inside Jack's sock. With the mercenaries' full attention on the money clip, the K'da risked pushing his paw out from beneath the cuff. A flick of his claws, and the sensor sailed upward.

Because he was listening for it, he heard the soft *clink* as the sensor's magnet connected it solidly to the lower part of the door.

"Get lost," Chips ordered. There was the sound of a light slap, and Jack staggered back a couple of steps. "Or I'll tell the cops you were the one who stole it in the first place."

"It's not fair," Jack muttered as he shuffled away. "Not *fair.*"

He crossed the street again and headed toward his doorway. But instead of settling back down for what was left of the night, he continued on along the street. "Uncle Virge?" he asked softly. "Did you get it?"

"I got it," Uncle Virge said with dark satisfaction. "Even with Draycos's sensor a little lower than where I'd wanted it."

Draycos grimaced. That was Uncle Virge, all right. He never missed a chance to try to make the K'da look bad in Jack's presence. "The low weight of the sensor makes it difficult to throw very far," Draycos pointed out stiffly.

"And I'm sure Uncle Virge was able to compensate," Jack soothed. Fortunately, he'd long since figured out what the other was trying to do. "Right, Uncle Virge?"

"I already told you I got it."

"Good," Jack said. "And for the record, Draycos, that money clip toss was perfect. Right where I wanted it."

"Thank you," Draycos said, feeling somewhat mollified. "Where exactly did you put the third sensor, if I may ask?"

"I slipped it up onto the back of Chips's holster," Jack told him. "So now the *big* question, Uncle Virge: can you code me a data tube that'll match their key well enough to get me inside?"

"Absolutely," Uncle Virge assured him. "And as a bonus, I can also make a blocker to get you through the cavity-wave alarm system just inside the door. Unless you'd rather disarm that one yourself."

"No, that's all right," Jack assured him. "Package deals are good."

"I just thought you might enjoy the challenge," Uncle Virge said. "It's clear you've still got the magic touch."

"Thank you kindly," Jack said dryly. "Just don't forget that that touch goes into retirement the minute Draycos's people are safe."

Uncle Virge gave a theatrical sigh. "I understand," he said. "Just a moment . . . ah. They've taken the money and dropped the clip into a wastebasket."

"Perfect," Jack said. "We'll be able to eavesdrop on the whole office."

"At least until they empty the trash," Uncle Virge said. "I presume you want me to get started coding the key?"

"Right," Jack said. "We'll spend the rest of today getting organized, and tonight we do it."

"You make it sound so easy," Draycos said.

"This time it will be," Jack assured him.

"*That'll* be a first," Uncle Virge muttered.

CHAPTER 2

During the long nights Jack had spent outside the Malison Ring office, the two mercenaries had always arrived between four-fifty and five-fifteen in the morning. Jack made sure he and Draycos were there at three-thirty sharp.

"Okay, buddy," he murmured to Draycos as they approached along the office's side of the street. "There are three security cameras covering the area around the front door, built into that low parapet on the roof. You think you can handle them?"

"I shall do my best," Draycos said. With a surge of weight, he leaped out the back of the boy's collar, his front paws pushing down on Jack's shoulders to give himself some upward momentum. There was a second, harder surge as his hind paws pushed down in the same places, and Jack looked up in time to see a flicker of gold scales disappear up onto the roof of the building they were passing.

He crossed to the far side of the street and continued on, rubbing briefly at his shoulders where the dragon had pushed off. In his early days with Draycos, that maneuver would probably have knocked him flat on his face. Now, he was so used to it he hardly even noticed. No doubt about it, he and Draycos were becoming a real team.

Just when that team might be about to dissolve.

Jack shivered, this time not from the cold night air. Only a couple of weeks ago, near the end of his time as a slave, Draycos had been doing his look-over-a-wall trick in two-dimensional form when he'd suddenly fallen completely off Jack's back, ending up on the far side of the wall he'd been looking through.

Fortunately, he'd come out in proper three-dimensional form on the other side. But that hadn't made the whole thing any less scary. By Draycos's own admission, no other K'da had ever managed such a trick before with their regular Shontine symbiotic hosts.

The fact that Draycos hadn't accidentally slipped off Jack's back since then wasn't any real comfort. Neither was the fact that the dragon insisted he'd never felt better in his life. The bottom line was that something unexplained had happened.

And if there was one thing Uncle Virgil had made sure to hammer into Jack's skull, it was that the unexplained was always something to worry about.

Was Jack's body somehow rejecting Draycos? That was the simplest possibility. It was also the most ominous. A K'da couldn't live away from a host for more than six hours at a time. If he tried, he would go two-dimensional anyway and disappear off into death. The rest of the Shontine refugees were on their way, but they were still almost three months out from the eastern edge of the Orion Arm. If it turned out that human beings like Jack could only act as temporary K'da hosts, Draycos would most likely be dead long before they arrived.

Ahead was the doorway that had been Jack's second home for most of the last week. He paused there, peering across at the Malison Ring office, determination settling into his stomach like a lead weight. If Draycos was going to die, there was probably nothing either of them could do to prevent it. But whatever happened, no matter what it took, Jack would see to it that the rest of the K'da and Shontine made it safely to their new home. He owed Draycos that much.

Across the street, a gold-scaled dragon head lifted into view over the roof parapet, the long snout turning sharply upward in silent signal. Peeling himself away from the wall, Jack hurried over.

Draycos dropped from the roof as Jack approached, landing in a crouch beside the door. "The cameras are disabled," he reported quietly. "There was also a fourth, hidden from the street, guarding the approaches to the other three. I dealt with that one first."

"Thanks," Jack said, pulling out the key he and Uncle Virge had created that afternoon. Mentally crossing his fingers, he slid it into the lock.

With a quiet snick, the lock popped open. "One down, one to go," he said, holding out his hand.

Draycos put a paw on his palm and melted back onto his skin, slithering his way up along his arm. Jack waited until the dragon had maneuvered himself into his usual position with his head curving around Jack's right shoulder, then eased the door open.

Even without Uncle Virge's warning the previous night, he would have known from the distinctive hum that a cavity-wave system was operating. Without the counterlock they'd put together, disarming it would have been tricky. With the counterlock, it was a piece of cake. Keying the device, he waited patiently until the hum faded into silence. "Uncle Virge?" he murmured.

"It's off," the computerized voice confirmed from Jack's left collar. "Watch yourself, lad."

"Right." Keeping alert for laser tags and other more subtle security traps, Jack headed in.

The office was similar to the Whinyard's Edge recruiting office he'd been in on Carrion a couple of months back, consisting of a single large room with several smaller offices opening off the side and back walls. Unlike the Edge recruiting office, though, each of the rooms here was decorated with a gold plate identifying its occupant. On the theory that mercenary leaders were as vain as the business and government types he and Uncle Virgil had scammed over the years, Jack picked out the door with the most elaborate plate and headed toward it.

He encountered two more barriers along the way, one a laser alarm, the other a pressure plate hidden beneath the rug. Both were easily avoided.

"Okay," he muttered under his breath as he examined the lock. It looked straightforward, but this was no time to get sloppy. "Draycos?"

"I am ready."

Turning around, Jack pressed his back against the door, feeling the subtle shift across his skin as Draycos curved his two-dimensional form to look "over"—the dragon's preferred term—the wall. Jack held his breath as the other moved around a little, wondering if he would lose his grip and fall off again.

But a few seconds later the dragon returned safely to his original position. "There are no extra locks or traps I can find," he reported.

"Good," Jack said, pulling out his lock pick. "This'll just take a second."

Two minutes later, Jack settled himself into a very expensive desk chair facing an equally expensive computer system. "Bingo," he said, switching on the machine. "Human designed, and with a modern operating system. This will do nicely."

The computer finished its start-up procedure. Leaning forward, Jack punched in the "sewer-rat" program Uncle Virgil had created for breaking into other people's computers.

It would be nice, he reflected, if Neverlin had been considerate enough to load the rendezvous information into the general Malison Ring computer network where anyone could get at it. But even if the conspirators hadn't been that careless, there were other tricks he could try.

One approach would be to download a list of worlds where the Malison Ring had troops and equipment, particularly the Djinn-90 starfighters they'd used against Draycos's advance team. With that information, he and Draycos could travel to the most likely jump-off points for the attack and search the local squads' computers for the rendezvous data. Or Jack could try loading a dump-tap into the system that would pull any messages to or from Neverlin and send copies to another computer where Uncle Virge could access it.

However he found the rendezvous point, he and Draycos would then have two choices. They could either try to beat the Malison Ring there and warn the refugee fleet or else turn everything over to StarForce and let them handle it.

And with thoughts and plans sifting themselves through Jack's mind, he was caught completely by surprise when the door across the room was abruptly slammed open.

He leaped to his feet. But it was far too late. Men in Malison Ring uniforms were pouring into the office, guns drawn and ready. "Don't shoot!" Jack called, holding his hands wide open, his heart pounding in his chest. Once before, he'd seen Draycos take out a room full of opponents. If he'd done it once, surely he could do it again.

But that time his opponents had been stupid enough to bunch up where the dragon's speed and agility gave him the advantage. This group, unfortunately, wasn't playing it that way. Instead of heading straight toward him, they spread out in both directions along the walls, staying well back.

"Jack?" Draycos whispered, his voice too soft for anyone but Jack to hear.

"No," Jack whispered back, keeping his lips motionless. "Uncle Virge, lock down."

The flood of mercenaries finally ended, leaving nine of them facing him. For a moment they stood motionless, staring at Jack in silence as if he were some kind of museum exhibit. Then, still without a word, the middle three men handed their weapons to those beside them and strode forward.

Quickly, efficiently, silently, they patted Jack down, relieving him of his comm clip, his key, his burglar equipment, his multitool, his belt, and his boots. One of the men, a sergeant, produced a handheld scanner from a belt pouch and ran it systematically over Jack's body. The second man had a set of handcuffs, and he and the third fastened Jack's hands securely behind his back.

The sergeant returned the scanner to its pouch and jerked his head over his shoulder. "Let's go."

The other two grabbed Jack's arms and marched him toward the door. The guards along the walls began to file out, adjusting their exit so that three of them ended up walking in front of Jack and his keepers while the other three walked behind them. Even with their prisoner in handcuffs, they kept their guns handy.

There was a tall man standing alone in the middle of the large room when Jack emerged from the office. His Malison Ring uniform was a lot flashier than those of the rest of the soldiers, with two rows of colored bars across his upper chest. "He's clean?" he asked as Jack and his three keepers approached.

"Yes, Commandant," the sergeant said. "Looks like he was trying to break into your computer."

The commandant turned cold fish eyes on Jack. "So desertion wasn't enough for you, eh?" he demanded.

Jack blinked. *Desertion?* "I'm not a deserter," he protested.

"No, of course not," the other said darkly. "Colonel Frost put out a blanket alert on a perfect stranger just for the fun of it. Sergeant, put him in the tombs while I call the colonel and see what he wants me to do with him."

"Yes, sir." The sergeant gestured, the two soldiers holding

Jack's arms gave him a shove, and the whole group continued on across the room to an unmarked double door.

The double door led to a long corridor with another set of double doors at the far end. The sergeant unlocked one of them and led the way through, and Jack found himself in a smaller version of the big room they'd just left. Most of the doors here were the normal wooden variety, but the one all the way across the room from the double doors was made instead of thin, crisscrossed metal bars. The sergeant walked the group over to the latter door and swung it open. "In here," he said.

Jack obeyed. The sergeant stopped him at the door, removed his handcuffs, and gave him a final shove into the cell. With a solid-sounding *thunk* the door slammed shut behind him. "Smit, Gargan—you're on watch," the sergeant said, gesturing the rest of the group back to the double doors. They filed back out, leaving two of the mercenaries standing guard on opposite sides of the exit where they could watch Jack's every move.

Taking a deep breath, feeling thoroughly disgusted with himself, Jack walked to the cot at the back of the cell and sat down.

Secret plots being what they were, he'd been pretty sure that Neverlin and his fellow conspirators wouldn't have shared the details of their scheme with the entire Malison Ring. But he really *should* have expected them to come up with a cover story that would get everyone in the group hunting for him.

Jack Morgan, Malison Ring deserter. So obvious.

"Jack?" Draycos murmured from his shoulder.

"Just a second," Jack murmured back, giving the cell a quick check. No obvious cameras or microphones, and the guards were too far away to eavesdrop. "Clear enough," he said. "Sorry, Draycos. After what happened on Brum-a-dum, I should have expected Neverlin to turn the whole hornets' nest loose on us."

"No apology needed," Draycos assured him. "Do you want me to eliminate the guards?"

Jack measured the distance across the room with his eyes. "I don't know," he said doubtfully. "There's an awful lot of ground to cover. We need a diversion of some sort."

"What do you suggest?"

Jack chewed the inside of his cheek. It would be dangerous, he knew. But then, what *wasn't* dangerous these days? "The room next door seems to be just a normal office," he said. "If you were able to slide off my back through the wall, you could maybe make some noise and see if they would come close enough for you to jump them."

Draycos didn't reply. "I know it's dangerous," Jack went on. "But right now I can't think of anything else to try. If you'd rather, I'm willing to wait a bit and see if we come up with something else."

"No," the dragon said. "If we are to make our escape, we must do so at once. Neverlin already knows about me, though it would appear he hasn't passed that knowledge on to the rest of the Malison Ring."

"But if they contact him and he spills the beans, it's all over," Jack agreed grimly. "First thing they'd do is move us someplace where none of these tricks would work."

"So let us do it," Draycos decided. "Put your back against the wall."

Jack shifted around and pressed his back against the side of the cell. He felt the dragon shift around on his skin, lifting his two-dimensional form through the extra dimension and leaning over the barrier.

For a moment nothing happened. Then, all at once, there was a sudden movement against Jack's back, and Draycos was gone.

Jack took a careful breath. There was no way of knowing whether or not the trick had been successful. Still, it had felt about the same as the time it had happened accidentally. He hoped that meant Draycos was all right.

Jack had just moved away from the wall when, across the room, the two guards quietly collapsed onto the floor.

Jack stared at them in disbelief. Draycos hadn't even made it out of the office yet. How could he have—?

And then, as Jack's suddenly sluggish brain tried to figure it out, he caught a hint of a familiar odor wafting toward him.

Someone was pumping sopor mist into the room.

Jack twisted back around, holding his breath as he pounded three quick times against the sidewall. If he and Draycos fell asleep before they could get back together, the commandant wouldn't need Neverlin or anyone else to tell him something strange was going on.

Jack had lifted his hand to hit the wall again when the universe went dark.

CHAPTER 3

The room beside Jack's cell was a cramped junior staffers' office, with desks and chairs for three people and a single window opening out the rear of the building. Draycos had only just started looking for something to attract the guards' attention when he heard Jack's pounding on the wall.

He leaped across the room and pressed one ear against the door. Had the mercenaries decided to begin the interrogation?

And then, seeping in under the door, he caught a whiff of something he'd smelled once back at the Whinyard's Edge training camp. It was sopor gas, a weapon used to put enemies to sleep.

Quickly, he took a deep breath, filling his lungs to full capacity before the gas could become thick enough to affect him. Then, carefully, he eased the door open a crack.

The two guards across the outer room were already asleep, lying crumpled on the floor. No one else was visible. Frowning, he pulled the door the rest of the way open and slipped around the corner to look into the cell. Jack was alone, and fast asleep.

There was no time now to try to figure out what was going on. He had to get Jack out of here, and the sleeping guards across the outer room were his best chance of doing that. If one of them had a key, he could perhaps get Jack out through the office window before he himself ran out of air.

He was crouching for a leap across the room when there was a click and the outer double doors began to swing open.

Draycos twisted around, darting instead back into the office. He flicked his tail at the edge of the door as he passed, trying to swing it closed.

But he missed, and then it was too late. He felt the subtle air currents as the far door swung all the way open, and heard the soft sounds of someone jogging quickly toward Jack's cell.

For a moment the footsteps seemed to falter. Then, they continued on.

Only now they seemed to be coming straight toward the half-open office door.

There was no time for anything clever. Draycos leaped to the far side of one of the desks, landing as silently as he could. He wormed his body past the chair and ducked out of sight.

He was barely in time. The steps paused, and the office door swung all the way open.

Draycos froze in place. Now, too late, he wondered if the intruder might have an infrared scanner that would penetrate the material of the desk. The other stood in the doorway for perhaps five seconds, and Draycos caught the slightly sinister hiss of a full-helmet gas mask. Then, to his relief, the footsteps headed away toward Jack's cell.

Silently, Draycos rose from his hiding place and padded back to the door. With the other's full attention on Jack, it was time for him to make his move. He eased one eye around the edge of the door—

And felt his tail stiffen in stunned surprise.

It wasn't Arthur Neverlin or one of his Brummgan thugs, as he'd first feared. Nor was it some local Malison Ring soldier who'd decided to go ahead and start Jack's interrogation on his own. It was, instead, possibly the last person Draycos would ever have expected to see again.

It was Alison Kayna.

A kaleidoscope of memories rippled through his mind as he ducked back out of sight. Alison had been the very best of the teenaged recruits whom Jack had joined in his infiltration of the Whinyard's Edge. She'd been smart, resourceful, and far more skilled than a raw recruit should have been. Especially one who was no older than Jack himself.

She and Jack had also been among the handful of those recruits who'd been marked for death. Only by working together had they managed to escape.

Now, against all odds, here she was in the middle of a Malison Ring office.

And for some reason she was trying to get to Jack.

The cell door snicked open. Draycos eased forward for another look, his brain and muscles frozen with indecision. He didn't have nearly enough air left for a long fight. But if Alison intended to harm his host, it was Draycos's duty to do whatever he could to prevent that.

Yet why would Alison want to hurt Jack?

There was another rustle of cloth, and Alison emerged from the cell, Jack's sleeping form slung over her shoulder in a variant of a Shontine hunter's lift. Staggering a little under his weight, she hurried toward the exit.

There was no way Draycos could follow them out, at least not without Alison spotting him. Fortunately, it also didn't look as if she intended Jack any immediate harm. That she could have done right there in the cell.

Which suggested that she'd come in here to help him escape.

There were a lot of questions Draycos didn't have answers for. But the ache in his lungs was an urgent reminder that he wouldn't be answering questions or doing anything else if he didn't get himself to fresh air.

A quick slash of his claws shredded the lock mechanism on the office window. It probably also set off a dozen alarms, but he doubted now that anyone in the building was in any condition to hear them. A tug on the sash and he was outside. Hitting the ground, he spun around and leaped upward onto the roof.

He paused there a moment to gasp in a few lungfuls of air. Then he set off toward the front of the building, wondering if there were other security cameras up here besides the four he'd dealt with.

But whether there were or not, he had no time to look for them. If Alison got Jack to a vehicle before he could overtake her, he might never see the boy again. Certainly not before his six-hour time limit ended and he died.

Fortunately, a burdened fourteen-year-old girl was considerably slower than an unburdened K'da. Draycos was at the parapet, searching the street and nearby buildings for signs of trouble, when Alison and Jack emerged through the front door.

There was a car parked in front of the building, a vehicle that hadn't been there when he and Jack had broken in. Alison hurried over to it, opened the back door, and rolled Jack off her shoulder onto the backseat. One of his legs twitched a couple of times, then kicked out to flop limply over the edge of the seat. Alison maneuvered it back inside and closed the door, then went around behind the car to the driver's side. With one last look around, she got in and reached for her door handle.

And Draycos leaped.

The timing had to be perfect, he knew, and once he was in the air there was nothing he could do to alter that timing. But warrior's luck was with him. Precisely as Alison slammed her door, he landed on top of the car, absorbing as much of the impact with his legs as he could.

He froze, muscles tensed, waiting for her to realize that the door had slammed with far more sound and vibration than usual. But with her full-helmet gas mask still in place, she apparently didn't notice. There was a hum as she activated the engine, and the car sped off into the night.

Draycos flattened himself against the roof, closing his eyes to slits to protect them from the wind rushing against his face. Digging his claws into the roof as deep as he dared, he held on. If any of Avrans City's citizens were wandering the streets at this hour, they were in for a remarkable sight.

Even if they weren't, he was already running out of time.

Alison was driving straight toward the spaceport, and even at this hour the port would be bustling with people.

He had until they arrived to get out of sight.

Easing the tip of his tail over the edge of the roof beside the rear window, he rubbed it across the plastic. Those leg twitches he'd seen had suggested that Jack was starting to wake up. If so, this should work.

If not, they were in trouble.

Something soft slammed up against Jack's back, and with a rather foggy jolt he woke up.

He opened his eyes to find himself staring in partial darkness at an even darker curved surface no more than three feet from his face. He tried to move his legs, and got a second shock as someone grabbed one of them and pushed it toward him. There was a slamming sound from that direction.

And then, all the blurry strangeness came into focus. He was lying on his back on the rear seat of a car, his knees pushed up toward his chest. Someone had apparently taken him out of the Malison Ring cell, and they were about to make a run for it.

Without Draycos?

Jack caught his breath, his hand darting into the opening of his shirt. The last thing he remembered was dropping the dragon through the cell wall into the office. Then the sopor mist had come in. . . .

Jack swiveled around onto his side, trying to force numb muscles to push himself into a sitting position. If he could get the door open, he might be able to get back in there and find his partner.

Too late. A shadowy figure opened the driver's door and climbed in behind the wheel, slamming the door hard enough to shake the whole vehicle. "Wait!" Jack said, his hand fumbling for the handle.

"Relax," a girl's voice came from the front seat. She pulled off a full-helmet gas mask and tossed it onto the seat beside her.

And Jack felt his mouth drop open. *"Alison?"*

"You were expecting the tooth fairy?" Alison Kayna countered. "Hang on."

She keyed the engine, and with a lurch they were off. "Wait a second," Jack protested, trying to get his brain working. If they left Draycos behind, the K'da would be dead in six hours. "We have to—I mean, I wasn't done in there."

"Trust me—you were done," Alison countered. "Or do you really want to be in there when their air system finishes cleaning out the sopor mist?"

"No, but—" Jack broke off as something flicked past the corner of his eye. He turned to look just as the end of a whip-like K'da tail brushed against the top of the plastic.

So that was why the car door had slammed so hard. Most of the sound and vibration had actually been that of a K'da poet-warrior landing on the roof.

Clever. Now it was time for Jack to be equally clever and get the dragon inside.

Fortunately, this one was a no-brainer. "Oh, geez," Jack said, fumbling at the window release. "Open the window—quick."

"What's the matter?" Alison asked, frowning back over her shoulder.

"I don't feel so good," he said, putting a little grunt on the last word. "Just get it open."

"Yeah, yeah, right," she said, her shoulder moving as she hit the control.

The window rolled down, and Jack leaned his head outside. As he did, he gripped the top of the door with his right hand as if steadying himself.

And felt Draycos grab the back of his hand and melt onto his skin.

They were safe again. At least for now.

He held his pose another few seconds, just for show, then pulled his head back inside. "Okay," he said, slumping onto the seat cushions. "False alarm."

"I'll leave it open anyway," Alison said pointedly.

"Fine," Jack said. "So what in blazes are you doing here?"

"That was *my* question," she countered. "Are you *trying* to make a career out of messing up my life?"

"Seems to me the last time I saw you I was helping *save* your life," Jack growled, annoyed in spite of himself.

"You have an interesting memory," she said. "The way *I* remember it, you didn't do anything for me I couldn't have done myself."

A set of K'da claws pressed in silent warning against Jack's ribs. He grimaced, but the dragon was right. This wasn't the time for an argument. "Yeah, whatever," he said. "So how exactly did I mess things up for you this time?"

"I was trying to join the Malison Ring," she said. "In fact,

I was having my final interview with them yesterday when I overheard someone saying you'd been spotted in the area."

"And you didn't think about maybe warning me?"

"I would, if I'd known where to find you," she said. "The last thing I wanted was for them to catch you and start asking questions, especially about your time in the Whinyard's Edge. So I came by tonight, hoping I could stop you before you walked into their trap."

"So what happened?"

"What do you mean, what happened?" she retorted. "I was waiting for you in back, that's what happened. I never figured you'd be crazy enough to walk in the front door."

Jack grimaced. "Yeah. Well . . . sorry."

She shrugged. "I'll live," she said. "Can I drop you some-where?"

"I've got a ship at the port," he said. "Docking slot E-7."

She nodded. "Fine."

For a few minutes they rode in silence. Jack wanted to ask Draycos if he was all right but couldn't risk Alison overhearing his mutterings. Still, from the way the K'da had moved along Jack's skin, he certainly seemed to be unhurt.

Ahead, Jack could see the elaborately carved archway marking the entrance to the spaceport. "Keep an eye out for large men with guns," he warned.

"Thank you," Alison said dryly. "That *had* occurred to me. If you don't mind, we'll just go to my ship—it's in D-2—and you can walk the rest of the way."

"That's fine," Jack said. "By the way, thanks for getting me out of there."

"No problem," she said. "You owe me one."

They passed beneath the archway. Jack watched carefully, but if the Malison Ring had been able to get any men to the port, they weren't being obvious about it. Certainly no one stepped out into the street in front of them and started shooting.

So he and Draycos had lost this round. But that was all right. There were a dozen more major Malison Ring offices scattered around the Orion Arm. As soon as Jack got back to the *Essenay* he'd get Uncle Virge looking for another good target. They would come up with another scheme for getting in, figure out a better disguise this time—

"Uh-oh," Alison muttered.

Jack snapped his attention back. "What?"

"Trouble," she said, nodding toward a rather decrepit-looking light freighter off to the left. A half-dozen men in business suits were visible nearby, walking around it or standing idly near the entry hatch.

"They don't look like mercenaries to me," Jack said.

"They're not," Alison said. "It's still trouble."

She drove past the turnoff, and Jack half-turned to peer out the back window. The loitering men didn't seem to have noticed them. One of them shifted position slightly, bringing his face more fully into the glow of one of the port's lights—

"Did they spot us?" Alison asked.

Jack found his voice. "Doesn't look like it," he said, forcing his voice to stay casual. "I hope you have a backup plan."

"I do, but not on this planet," Alison said grimly. "I don't suppose I could talk you into giving me a lift."

Jack hesitated. Even if Draycos's existence wasn't exactly a secret anymore, they still didn't want to broadcast the news to the whole Orion Arm. Besides that, he'd taken great pains for over a year now to keep Uncle Virgil's death a secret. And *that* one hadn't yet leaked out at all. Having a stranger aboard for even a few days would be begging for trouble.

But on the other hand . . . "Where exactly did you have in mind?" he asked.

"It's a planet called Rho Scorvi," she said. "Ever hear of it?"

"I don't think so," Jack said, searching his memory. "Does it have a real name?"

"The natives probably have their own name for it, but no one else does," she said. "It's about eighty light-years past Immabwi."

Jack grimaced. Immabwi was off toward the southern edge of the Orion Arm, not exactly in the mainstream of civilization. It was going to cost either a lot of time or a lot of fuel to get there. And he and Draycos didn't have any extra time to spare. "You sure I can't just fly you twice around the galaxy?"

"That's the nearest place where I know I can find some friendly transport," she said stiffly. "If it's going to upset your delicate schedule, forget it."

"Don't get huffy," he said. "I just hope you've got enough cash to get us there, that's all."

"Don't worry; I've got plenty of fueling credits," she said, patting her jacket pocket. "Always carry them with me, just in case."

"That's handy," Jack said. "Rich uncle?"

"Careless travelers."

Jack made a face. And here he was, trying hard to *stop* stealing from people. "So how come the guys back there are after you?"

"I never said they were after *me*," she said. "That ship belongs to some other friends—I've just been hitching a ride. They must be after *them*."

"Fine," Jack said. "So why are they after *them*?"

"How should I know?" Alison retorted. "Can we just get out of here? *Whoa*."

"What?" Jack asked, twisting around to look over his shoulder.

"Is *that* your ship?" Alison asked, pointing ahead.

"Oh," Jack said, relaxing again. "Yes. Actually, it belongs to my uncle."

"Your uncle's doing very well for himself," she said as she brought the car to a stop near the *Essenay*'s air lock hatchway. "That's, what, a Pergnoir-7 light personal transport?"

"Hardly," Jack said with a snort as he climbed out of the car. His legs still felt a little wobbly, but he should be able to make it into the ship without Alison's help. "It's just your basic run-of-the-line light freighter."

"If you say so," Alison said, sounding doubtful as she followed him into the air lock. "Sure looks like a Pergnoir to me. You sure giving me a ride will be all right with your uncle?"

"Don't worry; he's not here at the moment," Jack said, looking warningly at the air lock's camera/speaker/microphone module. He hoped Uncle Virge would take the hint and keep quiet. "He's off-planet on a job."

"Handy," Alison said. "When do you need to pick him up?"

"He'll let me know," Jack told her, heading for the cockpit. "Come on—you can get us our lift clearance while I crank up the systems. The sooner we get out of here, the better."

CHAPTER 4

Jack prepped the ship while Alison talked to the control tower, and a few minutes later they were heading up into the faint glow of the pre-dawn sky. Twenty minutes later, Jack keyed in the ECHO stardrive, and they were on their way to Rho Scorvi.

Alison had been impressed enough by her first look at the *Essenay*'s exterior. Jack's guided tour of the interior knocked her socks off.

"I don't believe this," she said for probably the fourth time as he took her into the dayroom. "A full-auto medic chair, a class-five food synthesizer, *and* a table repeater display. Your uncle poured a *big* bucket of cash into this thing."

"Like I said, he's good at what he does," Jack said.

"No kidding," Alison said. She turned the table on and off, watching as the wood-grain surface went transparent and then opaque again. "What sort of remote sensors do you have?"

"I'm not really sure," Jack said. "Computer?"

"We have a Calico 404 package," Uncle Virge answered. His voice was bland and emotionless, but there was a definite edge of quiet annoyance beneath the surface.

Jack heartily sympathized. Unfortunately, there wasn't a thing he could do about it. Even before they'd lifted, Alison had spotted the P/S/8 designation on the computer-interface board and recognized it as a model with personality simulation capabilities. At that point, Jack had had no choice but to allow—or rather, insist—that Uncle Virge talk to her.

He'd modified his normal voice, of course, going with something that sounded more like a standard P/S computer than the more colorful personality Uncle Virgil had left behind. But it was obvious that he wasn't happy with any of this.

It was equally obvious he was going to be having a long and unpleasant conversation with Jack the minute their new passenger was out of earshot.

"Extremely cool," Alison said, turning the table transparent one last time. "Can you access your InterWorld transmitter from here, too?"

Jack felt his breath catch in his throat. Ships this small, even luxury models, never had InterWorld transmitters aboard. How could Alison have guessed the *Essenay* had one? "What are you talking about?" he asked guardedly.

"Don't be cute," she said. "I saw the InterWorld directory tab on the list when you were pulling up Rho Scorvi's coordinates."

"A *directory*?" Jack repeated, thoroughly lost now. "What does a directory have to do with anything?"

"Because the InterWorld directory is part of the Inter-World access software," she explained patiently. "If you've got a directory, you've got the software. If you've got the software, you've got the transmitter."

"Or my uncle just wants to be able to look up numbers before he calls them," Jack countered. It was, he thought rather disgustedly, a pretty weak argument.

Alison apparently thought so, too. "Right," she said sarcastically. "Even though every spaceport and planet-based transmitter has its own directory. But fine. Let's ask. Computer—?"

"Never mind," Jack cut her off, half-lifting his hands in a gesture of surrender. The standard P/S/8 computer interface probably couldn't lie. Uncle Virge could, and in this case probably would, and the last thing Jack wanted was for Alison to catch him at it. "Yes, we've got a transmitter."

"Which is another five or six buckets of cash," Alison concluded, looking around the dayroom. "I hope you realize just how much money you're sitting on here, Jack Montana."

She brought her gaze back to him. "*If* that's your real name."

"Like 'Alison Kayna,' you mean?" Jack asked pointedly.

Her lip twitched. "Fine. None of my business. So where do I sleep?"

"You can use my uncle's cabin," Jack said. "It's down the hall on your left."

"You're sure he won't mind?" she asked. "I could just sleep here on the couch."

"He won't mind," Jack assured her. "Besides, I sometimes like to get up during the night and have a snack. I don't want to trip over you."

"Fair enough," Alison said. "If you don't mind, I'm going to go sack out for a while. It's been a long and fairly interesting night."

"Sounds like a plan," Jack agreed. "I think I'll catch some winks myself after I check the ECHO settings. Help yourself to anything you want—food or music or whatever. I'll get you some of my clothes, too."

"Okay," Alison said, heading for the door. "Thanks for the tour. And thanks for the ride. I appreciate it."

"I appreciate you getting me out of that cell," Jack said. "See you later."

He headed to the cockpit. "She still in her cabin?" he asked as he dropped into the pilot's chair.

"She's cleaning up in the bathroom," Uncle Virge said.

"Okay," Jack said, bracing himself. "Let's have it."

"Let us have what?" Draycos asked, lifting his head from Jack's shoulder.

"The objections, arguments, and how-dare-yous," Jack said. "Mouse got your tongue, Uncle Virge?"

"What are you expecting me to say, Jack lad?" Uncle Virge growled. "That this is as crazy a scheme as you've ever come up with? And given your record these past three months, that's a high standard for you to top."

"Number one," Jack said, holding up a finger, "she got me out of a tight jam."

"I thought getting you out of jams was what your tame K'da poet-warrior was for."

Draycos stirred against Jack's skin. "He *could* have gotten me out, yes," Jack said hurriedly before the dragon could speak. "Alison got there first. I owe her."

"So buy her a liner ticket to Rho Scorvi and send her on her way."

"Number two," Jack said, lifting another finger, "I never did find out what kind of game she was playing back at the Whinyard's Edge training camp. Given that whatever it was nearly got both of us killed, it might be nice to see if I can wheedle it out of her."

"She was running a scam, of course," Uncle Virge huffed. "Just like you were."

"And third," Jack said, lifting one final finger, "the people she was avoiding back at her ship were from Braxton Univer-sis."

There was a short pause. "Are you sure?" Uncle Virge asked, his huffiness suddenly gone.

"Positive," Jack said. "I saw one of them back on the *Star of Wonder*. His name's Harper, and he's one of Cornelius Braxton's more trusted bodyguards."

"Are you suggesting *Braxton* is interested in this girl?" Uncle Virge asked.

"If not him, then it's someone else high up in the corporation."

"Or they could merely be interested in Alison's friends," Draycos suggested. "The ones she said she was riding with."

Jack shook his head. "There aren't any friends. That ship is hers."

"Are you certain?"

"Trust me, I know a lie when I hear it," Jack said. "The point is that if Braxton is interested in her, maybe we should be interested, too."

"Seems to me it's just one more reason to cut her loose at the first stop," Uncle Virge said darkly. "Or had it occurred to you that there's just one person at the top of Braxton's interest list right now?"

"Arthur Neverlin," Jack agreed. "But if Alison is working for him, why did she spring me just now?"

"Maybe he wants to give us some rope," Uncle Virge suggested. "A little running room to see how much we know. It just seems to me that the timing of this little rescue is awfully convenient."

"True," Jack had to admit. "Still, if she *did* overhear them yesterday, it wouldn't have taken her any time at all to put something like this together. We know she's partial to sopor mist—she probably had everything she needed already aboard her ship."

"I still think she's here to worm out your secrets," Uncle Virge insisted.

"Or perhaps she hopes you'll lead her to your uncle," Draycos put in thoughtfully. "Recall that on Brum-a-dum they were still trying to use you to get to him."

"They were, weren't they?" Jack said slowly, thinking back to that conversation. Unless they just wanted revenge . . . but Neverlin didn't seem the type to waste time with revenge. Not his own time, anyway. "Granted, Alison could be all of that. Even so, I think our best bet is to hold on to her, at least for a while. How does that saying go? Keep your friends close, and your enemies closer?"

"That's the one," Uncle Virge said with a sniff. "And if you ask me, it's a very stupid saying. *I* say keep your enemies as far away from you as you can."

"And your friends?" Draycos asked.

"Better to make do without them," Uncle Virge retorted.

Jack sighed. In Uncle Virgil's world, people had always fallen into one of two categories: the ones he could use, and the ones he couldn't. "Friendship," "affection," "trust"—those might as well have been alien words as far as he was concerned.

Maybe Jack himself had been an exception. Then again, maybe he hadn't.

But things were different now, he reminded himself firmly. He *did* have a friend—Draycos—and he was going to make that friendship work.

And part of that process was for him to earn the dragon's respect, which meant keeping his promises. "No one's suggesting we have to become Alison's best friends," he told Uncle Virge. "But we *are* going to take her to Rho Scorvi. Period."

"Whatever you say, Jack lad," Uncle Virge said with a theatrical sigh. "Would it strain the duties of a proper host if I at least kept an eye on her?"

"Of course not," Jack said.

"I agree," Draycos seconded. "Keeping a promise does not require one to abandon caution."

"Then we're in agreement," Uncle Virge said with false cheerfulness. "How wonderful for us all."

"Don't be snide," Jack admonished him, climbing out of the pilot's seat. "And while you're being all vigilant, I'm going to get some sleep."

"Fine," Uncle Virge said. "Incidentally, I trust you realize there's one other option."

"About . . . ?"

"About those Braxton Universis men," Uncle Virge said,

his voice going a bit darker. "It could be they were looking for *you*."

"Why would they seek him?" Draycos asked.

"Because he's crossed paths twice now with Arthur Neverlin," Uncle Virge reminded him.

"And both times Neverlin has come out the worse for the exchange," Draycos reminded him.

"True, but Braxton may not realize that," Uncle Virge said. "If *I* were him, and I saw two people keep running into each other, I'd wonder if there were dots that needed to be connected. At the very least, he might want to borrow Jack for a nice cozy chat somewhere."

"Which I really don't want to do right now," Jack said. "Actually, Uncle Virge, that *had* occurred to me. But I don't see much I can do about it."

"I just wanted to make sure we were all on the same page," Uncle Virge said soothingly. "Good night, Jack. Sleep well."

CHAPTER 5

The trip, including fueling stops, took eight days.

It wasn't nearly as bad as Jack had expected it to be. Alison kept mostly to herself, coming out of her cabin for meals and sometimes to play games on the dayroom computer terminal. Other than that she spent most of her time sleeping or writing in a small notebook she always kept with her.

She didn't poke or pry around the ship in the middle of the night, either. Jack had half-expected her to try that. Uncle Virge was clearly annoyed that she didn't.

Twice she accepted Jack's invitation to pair up for one of the two-player games he hadn't played since Uncle Virgil's death. He beat her both times, but by a much smaller margin the second time. Clearly, she was a fast learner.

For all her hermit tendencies, her mealtime conversation was bright and cheerful. But it was mostly empty words, the sort of chatter Uncle Virgil had taught Jack how to do when he wanted to fill time without actually saying anything. Jack's efforts to get past the surface froth got him nowhere.

Which was extremely irritating, and not just for Jack. By the fourth day Uncle Virge, who was as frustrated at Jack's failures to dig anything out of the girl as Jack himself was, began pushing for Jack to let him have a go at her.

It was a ridiculous suggestion, of course. Even if Uncle Virge was careful with his voice and mannerisms, Alison would be bound to notice the sudden change in the computer's personality. But he kept pushing, until Jack finally had to give him a direct order not to bring it up again.

That stopped the demands. But it did nothing to lower the tension. Between Uncle Virge's sulking and Alison's useless conversation, Jack was thoroughly sick of both of them by the time they finally reached Rho Scorvi.

"There," Alison said, pointing out the cockpit canopy at a large, dark green forest at the edge of a wide plain. "That's where they'll be putting down."

"Nice," Jack commented, studying the area. The forest was about a hundred miles across, lying mostly to the east of a range of snow-covered mountains. A churning river rolled down the slopes, widening as it went, cutting through the center of the forest and then continuing eastward across the plain. "If you like that sort of thing."

"I take it you don't?"

"I prefer my nature in nice, neat layer gardens," Jack said. "So what are they coming here for?"

"There's a colony of nomads that travel around the edge of the forest," she said. "My friends are supposed to be doing some trading with them."

"What kind of trading?"

"Some kind of wild herbs, I think," Alison said. "I'm a little foggy on the details. The Erassvas—those are the natives—hang around the edge of the forest picking fruit, digging up roots, and pulling edible bark off the trees. They get clothing materials from other plants."

"Hunter-gatherer types, then?"

"Right, minus the hunter part," Alison said. "They're nomadic, too. Once they've cleared out an area, they move on around the edge of the forest. By the time they've made a complete circle, it's been a couple of years and the stuff's all grown back."

"Sounds like your basic Garden of Eden," Jack suggested.

"More or less," Alison agreed. "They just have to make sure they don't go too deep into the forest, where all the nastier creatures live."

"How nasty?"

"I don't think anyone knows," she said. "No one's ever seen them, except maybe the Erassvas, and they're not talking. But there are legends, and the handful of researchers who've gone into the forest have found and documented some very intriguing claw marks on trees and even on some of the big rocks."

Jack winced. That sounded ominous. "Lucky for us, we aren't going in there," he said, keying in the landing sequence. As he did so, there was a quiet beep from the board. "Computer?" he asked, frowning.

"Another power glitch," Uncle Virge confirmed. He was still trying to sound like a normal P/S computer, but Jack could hear the tightness in his voice. "Still unable to locate the source."

Jack drummed his fingers thoughtfully on the edge of the control board. This was the third time since leaving Bigelow that this mysterious power dip had happened, as if some system aboard the *Essenay* had suddenly decided to take an extra helping of power without telling anyone. Uncle Virge had run the diagnostics a dozen times but hadn't found anything out of place. "Any ideas?" Jack asked, looking over his shoulder at Alison.

She shook her head. "I just hope it's nothing serious."

"Well, you won't have to worry about it much longer," Jack said. "Computer, do you have a line on those nomads yet?"

"I'm picking up a group of beings at the southern edge of the forest," Uncle Virge said. "I'm not sure how many—the forest canopy is scrambling the infrared readings."

"That's probably them," Alison said. "There shouldn't be anyone else around. I'll go get my stuff together."

"Need any help?" Jack asked with just a touch of sarcasm. At their first fueling stop, at Jack's suggestion, Alison had gone off to do some shopping. From the size of the two travel bags she'd lugged back to the *Essenay,* he figured she'd decided to get started on next year's wardrobe.

"I can manage," she assured him. If she'd noticed the sarcasm, she didn't mention it. "See you."

She left the cockpit. "You really can't track this power glitch?" Jack asked when she was out of sight.

"No, and it's driving me crazy," Uncle Virge said irritably. "It's like there's an intermittent power drain somewhere. Probably in the ECHO."

"Why in that particular system?" Draycos asked.

"Because the only time it shows up is when we come back into normal space," Uncle Virge said. "There's a pulse in power utilization right as we shut the ECHO down; then a few minutes later we get this dip effect, like something is sucking up extra power."

"Could it be a problem with the cooldown?" Jack suggested. "Some wire contracting too fast and making contact where it's not supposed to?"

"If it is, it's not showing on the diagnostics," Uncle Virge said. "I'm probably going to have to do a systematic shutdown to isolate it. But I don't think we want to hang around this rock while I do that."

"On the other hand, we may have the necessary time to spare," Draycos said. He jabbed his tongue toward the sensor display. "I see no sign of any ship."

"So?" Uncle Virge asked.

"If her friends have been delayed, Alison may be marooned," Draycos said patiently.

"All Jack promised was to bring her here," Uncle Virge said tartly. "He never said we'd stay and hold her hand."

"We cannot simply fly away and abandon her," Draycos insisted.

"It's none of our business," Uncle Virge insisted right back. "Besides, there's half a chance she won't *want* us to see who it is who comes to get her."

"Can we just get down there?" Jack interrupted. "We can decide later whether or not to throw her a going-away party."

The winds sweeping over the mountains made the approach trickier than Jack had expected. But Uncle Virge was equal to the task, and soon they had passed over the snow-covered peaks and were flying over the river on their way to the forest below.

"Interesting," Draycos commented, the side of his triangular head pressed against the canopy as he tried to look straight down. "I do not believe I have ever seen water quite so chaotic."

"They're called rapids," Jack told him. "Fast and shallow water running over big rocks just below the surface."

"Actually, the only rapids I spotted are higher up the mountain," Uncle Virge said. "The water along here is really pretty deep."

Jack frowned. "Then what's causing all the white water?" he asked, maneuvering the *Essenay* a few yards to the side to give him a better view of the river.

"Probably have some underwater springs coming in under pressure," Uncle Virge said. "I can't tell for sure—there's a lot of silt churning around down there throwing off my sensors."

"So it's like a free-flowing spa tub?" Jack suggested.

"A free-flowing spa tub for walruses," Uncle Virge said. "That water's mighty cold."

"I wasn't suggesting we take a dip," Jack assured him, turning his attention to the forest. Close up, it looked even darker and more ominous than it had from low orbit. "You spotting any technology at all down there?"

"None," Uncle Virge said. "As far as I can tell, this place is as primitive as you can get in the Orion Arm."

"I guess Gardens of Eden are supposed to be that way," Jack said, shifting his eyes to the more cheerful-looking plain at the forest's southern edge. "Well, let's get to it. The sooner we drop Alison, the sooner we can get back to the job of rescuing Draycos's people."

Given their apparent lack of technology, Jack had half-expected the colony of Erassvas to scatter in panic as the *Essenay* flew past overhead and then settled to the ground a hundred yards from the forest.

Not only did they not scatter, but most of them didn't even bother to look at the big metal bird that had invaded their territory. "Certainly are calm types," Uncle Virge commented as Jack shut the ship's systems down to standby.

"It's better that than the alternative," Jack said. "Draycos, can you see all right?"

"I am fine," the dragon assured him. "And I can hear and smell, as well. If there are any predators nearby, I should detect them before they become a threat."

He pushed against Jack's shirt as he lifted his head from Jack's shoulder. "Or is that not what your question meant?"

"Yes, it was," Jack said, grimacing. Sometimes the dragon read his mind a little *too* well.

Alison was waiting at the air lock, her two travel bags at her sides. "I'm told there are enough traders and mining speculators poking around these colonies that there should be at least one or two Erassvas in the group who speak English," she told Jack as he keyed the outer door. "You might want to let me do the talking, though."

"Be my guest," Jack said, gesturing her to go ahead of him.

"Thanks." She gestured at the tangler Jack had belted at his waist. "And you'll want to keep that in its holster, too."

"It's just a tangler," Jack said.

"With shock rounds?"

"Low-current variety only," Jack assured her. "Just enough juice to stun most beings without damaging them."

"Good," Alison said. "Keep it in its holster anyway."

The Erassvas hadn't been much interested in the *Essenay*'s approach. They were just as uninterested in the two humans walking across the hairlike grass toward them. A couple of the aliens looked up but then returned calmly to their work of picking berries off the colorful vines that grew up the sides of the trees.

"What?" Alison asked.

"What do you mean, what?" Jack growled.

"You were muttering something."

"Oh." Jack hadn't even noticed he was speaking. "I was just thinking."

"About . . . ?"

He gestured at the Erassvas. "I did some berry-picking work a while back. It wasn't very pleasant."

"Ah," Alison said. "Well, in the future, if you want to talk to yourself, talk a little quieter."

Clamping his jaw firmly shut, Jack kept walking. Focusing his attention on the aliens, he tried to force back the memories of the Brummgan slave camp.

The Erassvas were actually quite human looking, if bald, pale-skinned creatures who looked like overweight sumo wrestlers could be said to look human. The twenty children Jack could see were already starting to fill out, while the thirty or forty adults were just plain huge. It was a wonder that their stubby legs could even carry all that weight.

But apparently they could. The Erassvas seemed quite comfortable as they moved back and forth among the trees, picking berries and either eating them right there or else putting them into one of the massive pockets in the heavy greenish-brown robes they wore wrapped kimono-style around their bulk.

Their arms were as strong as their legs, too. Jack watched as an adult weighing at least three hundred pounds hauled himself up on one of the branches, chin-up style, to check out a vine running along the top.

One of the few aliens who had bothered to watch the *Essenay*'s landing looked over again as the visitors approached. He looked them up and down, then detached himself from the group and waddled over to meet them. "A noon sun and satisfied belly to you," he greeted them in heavily accented English. His smile was wide, seeming to split his face in half, and his eyes were half-closed and rather dreamy looking. "I am Hren."

"A noon sun and satisfied belly to you, as well," Alison said, bowing her head toward him. "I'm Alison. This is Jack."

"Fine names for ones so young," Hren said approvingly. "Have you come to join in our midday song?"

Jack glanced at the sun, which wasn't even close to being overhead. The Erassvas apparently scheduled their rest breaks early. "I'm afraid not," Alison said. "I've come to meet up with two others of our people."

"None such has been seen here for many songs," Hren said, some of the dreaminess going out of his eyes as he frowned thoughtfully at her. "Are you sure you do have the right place?"

"I'm sure," Alison said. "But they may have been delayed. Would you mind if I waited here for them?"

"Your company would be as sweet as a *bishti* berry," Hren said. "And since you are here, will you not please join us in our midday song?"

He looked at Jack. "You, especially, would be most heartily welcome."

Jack frowned, throwing a sideways look at Alison. "Me?"

"Yes," Hren said, smiling knowingly. "Because of—" He broke off, waving a hand at Jack's chest. "But come," he went on, looking at Alison. "You all are welcome."

"We *all*?" Alison asked. "Don't you mean we *both*?"

A slight frown creased Hren's face. "Perhaps I use the wrong word," he said. Puckering his lips, gazing out into space as if in deep thought, he reached a wide hand to the front of his robe. For a moment he flapped it in and out as he fanned air onto his torso. Then he let go, leaving it partway open at the neck.

And Jack froze. Starting from the big Erassva's right collarbone and curving around over his shoulder to his back was a wide green-and-brown tattoo. An image of a large, serpentine creature.

Only it wasn't just any serpentine creature. And it wasn't a tattoo.

It was a K'da.

"Thank you for the offer—" Alison was saying.

"Yes," Jack cut her off. "We would be honored to attend your song."

CHAPTER 6

Hren led the way toward the forest, Jack following behind him with Alison bringing up the rear. She hadn't said a word about Jack's abrupt decision, and he didn't have a clue as to what she thought of it. But at the moment, he didn't really care.

There couldn't be K'da here. There *couldn't*. Draycos had told him the refugee fleet was coming from an entirely different arm of the galaxy. It had taken the advance team nearly two years of hyperspace flight to get here.

But if that wasn't a K'da wrapped around Hren's body, it was a terrific imitation.

Had Draycos spotted the tattoo? Jack didn't dare ask, not with Alison right behind him. But he could feel the dragon shifting restlessly, and a couple of times he twitched as sharp claws brushed against his skin. Either Draycos had indeed seen the K'da or else he was a lot more agitated by Jack's decision to join the Erassvas' midday song than even Alison was.

Or maybe he had smelled the other K'da. Did K'da give off an aroma when they were in their two-dimensional form? Somehow, the subject had never come up.

"The Phookas will be gathering in the forest for the morning celebration," Hren said as they reached the other Erassvas.

"Phookas?" Jack asked.

"Our friends," Hren said. He gave Jack another knowing smile, like a child with a secret. "They usually hide when there are strangers near. But you are different. You they won't mind."

He gestured toward a wide path that had been worn in the grass between the trees. "Please. Join them."

"Thank you," Jack said, bowing the way Alison had earlier.

Hren smiled again and headed back to the outer edge of the forest to rejoin his fellow berry pickers. Squaring his shoulders, Jack started toward the path.

And stopped short as Alison grabbed his sleeve. "Wait a second," she said in a low voice. "Are you forgetting what I said about there being big, nasty predators in there?"

"You said the legends put them in the deep parts of the forest," Jack reminded her.

"Legends are sometimes a little off in their geography," she countered. "You want to rely on that tangler of yours to deal with them?"

Jack thought about the K'da spread across his back. "We'll be okay," he said. "Trust me."

She snorted. "I'd love to." Bending down, she popped open one of her travel bags. "Fortunately, that won't be necessary."

And as Jack gaped in astonishment, she pulled a small Corvine 4mm pistol from the bag. "What the—?"

"What the what?" she asked as she pulled out a holster and spare ammo clip and fastened them to her belt. "I like to bunker my bets a little." She checked the Corvine's clip and safety, then settled the weapon into her right hand and picked up the bag with her left. "You can take the other bag."

Jack rolled his eyes. "Oh, *may* I?"

"Don't be snide," she said, starting toward the path. "And stay close."

The path snaked its way through several rows of trees and bushes. The bushes in particular showed how the trail had been formed, their branches bent and broken on both sides by the stream of wide-bodied aliens who had pushed their way through during the past few days or weeks. Passing between two final bushes, Jack and Alison stepped into a large clearing.

And Alison came to a sharp halt. "Mother-of-pearl," she breathed.

Jack nodded in silent agreement. All across the clearing, digging methodically into fallen trees or poking among the bushes or just wandering around in the sun, were K'da.

K'da of all sorts, too. Draycos had mentioned that his people came in many different color combinations. But Jack, with only the one example, had naturally come to think of them as gold-scaled dragons.

This group covered pretty much the whole rainbow. There were K'da with dark red scales, dark green ones, blue ones, and another of the brown-and-green ones like Hren was carrying. One of them, particularly striking to Jack's way of thinking, was all gray with shining silver eyes.

"Jack, they're *dragons,*" Alison whispered. "They're real, live *dragons.*"

Jack nodded. "Sure looks that way."

"But this can't be," she protested. "How could they—I mean, how come no one's ever seen them before?"

Maybe because they're usually wrapped around Erassvas bodies? "Why would they?" he said instead. "You said the only people who come here are miners and traders."

"None of whom would bother with the forests," she conceded reluctantly.

"*And* Hren said they usually hide from strangers," Jack reminded her.

"Right," she agreed, her voice going suddenly thoughtful. "So how come we're different?"

Because Hren's figured out I've got one wrapped around my body, too? "No idea," he lied.

He felt her eyes on him. "If you say so."

"I say so." Jack took a deep breath. This might be risky, but he needed to make sure this wasn't some kind of weird look-alike species. "Stay here. I'm going to get a closer look."

"Oh no, you don't," Alison insisted, bringing her gun up. "They've got teeth and they've got claws, and I'm betting they're every bit as fast as they look."

"They also seem very well fed," Jack pointed out. "Most predators don't kill when they're not hungry."

"Jack—"

"Just stay here and keep an eye on them, okay?" Jack cut her off. Without waiting for more argument, he strode off toward the dragons.

He was halfway there when it belatedly occurred to him that even if they *were* K'da, they might not be civilized. "Draycos?" he muttered, slowing down his pace a little. "What do you think? Are they all right?"

There was no answer. "Draycos?" he repeated. "Come on, buddy, wake up."

"Look at them, Jack," Draycos murmured darkly.

Jack glanced down into his shirt. "What?"

"I said look at them," Draycos said, his voice going even darker. "Lying around, not watching for danger or threat, digging grubs—*grubs*—out of dead wood."

A chill ran up Jack's back. He studied the multicolored dragons as they wandered around, trying to see in them the powerful, clever, deadly poet-warrior that was Draycos. "But they *are* K'da, aren't they?"

"No," Draycos said bitterly. "Not K'da. Not anymore."

"They are *animals.*"

Over the next half hour the Erassvas gradually filtered into the clearing, lowering themselves in wide heaps onto the grass around the edges. Once settled, they began pulling out the berries they'd been stashing away in their pockets.

And as they ate, the group of K'da did a little dance. A nice, simple, pathetic little dance.

"Maybe they're not real K'da," Jack suggested hopefully as he sat against a tree a short distance away from the Erassvas. "You said yourself they don't smell quite right."

"No, they are K'da," Draycos told him. His earlier anger and bitterness had passed, leaving an even more disturbing emptiness behind. "The change in odor is most likely a result of their diet. A diet of *grubs.*"

Jack winced. There was something about that part in particular that seemed to really bother his partner. Was it because these K'da were no longer true hunters? "Well, at least we now know where you came from," Jack said. "The race of slavers who kidnapped your people all those years ago must have missed a few."

Draycos snorted, a breath of hot air brushing across Jack's chest. "If this was our original home, then our storytellers are liars," he said flatly. "These Erassvas are hardly the proud and noble Dhghem spoken of in so many songs. They are primitives. And they are primitives by choice."

Jack looked over at the robed mounds of flesh munching placidly away at their handfuls of berries. Draycos was right, of course. The Erassvas had clearly had enough contact with the rest of the Orion Arm to learn English, and yet didn't have a single bit of the galactic community's technology. "Some people like their lives just the way they are," he offered.

"And they have no ambition?" Draycos bit out. "No self-pride? No desire for a better life for themselves and their offspring?" His tongue flicked out, tickling briefly against Jack's skin. "What happens here when there is rain or snow? What happens when there is disease or predator attack?"

Jack suppressed a sigh. There were counterarguments for each of those, of course. Some people didn't mind getting wet, while others didn't have much trouble with disease or predators.

But then, this wasn't really about the Erassvas. "Okay, so the K'da here aren't as sophisticated as you are," he said as soothingly as he could. "That doesn't mean anything. There are backwoods cultures all over the Orion Arm that are still composed of intelligent, rational beings."

Draycos didn't answer. "Draycos?" Jack prompted. "Come on, buddy. It's not that bad."

Still no answer. With a sigh, Jack gave up.

A motion to his left caught his eye, and he looked up as Alison came out of the trees into the clearing. "Enjoying the show?" she asked, sitting down beside him.

"Actually, dance never really did much for me," he said. "How's your head count going?"

"Finished, I think," she said. "Including children, there seem to be about two hundred Erassvas in this particular troop. About half of them are working the vines on the far side of those bushes."

"They don't like the dancing?"

She shrugged. "Maybe the Phookas will do a second show. Speaking of which, I count fifty of them, including the six who are across with the other group."

Which wouldn't include any who might be currently riding various hosts' bodies. But Jack couldn't exactly point that out. "I don't see any young Phookas," he said instead. "You suppose all of the ones here are male?"

"You're welcome to try to find out," Alison said dryly. "Me, I'm staying here. Let me see that tattoo of yours."

The sudden change in subject caught Jack by surprise. "What?"

"Your tattoo," she said patiently. "You didn't have it taken off, did you?"

There was, unfortunately, no way around it. Suppressing a grimace, Jack unfastened his shirt and pulled it open, exposing Draycos's head to view.

"Interesting," she said, studying Jack's shoulder and then looking over at the performing K'da. She looked back at Draycos, back at the K'da. "You realize your tattoo is the spitting image of a Phooka?"

"Really?" Jack asked, feigning surprise. He looked cross-eyed down at his shoulder, as if trying to get a good view of the image there. "Yeah, there *is* some resemblance, isn't there?"

"Resemblance, nothing," she countered. "It's the same head, same snout, same scale pattern. You've even got a sort of flattened version of that spiny crest that goes over their heads and down their backs."

"I'll take your word for it," Jack said, still pretending he couldn't quite focus on his tattoo. "Huh. That's funny."

"More than just funny," Alison said. "Where did you say you got that done?"

"I didn't say," Jack said. "If you must know, it was in a little shop in New Paris on Gaullia."

"Mm," Alison said, looking again at the dancing K'da. "I wonder how the artist could have known about Phookas."

"Maybe he knows some Erassvas," Jack said. This really wasn't a topic he wanted to get into. "Or maybe he just had a good book about dragons. So where are your friends?"

"My friends?"

"The people you said you'd be rendezvousing with."

"Oh. Them." Alison peered up at the small patches of sky

that could be seen through the tangle of tree branches. "Not here, obviously."

"No kidding," Jack said. "You sure you've got the right place?"

"This is definitely it," she assured him. "They could just be late." She made a face. "Or *they* could have gone to the wrong spot."

"I don't suppose you thought to bring a comm clip."

"Actually, I did," she said, a little coolly. "And I've already tried. If they're here, they must be out of range."

"How about we run it through the *Essenay*'s comm?" Jack suggested. "It's got a lot more range. In fact, why don't we just go ahead and pop the ship into orbit? That way we can cover half the planet at a single gulp."

"Worth a try," Alison agreed, getting to her feet and brushing some stray leaves off her jeans. "Is there any trick to starting up the engines?"

"There's no trick," Jack said. "There's also no need." He tapped his comm clip. "Unc—computer?"

"Computer," Uncle Virge's voice came back instantly.

"I need you to take the ship into low orbit and do an ID broadcast," Jack said. "Alison's comm clip frequency is—" He looked up at her and raised his eyebrows.

"Why don't I just go aboard and plug it in?" she suggested. "I don't like giving comm clip info to strangers."

"And *I* don't like strangers alone in my ship," Jack countered. "Just give me the frequency, okay?"

"Fine," she said crossly, digging a comm clip from inside her shirt and tossing it to him. "Whatever."

Jack caught it and peered at the markings on the back. "Okay, here it is." He read off the frequency and pattern specs. "Start with a parabolic upper-atmosphere dip," he went on, tossing the clip back to Alison. "If you don't get an answer, expand it to a complete orbit."

"Acknowledged," Uncle Virge said hesitantly. "With all due respect, Master Jack—"

"Carry out your instructions," Jack cut him off. Normal P/S computers never argued with their owners. Uncle Virge, in contrast, never seemed to do anything but. Even if Alison hadn't been standing right there listening, Jack was in no mood to listen to the computer personality's objections. "Alison, what message should he send?"

"Just the word 'winderlake,' " she said. "If he hears the response 'harborlight,' mark the location and let me know."

"You get that?" Jack asked Uncle Virge.

"Acknowledged."

"Then get going." Jack tapped off the comm clip and gestured to the ground beside him. "Might as well get comfortable," he told Alison. "This could take a while. You tried the berries yet?"

"No, and I don't think you should, either," she said, reluctantly sitting down again. "There's something about the Erassvas' eyes that weirds me out a little."

"Yeah, I noticed that, too," Jack said. "You think there's some kind of mild narcotic in the berries?"

"Or maybe not so mild," Alison said. "And if it's strong enough to affect people their size, it would probably kill either of us. If you're hungry, I've got ration bars in my bag."

"Maybe later." Beyond the trees, he heard the hum as the *Essenay* lifted into the sky. "What are you going to do if they're not here?"

She shrugged. "Wait, I guess," she said. "That's why I bought all that camping gear." She gestured at her bags. "You don't have to wait with me if you don't want to."

"I don't, and I wasn't planning to," Jack said, feeling a twinge of guilt. He knew how Draycos would feel about abandoning a companion in the middle of nowhere, even a companion as loosely connected as Alison. "But I might stick around another day or two, anyway."

"Well, don't mess up your schedule just for me," she said. "Ah—show's over." She gestured toward the center of the clearing, where the Phookas had finished their dance and were wandering away back into the forest. "Let's see if the rest of the Erassvas come in for a second performance."

"Looks to me like the cast is leaving the stage," Jack said. "Maybe there's a dinner theater later for the—"

"Jack!" Uncle Virge's voice came suddenly from the comm clip. "Incoming ships: one Kapstan long-range transport and two Djinn-90 pursuit fighters."

Jack's breath caught in his throat. *Djinn-90s?* "Get out of there," he snapped. "Go to ground and hide."

"Too late—they see me," Uncle Virge said grimly. "I'm getting a signal—"

There was the click of a relay. "Hello, Jack Morgan," a dark voice said. "And your slippery uncle Virgil Morgan, too, I presume?"

Jack's first impulse was to lie, to use all of Uncle Virgil's training to convince them that they had the wrong person. The *Essenay* was running under a false ID, after all. Maybe they weren't really sure it was him.

But no. Neverlin's allies had had plenty of opportunity at Brum-a-drum to record the *Essenay*'s description and parameters. They knew they had the right ship.

And that voice wasn't showing a single scrap of doubt. Lying about it would just be a waste of effort. "Uncle's not here at the moment," Jack said instead. "Can I take a message?"

"Ah," the voice said. "So you're the boy who's been causing my friend Mr. Neverlin such trouble."

"Mr. Neverlin hasn't exactly been giving me a free ride, either," Jack countered. "And you are . . . ?"

"Colonel Maximus Frost of the Malison Ring," the voice said. "And I'm very much looking forward to meeting you."

CHAPTER 7

The comm clip went silent. Jack found himself staring down at nothing, his throat tight, his stomach twisting into a knot of fear and anger.

It couldn't be. How could the mercenaries possibly have tracked the *Essenay* across the Orion Arm to this fifth-rate planet? How could they possibly have known where to find him and Alison?

Alison.

Alison, who'd been so conveniently on the scene to spring him from their trap. Alison, who'd noted and even commented on the *Essenay's* InterWorld transmitter.

Alison, who'd talked him into coming to this nice little out-of-the-way system in the first place. A place where he and Draycos and the *Essenay* could quietly disappear.

Jack turned to look at her, expecting to see her Corvine pistol leveled at his stomach, a triumphant smile on her face.

But the gun wasn't pointed at him. And her face was as taut and horrified as he'd ever seen it. "Alison?" he asked carefully.

She twitched; and as if a mask had suddenly dropped into

place, the fear vanished from her expression. "I think we've got trouble," she said.

"No kidding," Jack growled, scrambling to his feet. Dodging between and around the strolling Erassvas, he sprinted back down the path to the edge of the forest.

It was as bad as he'd expected. In the distance over the mountains he could see the *Essenay* swooping and dodging through groups of wispy clouds. The two Djinn-90s were right on its tail, their lasers flashing as they tried to bring it down. "Uncle Virge?" he called. "How are you doing?"

"I'm open to suggestions," the computer's voice came back.

"Try a *mirm preah* maneuver," Draycos said, his head rising from Jack's skin and pressing against his shirt as the dragon gazed out at the distant battle. "Break to your right . . . *now.*"

The *Essenay* twisted sideways, dipping lower toward the mountains below. The two pursuit fighters shifted course to stay on it, and then suddenly the *Essenay*'s nose dropped and the ship dived straight down.

Jack caught his breath. But even as the Djinn-90s dived after him, Uncle Virge brought the nose sharply up again and spun the ship nearly a hundred eighty degrees around to point straight back at his attackers.

They reacted instantly, wrenching away to either side to avoid ramming at full speed into the larger ship. But for one of them it was too late. A double burst from the *Essenay*'s meteor-defense lasers caught it squarely in the nose as it maneuvered, shattering it into a ball of flame. The other fighter was luckier, managing to dodge away from the short-range missile Uncle

Virge fired at it. The *Essenay*'s lasers flashed at it as it fled, but before they could get a good target-lock the Djinn-90 vanished out of sight behind one of the mountain peaks.

"One down," Uncle Virge said as the *Essenay*'s path curved around toward the forest. "Let's see if I can get back there and pick you up before he comes around the other side."

"We're ready," Jack said. There was the rustling of bushes behind him, and he glanced over his shoulder to see Alison jog into view. "Make it fast."

But Uncle Virge didn't make it fast. In fact, he didn't make it at all.

It happened all at once, with perfect timing and coordination. From high in the sky the Kapstan transport Uncle Virge had mentioned earlier suddenly dropped into view through the clouds, the sun glinting off its stubby wings, its belly weapons raining laser and particle-beam fire down on the *Essenay*. At the same time, the remaining Djinn-90 reappeared from behind the mountains, zigzagging through the peaks as it charged toward the *Essenay*'s right flank.

Two armed ships . . . and the *Essenay* was caught between them.

Jack clenched his hands into fists, vaguely aware of Draycos's claws tightening reflexively against his skin. Uncle Virge was trapped like a rat in a cage. If he didn't surrender, and fast, the two attackers would cut the ship in half.

"The Saga of Fristra," Draycos said suddenly, his head melting back onto Jack's skin. "*Min kly,* then the Saga of Fristra."

Jack blinked. "What—?"

"Jack?" Alison demanded as she came up beside him. She peered up at the mountains, shading her eyes with her hand. "Uh-oh."

"*Min kly,* then Fristra," Uncle Virge acknowledged, his voice tight. "See you, Jack lad."

"What's a *min kly*?" Alison asked, throwing a frown at Jack's comm clip.

Jack was still trying to think up a good answer to that when the *Essenay* twisted suddenly like a hooked fish, spun to the side, and raked the incoming Djinn-90 with a full salvo from its lasers. Half-hidden by the brilliant flashes, a pair of missiles arrowed out in a one-two punch.

The first missile exploded against the side of the mountain as the fighter passed, blanketing the attacker in a flow of shattered ice and rock. The second arced straight into the middle of the avalanche. There was another ball of flame, and now only the Kapstan was left.

But the maneuver had cost the *Essenay* dearly. Its sideways skid had robbed it of most of its forward momentum, and Jack could see Uncle Virge fighting for stability in the churning mountain winds. Even as the transport dropped lower, its attack intensifying, the *Essenay* rolled over and plummeted toward the cliffs below. It disappeared behind a peak—

And there was one final violent explosion. The Kapstan veered sharply away, bouncing as it was buffeted by the blast.

Jack stared at the fading light and smoke, his pulse pounding in his ears. "Uncle Virge?" he whispered toward his comm clip. "Uncle Virge?"

There was no answer. In the distance, the Kapstan's pilot

had gotten the transport back under control and returned to the area above the final explosion's fading glow. Slowly, it circled the area, its weapons silent.

Which could only mean that Colonel Frost no longer had anything to shoot at.

Dimly, Jack felt his muscles starting to shake, his vision blurring with tears. Uncle Virge, the *Essenay,* everything he'd known since he was three years old—it couldn't all be gone. Not here. Not now.

He jerked violently as a hand suddenly touched his shoulder. He turned, trying to see through the tears. "Come on," Alison said quietly.

"Where?" Jack asked, his voice quavering. It was a sign of weakness Uncle Virgil had always hated, but Jack no longer cared.

"Into the forest," Alison said. "We have to get under cover."

"Why?"

"Because they'll be coming here next," she said patiently. Her face was tight, and he could see an edge of fear lurking at the corners of her eyes. But her voice was calm and determined. "They'll have tracked the transmission from your comm clip."

"So what?" Jack demanded bitterly.

"So I don't know about you, but I'm not ready to give up just yet," she countered, some of her control starting to crack.

Jack shook his head. "It's finished, Alison," he said quietly. More finished than she would ever know, in fact. Jack, Draycos, the K'da and Shontine—they were all dead.

"Snap out of it," Alison ordered tartly, slapping him none too lightly across the back of his head. "Okay, your ship's gone. I'm sorry. But it's a long way from being finished. My friends—remember? My friends are coming to get me."

Jack swiped at his eyes with his sleeve, a cautious flicker of hope stirring inside him. "Okay," he said, taking a deep breath. "I'm all right."

"That's better," Alison said. "Come on."

She got a grip on his arm and started pulling him back toward the path. "Where are we going?" Jack asked.

"I've got camping gear in my travel bags, enough for a couple of weeks if we're careful," she said. "We break it out, pack it for travel, and find someplace to hole up."

"What if they find us?"

"Then we do what we can," she said. "It's still better than being caught out here in the open."

Jack took another deep breath. She was right, of course. But the shock of losing the *Essenay* still pressed like a strangle cord across his mind. It was hard to think about anything else, even survival.

But Draycos wouldn't be nearly so handicapped. If Jack could just talk with him a moment . . .

They reached the first turn in the path. "Go ahead and start packing," Jack told Alison, waving her ahead as he slowed down. "I need to do something first."

She frowned. "Like what?"

"It'll just take a second," he promised. "Go on; get going."

She hesitated, then nodded. "All right, but hurry. And stay under the trees."

She turned and disappeared around the turn. "Probably thinks I need to cry about the *Essenay*," he muttered, looking down at Draycos.

"Jack—"

"No, it's all right," Jack cut him off. "The *Essenay* was just a thing. In the great grand scheme, things aren't important." He swiped at his eyes again. "And Uncle Virge was just a computer program. I did my crying for the real Uncle Virgil a year ago."

"I understand," Draycos said. "However—"

"Jack?" Alison's voice wafted over the bushes. "Come on, move it."

"Coming," Jack called back. "What I need to know right now," he said, lowering his voice again, "is whether or not it's safe for us to stay with Alison."

"Yes," Draycos said without hesitation. "I do not know why, but I believe we can trust her. At least, for the moment."

Which wasn't to say she wasn't working some private agenda of her own, Jack reminded himself. Somewhere along the line, that agenda could easily branch off from his.

Still, there *had* been that look on her face when Colonel Frost came on the comm. She apparently didn't want to see him any more than Jack did. "Close enough," he told the dragon, starting forward again. "Let's do it."

"Jack—"

"Later," Jack said as he reached the clearing and again threaded his way through the lethargic Erassvas.

Alison was busily stuffing the contents of the two travel bags into a pair of lightweight backpacks when he reached her. "You get your booby trap set?" she asked.

"Booby trap?"

"Isn't that what you stayed behind for?" she asked, frowning up at him briefly before returning to her sorting. "To slow them down a little?"

"I was going to," Jack lied. Clearly, his brain was still only working at half speed. "But I figured the Erassvas might get caught before Frost's thugs got here."

"Probably right," she conceded. "Maybe we can do something further on. Give me a hand."

"Sure." Jack dropped to his knees and started sorting a pack of ration bars into the two bags.

And as he did so, he felt a breath of hot air on the back of his neck. Twisting his head around, he found himself nose to muzzle with the gray-scaled K'da he'd noticed earlier.

Out of the corner of his eye he saw Alison snatch her gun from its holster. "Easy," he said quickly. For a long moment the silvery eyes stared into his, as if the K'da was trying to work out who exactly this new creature was and what it was doing in its nice quiet forest. Then, the eyes blinked slowly, and the head turned away, and the K'da wandered off.

Alison let her breath out in a huff. "I sure hope you're right about them being well fed," she said, setting the gun down on the grass beside her.

Jack gazed at the gray dragon as it sniffed along the edge of a fallen tree, an uncomfortable feeling stirring inside him. If Frost was one of Neverlin's partners, he would know all about K'da. Including the fact that Jack had one with him.

Which meant that when Frost and his men saw the Erassvas and their little group of Phookas . . .

"You think we can get this done *today*?" Alison's voice cut into Jack's musings.

"Sorry." Shaking the thought away, he got back to his packing.

But the thought refused to leave. Frost, Neverlin, the K'da . . . and by the time Jack and Alison had the backpacks sealed, he knew what he had to do.

"Okay," Alison said, hoisting her pack onto her shoulders and bouncing it once to settle it into place. "I thought we'd head west to the foothills we saw from orbit. They looked pretty rocky—there should be some caves in there where we can hole up."

"Sounds good," Jack said, bracing himself. Alison was not going to like this at all. "But we're taking the Phookas with us."

To his mild surprise, she didn't explode in anger or disbelief. She just stood there, one hand gripping her backpack strap, staring at him. "And how exactly do you propose we do that?"

It was, Jack decided, a very good question. Unfortunately, he hadn't yet come up with an answer for it. "I'll go talk to Hren," he said, taking a couple of steps back and turning around. He spotted the big Erassva at the far side of the clearing and headed in that direction.

"Jack, what are you doing?" Draycos asked from his shoulder.

"You want to leave your fellow K'da to the mercenaries?" Jack asked.

"Perhaps they would be better off dead," Draycos muttered, his voice dark.

Jack looked down at him. "You really believe that?"

Draycos sighed, a touch of warm dragon breath across Jack's chest. "No, of course not," he said reluctantly. "What is your plan?"

"Still working on it," Jack said between clenched teeth. Fifty K'da wandering around, plus however many were currently riding their Erassva hosts. Call it sixty or seventy. If he wanted all the K'da, that meant sixty or seventy Erassva hosts as well, all of them bulling their way through the forest. It would leave a trail Frost's men could follow in their sleep.

Unless . . . "Draycos, how long does a K'da have to stay on his host?" he asked.

"He can stay on as long as he wishes," Draycos said, sounding puzzled.

"I know he *can*," Jack said. "But how long does he *have* to? An hour? Two hours?"

"No more than an hour to fully recover," Draycos said, suddenly thoughtful. "Perhaps less."

"So that means each Erassva should be able to carry seven K'da," Jack said, trying to work it out in his still-sluggish mind. "One hour on, six hours off."

"Yes, that may work," Draycos said slowly. "Though it would be safer to include a margin of error."

"Okay, we'll put six with each Erassva then," Jack agreed. "Any idea how many there are?"

"Sixty," Draycos said. "I counted them."

"So we'll need ten Erassvas," Jack concluded. "Unless you think I should take a few of them myself."

"We would still need ten Erassvas," Draycos said. "Besides, I must be free to act at any time."

"Point," Jack agreed with a shiver. Even with a poet-warrior of the K'da on their side, the odds here weren't looking very good.

"Of course, that also assumes we can make the Phookas understand all this," Draycos went on. "That may prove difficult."

"Maybe Hren can help," Jack suggested. "They must have some way of communicating with them."

"Perhaps," Draycos muttered. "Assuming Hren himself understands."

CHAPTER 8

Hren, of course, didn't.

"You want to take our *Phookas*?" the big Erassva asked, blinking his eyes a half-dozen times as he stared at Jack. "But why?"

"Because there are bad men who want to hurt them," Jack said for the third time. "I want to take them into the forest where they'll be safer."

"But why would anyone want to hurt them?" the big Erassva persisted, still blinking. "They don't hurt anyone."

"I know that," Jack said. "As I said, these are bad men."

One of Hren's hands slipped into his robe and began restlessly stroking his shoulder where the K'da head draped over his skin. "Yet you are a good man?"

"I try," Jack said, feeling sweat collecting beneath his collar. They didn't have time for this. "You have to believe me when I say I care as much about your Phookas as you do."

Hren shook his head slowly. "They cannot go alone," he said, his forehead creased with concentration. "Not even with you."

"Yes, I know," Jack said. "I'll also need ten Erassvas to come with us. Maybe you'd be willing to be one of them?"

For a long moment Hren stood without speaking, still stroking his K'da as he gazed out into space. Then, abruptly, the look of concentration disappeared. "Then we must go at once," he said, hauling his bulk to his feet. "I will gather the other"—he held out his hands, frowning hard at the fingers—"the other nine," he concluded. "We will meet you there." He pointed to the far side of the clearing, where Jack could see the entrance to another path.

"Thank you," Jack said. "One other thing. My friend Alison must not be allowed to see how the Phookas come onto and off of your skin."

"Why not?"

"Because she won't understand," Jack told him. "The whole thing may terrify her, and cause her to abandon us and run off. We can't let that happen, for her sake as well as ours. Can you make sure the Phookas and other Erassvas understand that?"

Hren eyed Jack closely. "You have many secrets, young Jack," he said. "Perhaps too many. Very well. I will make the arrangements."

Alison was still standing where Jack had left her. "Well?"

"He's coming," Jack said, grabbing his pack and hoisting it onto his back. Settling it in place, he walked over to a pair of K'da who were probing with their muzzles at the base of a patch of reedy plants. "And he's bringing a few more of the Erassvas to help."

"To help with what?" she called after him. "Breaking trail?"

"They'll meet us at that path," Jack said, ignoring the comment. The two K'da, he saw now, were busily gobbling down some small lizards they'd flushed from the reeds. "Okay, Phookas," he said soothingly, waving his hands in a sweeping motion that probably looked as ridiculous as it felt. "Time to go. Come on—that way."

The two dragons paused in their meal long enough to bring their heads up and look blankly at him. Then, without budging an inch, they returned their attention to the lizards. "Draycos?" Jack muttered. "You people have a 'mush' command or something?"

"Try pulling gently against their crests, at the point where they descend from the back of the head down the neck," Draycos suggested.

"Okay," Jack said doubtfully. Stepping between the two K'da, he got a hand behind each of their crests. Trying not to think about Uncle Virgil's old warning about never bothering a dog when it was eating, he gingerly applied some pressure.

The two K'da looked up again, and Jack had the distinct feeling that they were mildly surprised at the liberty he was taking with them. But neither seemed inclined to run or, more important, to bite.

"A little harder," Draycos said.

Setting his teeth, Jack did so. This time, to his amazement, the K'da stood upright and began walking in the direction he was pulling. "I'll be fraggled," he muttered, keeping the pressure steady as he settled in between them.

"So that's the technique, huh?" Alison said from behind him.

"It'll do for a start," Jack said, looking around. Unfortunately, it was going to take way too long to get sixty K'da moving this way. "What we need is the head Phooka," he said, searching his memory. Uncle Virgil had often used animal and nature examples and analogies in his training. "The bellwether, I think it's called."

"The one everyone else follows," Alison said, nodding. "Great. Any idea how we figure out which one that is?"

"Give me a minute," Jack said, doing a slow turn to give Draycos a good look. "Mm?" he murmured toward his shoulder.

"There," Draycos murmured, his tongue lifting slightly from Jack's skin to point at a large emerald green K'da with three smaller dragons of different colors following closely behind him. "Try him."

"Let's try him," Jack said, pointing to the green dragon.

"I'll go," Alison volunteered. "You might as well get those two on the path."

She headed off. "Jack, I must speak to you," Draycos said as the boy got his two K'da moving again. "We cannot follow Alison's plan of hiding in the foothills."

"Why not?" Jack asked.

Draycos hesitated. "Because there is a chance the *Essenay* is still intact and functional."

Jack felt his chest tighten. "Why didn't you say so before?" he demanded.

"I tried, but you gave me no opportunity," the dragon said.

"Do you remember my telling Uncle Virge to use the Saga of Fristra?"

Jack nodded. "You called out one of your fancy K'da maneuvers, then said that."

"Correct," Draycos said. "Fristra was a young Shontin who was trapped by enemies at the edge of a grassy cliff. With no other hope of escape, he set fire to the grass, and under cover of the smoke leaped into the river below."

"That last explosion, and then the ship disappeared," Jack said slowly, thinking back. "And he was just about over the river, wasn't he?"

"Yes," Draycos said. "The questions are two. First, could the *Essenay* survive such a dive into the water? And second, would it be able to conceal itself afterward from the transport's sensors?"

"Yes to the first, I think," Jack said, his pulse pounding with new hope. He should have known Uncle Virge wouldn't have gone so easily. "The *Essenay* was pretty tough to begin with, and Uncle Virgil put a lot of money into building it up. And I'd say a probable yes to the second, too. You've seen the chameleon hull-wrap in action. It's as close to invisibility as you can get."

"Yes, I know," Draycos said. "My question was whether the hull-wrap would work in water, or whether there would be some sort of bubble effect that would be detected."

"No idea," Jack admitted. They reached the edge of the clearing and he shifted grips on his two K'da to guide them through the opening in the bushes. "As far as I know, Uncle Virgil never tried hiding in water. But remember how busy that river is. All that churning white water and floating silt would work in his favor."

"Agreed," Draycos said. "Then we are left with only the question of what precisely Uncle Virge will do once Colonel Frost turns his attention to us."

"Well, he won't just charge to the rescue, that's for sure," Jack said, chewing at his lower lip. "That Kapstan can probably outgun him four to one. My guess is that he'll stay underwater and try to move downriver."

He looked down at his chest. "Which is why you don't want to hole up in the foothills, isn't it?" he said with sudden understanding. "You want us to make for the river and try to link up with the *Essenay* there."

"Exactly," Draycos said. "Provided Alison's friends don't arrive first, of course."

"Yeah, well, I'm not going to hold my breath on that one," Jack said grimly, trying to remember the geography they'd seen on their way in. The river cut straight through the middle of the forest, which meant that as long as they kept going north they were bound to hit it.

That was the good news. The bad news was that he also remembered it being a good fifty-mile trek.

Fifty miles of unknown territory and unknown dangers, with sixty barely sentient K'da and ten wide-bodied Erassvas to drag along with them.

"Gangway." Alison's voice came from behind him. Jack turned, and saw her guide the green dragon through the bushes.

And behind them in more or less single file was the rest of the herd.

The herd. Jack felt an unpleasant shiver run through him. Draycos had so often pointed out what a proud and noble people the K'da were. Yet here, through some horrible twist of fate, they'd been reduced to something no better than animals.

Maybe Draycos had been right. Maybe they *would* be better off dead.

"Well?" Alison prompted.

Jack took a deep breath. "Right," he said. Stepping to the other side of the green dragon, Jack got a grip on the K'da's crest. "Let's go."

The first hundred yards were easy. The Erassvas had obviously been all through this area; the path meandered around in what Jack was starting to realize was typical Erassva fashion. A dozen somewhat narrower trails led off the main path in various directions where one or two of the big aliens had gone exploring for berries and other food.

At the end of that hundred yards, though, the trail came to an abrupt halt at the edge of a twenty-foot cliff. "Well, we needed to head west sometime anyway," Alison said as she and Jack surveyed the drop-off. "Let's go back to that last left-hand bunny trail and see how far it'll take us."

"Sounds good," Jack agreed. He hadn't had a chance yet to tell her about the change in their travel plans, but there would be time for that once they'd gotten past this cliff. "Go ahead and check it out. I'll bring Greenie and follow—"

"Jack?" Colonel Frost's voice came suddenly from his left shoulder. "Can you hear me?"

"Don't answer," Alison said sharply.

"I know," Jack said, double-checking that the comm clip's transmitter was still off.

"I know you can hear me, Jack," Frost went on. "I'm sorry about your uncle—I really am. Please believe me when I say that we really did want him alive. But he took one gamble too many. I'm afraid he and your ship are both gone."

Jack set his teeth firmly down on his tongue. Frost was trying to goad him into talking, he knew, hoping for some anguished cry of anger or denial or defiance that could be traced.

But he wasn't going to fall for it. Draycos's trick had worked, he told himself firmly, and the *Essenay* was safe. It had to be.

"Just one of the many hazards of carrying missiles aboard a ship that was never designed for them," Frost said. "Those were highly illegal for you to have, by the way."

Jack looked surreptitiously at Alison. She was gazing back at him, a thoughtful look on her face that he didn't care for at all.

"Sadly, there's nothing any of us can do about that now," Frost said. "Except, of course, to make sure you and your K'da don't suffer his same fate."

"Better turn it off," Alison said. "Out here in the middle of nowhere, even electronics as small as a comm clip can sometimes be detected."

"Yeah, that part of Sergeant Grisko's training I remember," Jack said. He switched off the comm clip, cutting Frost off in midsentence. "We'd better get out of here."

"Right," Alison said. "You take Greenie and get everybody

moving down the path. I'll hang back a ways and play rear guard."

Beneath Jack's shirt, K'da claws brushed lightly but urgently at Jack's skin. "Better idea: you take them," he said, thinking fast. "Now that we're out of the main Erassva stomping grounds, I can go ahead and set that booby trap I was going to use earlier."

A slight frown creased her forehead, but she nodded. "Okay, but don't be too long," she said. Getting a grip on the green K'da's crest, she turned him around and started maneuvering her way back though the crowd of K'da and Erassvas that had gathered behind them.

"Is something wrong?" Hren asked as Alison and Greenie reached the side trail and started along it. He didn't seem particularly worried, merely curious.

"A small change in direction," Jack assured him as he passed the other. "Stay with Alison and help her keep the Phookas together."

"I will," Hren promised.

Jack reached the back of the crowd and continued on. A wide S-curve later he was out of their sight. "Okay, buddy, we're on," he murmured.

There was a surge of weight against his shoulders, and Draycos leaped out of his shirt. "What is the plan?" the dragon asked, his gold scales glistening in the sunlight filtering through the mass of branches high above them.

"The plan is to keep Frost and his band of pirates from catching us," Jack told him grimly. "I just wish I really had something to use as a booby trap, like Alison thinks I have."

"You do," Draycos said. "You have me."

"Yeah, I figured you'd say that," Jack said grimly. "Problem is, they know about you now. That means no more sneak attacks."

"Perhaps," Draycos said calmly. He rose partially up on his hind legs, his neck stretching upward as he tried to look past the bushes and branches. His tongue flicked in and out of his mouth a few times as he smelled the air. "I may yet have a few surprises for them. What will you do while I am gone?"

Jack made a face at the other's implied order that he stay back here where it would be safer. But Draycos was right. He hardly needed Jack's help at this sort of thing, and the boy would just be in the way. "I thought I'd try to hide the spot where we left the path," he said.

"Good," Draycos said. "I will be as quick as I can."

Turning, he headed back toward the clearing, moving like a whisper of breeze through the grass and bushes.

Taking a deep breath, Jack moved to the side of the path and began gathering loose branches and small shrubs to hide their path. "Warrior's luck," he murmured to the empty air.

CHAPTER 9

Like most forests Draycos had seen, the ground here was covered with grasses, reeds, and dead leaves. Even Jack and Alison, who were trying to be quiet, had made considerable noise as they'd worked their way through the undergrowth. The Erassvas, who seemed to have no concept of the danger they were in, had sounded more like a set of brush-clearing machines.

Draycos himself knew several techniques for moving quietly. Trouble was, most of them involved slow stalking and right now he needed speed as much as he did silence.

Fortunately, with the trees as close together as these were, there were ways of traveling that would allow him to have both.

He leaped straight upward, grabbing onto the trunk of the nearest tree with his claws. His next leap cleared a row of bushes and landed him on a thick branch two trees over. He trotted along that branch to the trunk, then out again along another even thicker branch until he had a clear path to the next tree.

Two minutes and eleven leaps later, he had made it back to the edge of the clearing.

He was just in time. At the far side, six men in combat suits were marching in a two-by-two formation along the path Jack and Alison had first taken into the forest. As they reached the clearing, their guns swept warningly across the lounging Erass-vas. Fortunately, the aliens made no sudden moves, hostile or otherwise. A few of them gazed curiously at the invaders, but most ignored them completely.

Draycos eased his way a little farther around the side of the tree trunk he was clinging to, studying the mercenaries as they headed for the clearing's center. They were walking openly, al-most carelessly, with no attempt at caution or concealment.

Yet Arthur Neverlin knew Draycos had survived the Iota Klestis ambush. More than that, he'd seen the K'da poet-warrior in action. Could he have failed to warn Colonel Frost?

Draycos's jaws cracked open in a tight smile. No, of course Frost knew. Those six soldiers marching across the clearing weren't the attack force at all.

They were the bait.

Draycos took another, more careful look. This time he saw them: two pairs of camouflaged soldiers slipping quietly through the forest a few feet outside the edges of the clearing, one pair on each flank. An attacker careless enough to throw himself at the men in the clearing would find himself in a deadly crossfire.

The six mercenaries reached the center of the clearing and stopped, looking around and quietly talking among themselves. The two outrider pairs stopped, too, standing back-to-back and watching for trouble.

Back-to-back was a good defensive formation. Unfortunately for them, Draycos also knew how to deal with that one. Fixing their locations in his mind, he started to climb farther up the tree.

And then, from behind him came a soft crunch of leaves.

He twisted his head around, legs tensing for a powerful thrust that would shove him away from the tree and out of the line of fire.

But it wasn't a Malison Ring soldier back there. Nor was it Jack or Alison.

It was one of the K'da.

Draycos hissed between his teeth. He'd noticed this particular K'da the minute Jack had entered the clearing earlier. She was beautiful and graceful, with the gray scales he'd always wished he'd been born with. She reminded him strongly of one of his best friends when he was growing up, a friend named Taneem who had later died in a Valahgua attack.

But Taneem had been smart and funny and kind. The bright silver eyes now turned up toward him held none of those qualities.

He took another look around the side of the tree. The soldiers were still talking together, but he knew that wouldn't last much longer. If he didn't go now, he wouldn't have time to get into position once they all started moving again.

He turned back to the gray K'da. She was still watching him, her head cocked slightly to the side as if trying to work out why in the world this golden stranger was hanging on to a tree when all the really tasty grubs were on the ground. If Draycos headed off to the attack, the main group of soldiers would reach her before he could get back.

And bait or not, they certainly had live ammunition in their weapons.

Perhaps they would be better off dead. Draycos had said that earlier to Jack, and he was still wincing at the callousness of his words. If they had been any other species of nonsentient animal, he would certainly have treated them with compassion and care. How could he do less for his own people?

Even if they were his people in name only?

Climbing down the tree, he padded as quietly as he could to the silver female's side. "We have to go," he said.

Her silver eyes blinked at him, but otherwise there was no response. "We have to go," Draycos tried again, switching this time to the K'da language. Still nothing.

With a sigh, he flipped his slender tail up to catch her at the spot behind her crest that he'd shown Jack. "Come," he said, and started down the path.

He'd expected her to resist. To his mild surprise, she followed him willingly.

Early in their relationship, before Draycos had discouraged such talk, Jack had occasionally referred to him as his pet dragon. Now, it seemed, Draycos had picked up a pet dragon of his own.

They reached the left-hand path where Alison had taken the group, to find that the opening had vanished behind a wall of freshly cut bushes supported by a few large branches. Clearly, Jack had been busy in his absence.

Still, a good woodland tracker would have little trouble spotting the camouflage. Draycos would have to do something about that. "Go—over the top," he instructed the silver K'da, unhooking his tail from her crest. "Go on—jump."

She frowned, peering closely at his eyes. "Jump over the barrier and join the others," he repeated, fighting hard to keep his voice steady. The clock was counting down here, and he still had a lot of work to do. "Go on. *Go.*"

Her frown cleared. With an effortless bound, she leaped over Jack's barrier, landing beyond it with a crunch of grass and leaves that made Draycos wince. But at least she was gone.

A few feet down the main path another side path headed off to the right. Draycos moved a couple of paces down it and sliced off a pair of good-sized bushes. Dragging them back to the opening, he propped them up to block the path. He interwove some branches through them to keep them from falling over, then arranged some leaves at their bases to hide the slashed ends.

The Malison Ring soldiers were probably smart enough to spot Jack's camouflage. But they were also probably smart enough to be suspicious of it. With this second and considerably less obvious barrier a few feet farther along, they might conclude that Jack's was merely a decoy.

Draycos put a few more finishing touches on his camouflage, making sure it was better than Jack's but still detectable if they looked closely enough. Then, leaping into the trees, he headed back to the clearing.

The soldiers had finished their consultation and were on the move again. Unfortunately, whether through luck or tracking skill, they were heading straight for the path the group of K'da and Erassvas had taken. Even with the barriers he and Jack had erected, it wouldn't take the soldiers long to catch up to the refugees.

Draycos would just have to slow them down a bit.

The main force paused as they reached the entrance to the path, giving the two pairs of outriders time to work their way into new flanking positions. Then, guns held ready across their chests, they headed in.

For a moment Draycos studied their movements. The outriders were moving through the undergrowth nearly as quietly as a K'da warrior could have, keeping in sight of both the main force and each other. The second of each pair seemed to be trying to walk in the footsteps of the first, minimizing the chances of snapping a dry branch hidden beneath the leaves.

Each pair was also staying far enough apart that a K'da dropping on them from above couldn't take out both with a single attack. Clearly, they were well trained and well-informed.

But they weren't informed quite well enough. Easing down from his tree, Draycos headed into the forest to prepare his attack.

He was curled out of sight beneath a fan-shaped group of wide-leaf ferns when the two left-flank outriders arrived.

He let the first pass him by without interference. Then, as the second stepped into range, he reached out a paw and stabbed a claw neatly through the heel of the soldier's left boot.

The man gave a strangled gasp as his leg collapsed beneath him. "What?" his companion demanded quietly, hurrying back to his side.

"My ankle," the first ground out, crouching down to clutch at his heel. "Something bit me, right through my boot."

"You mean like a snake?" the other said, starting to take a hasty step back.

But he was too late. Reaching behind him, Draycos jabbed him in the same spot.

Either this one didn't handle pain as well as his companion or else Draycos's claw had found a more sensitive spot. Instead of a stifled gasp, the man let loose with a full-bodied bellow as he dropped to one knee.

"Alki, you idiot," someone snapped from the path. "Shut up—"

"We got trouble, Lieutenant," the first outrider called back, his voice taut with pain. "Snake or something. We both been bit."

The lieutenant swore. "Get back here," he ordered. "Imre, Quars—go help them."

Two of the main force left the path and pushed their way through the bushes. They reached the injured men and slung their weapons over their shoulders to leave their hands free to help them up.

And as they did, Draycos leaped straight up through the concealing ferns into view.

There was just enough time for the soldiers' eyes to widen in shock; and then K'da paws slapped hard against the sides of their necks beneath their helmets, dropping them unconscious to the ground. Draycos slapped his tail across the throat of one of the two men he'd first hit, sending him flying, then pawslapped the other.

But quiet or not, his attack hadn't gone unnoticed. "There!" one of the remaining four soldiers in the main group shouted as Draycos landed back on the ground. "There he is!"

"Fire!" the lieutenant snapped.

And as the four men swung their weapons around toward him, Draycos deftly inserted the tip of his tail through the trigger guard of the nearest fallen soldier's gun and squeezed the trigger.

The gun wasn't aimed at anything in particular, certainly not at any of the remaining men. But to soldiers with trained combat reflexes, the sound of nearby gunfire was all it took. As the first chattering salvo of slugs tore into the landscape, the remaining soldiers of the main group forgot their own weapons and dived for cover. Draycos fired a second salvo, just to encourage them to keep down, then unhooked his tail and slipped away into the forest.

He'd made it perhaps ten yards before the soldiers behind him pulled themselves together enough to begin raking the forest with fire of their own. But the shots were wild, and none of them even came close.

If they followed immediately, he knew, they would have a good chance of catching both him and the rest of the group ahead. But he also knew that they probably wouldn't. Four of their number were down, two of them with ankle injuries serious enough to put them out of action for days or possibly weeks.

And even people bent on genocide wouldn't be foolish enough to go charging madly into a dense forest full of unknown dangers and proven enemies. They would deal with their injured, regroup, and rethink their strategy. Only then would they try again.

He'd bought Jack and Uncle Virge some time. Hopefully, it would be enough.

. . .

A few yards beyond the low cliff they'd had to detour around, the band of tightly packed bushes began to thin out. By the time Jack caught up with Alison, the brush had cleared out enough that the group no longer had to travel in single file.

Of course, that also meant anyone coming up from behind would see them from a lot farther away. Trying not to think about the eyes—and guns—that might be lining up on his back, he passed through the throng of Erassvas and K'da to the front.

Alison looked back as he came up beside her. "Well?"

Jack shrugged. "Did my best. We'll see what happens."

"I guess." She measured him with her eyes. "So what exactly are these Erassvas and Phookas to you, anyway?"

It was a question Jack had known she would eventually ask. Unfortunately, he still didn't have a good answer to it. "What do you mean?" he stalled.

"What do you mean, what do I mean?" she retorted crossly. "You and I would be twice as far along right now if we weren't dragging these lotus-eaters and their entertainment herd along with us. I repeat: what are they to you?"

"I wish I could explain," Jack said with a sigh. "But I can't." He hesitated. "You don't have to stay if you don't want to."

He kept walking, his eyes forward, not looking at her. But he could feel her gaze on him. "Don't think I'm not tempted," she said at last. "But I saw how you handled forest duty back on Sunright. You wouldn't last an hour out here without me."

She gestured over her shoulder. "Especially not with a transport full of Malison Ring soldiers on your—"

She broke off as a stutter of gunfire erupted from somewhere behind them.

Jack spun around, his heart seizing up. But there was no sign of pursuit. A second burst sounded through the trees and bushes, followed by a much longer sustained chatter of fire.

Finally, almost reluctantly he thought, the weapons fell silent again. This time, they stayed that way.

"Mother-of-pearl," Alison breathed. "What kind of trap did you *set* back there?"

"Like I said, I did my best," Jack said, trying to keep his voice steady. If Draycos had been killed . . . but he wasn't going to think about that. "You were saying something about me not lasting an hour out here?"

He had the immense satisfaction of seeing some actual embarrassment flicker across her face. "Okay, so maybe I was wrong," she admitted. "In that case, how about you take Greenie here for a while, while I go back and take rear guard?"

"Good idea," Jack said, getting a grip on the green K'da's crest. "You spot any trouble, just whistle."

CHAPTER 10

Draycos was waiting for him another hundred yards ahead, hidden behind a particularly large tree. "You all right?" Jack asked anxiously as he stretched his hand behind the tree, glancing back first to make sure Alison wasn't watching.

"I am fine," the dragon assured him. He touched a paw to Jack's hand and vanished up his sleeve. "Four of the enemy have been neutralized, at least temporarily."

"Great. Tell me about it."

He listened as the dragon gave him a quick summary, the gold-scaled head draped as usual across Jack's right shoulder. "Good job," he said when the other had finished. "Hamstringing those first two was especially smart. It'll take a week of regrowth treatment before they can do anything but hobble."

"Thank you," Draycos said. "Unfortunately, I will probably not be able to use such a trick a second time."

"That's okay," Jack assured him. "Now they'll have to keep an eye on what's going on above them, around them, *and* below them. That's bound to slow them down a little, and every bit helps."

"Agreed," Draycos said. "Has the first K'da switch taken place yet?"

Jack nodded. "About ten minutes ago."

"How did Alison react?"

Jack glanced back again. "Actually, I don't think she noticed."

"How could she not?" Draycos countered. "She is right in back where she can see everything."

"I know, but everyone was very cool about it," Jack told him. "The next batch of K'da just sort of drifted over to their chosen Erassvas; then they went up one sleeve while the old batch came out the other. Very slick. I'd told Hren to keep it a secret, but I hadn't really thought he and the others could pull it off."

Draycos was silent a moment. "We can hope they will continue to be as capable," he said, sounding doubtful. "Still, now that I'm here, we can take rear guard while Alison leads. That way, she will be facing away from the K'da for the next transfer."

"If she'll let me," Jack warned. "Don't forget, she's the one with the gun."

"You do not need a gun," Draycos pointed out. "You have me."

"I know that, but Alison doesn't," Jack reminded him.

"You will find a way to convince her," Draycos said. "I have confidence in you."

"Thanks," Jack said. "Any ideas on what we do when it's Greenie's turn, by the way?"

"Greenie?"

"Our leader of the pack," Jack said, nodding at the green K'da padding along beside him. "Alison's bound to miss him. Especially if she's the one leading him at the time."

"That would certainly make her wonder," Draycos agreed with the first touch of humor Jack had heard from him since they'd arrived on this world. "We will have to call a rest break when that time comes."

"I suppose that'll work," Jack said. "Any chance you can give me some warning before he needs a host?"

"I can do that," Draycos assured him. "Tell me, did Taneem return safely?"

Jack frowned. "Who?"

"I mean the gray-scaled K'da."

"Oh—him," Jack said, looking around.

"Her," Draycos corrected. "She is a female."

"Ah," Jack said. He'd wondered earlier whether there were any females among the group. "Yeah, there she is—over to the left." He half-turned his torso so that Draycos could see her through the opening in his shirt. "Looks okay to me."

"Good," Draycos said. "She followed me, and I had to send her back."

"Did she give you trouble?"

"I doubt any of these beings are capable of giving genuine trouble to anyone," Draycos said scornfully. "I was merely concerned that she had returned safely."

"Ah," Jack said, nodding. "You called her Taneem?"

There was a short silence, and he had the odd impression that Draycos was actually embarrassed. "She looks very much like someone I once knew," the dragon said at last, reluctantly. "I apologize for the confusion."

"No, that's all right," Jack assured him. "We can call her Taneem if you want to."

"I do *not* want to," the dragon growled. "My Taneem was nothing like this. I do not wish her name associated with these . . . creatures."

"Okay, fine," Jack said hastily. "I'm sorry I even brought it up."

He felt the dragon move restlessly against his skin. "I am sorry in turn," Draycos said more quietly. "I will try not to— just a moment."

"What?" Jack asked, coming to an abrupt stop. He knew that tone, and it usually meant trouble.

"Something ahead," Draycos said. His tongue flicked out through Jack's shirt as he tasted the air. "Animals. Many of them."

"A herd of something?" Jack asked hopefully.

"Or a pack of something," Draycos said grimly. "There is no way to tell whether or not they are predators without seeing them."

Jack looked over his shoulder. He could see Alison through the trees, but her attention was on something off to her right. "Clear," he told Draycos, putting his hand around the side of the nearest tree. "Go."

Draycos shot out of his sleeve, his claws catching the tree trunk in a solid grip as he passed. Scampering up the trunk like a giant golden squirrel, he vanished into the foliage above.

"Jack?" Alison called. "You'd better come see this."

"Coming," Jack said. Giving Greenie a pat on the flank, he headed back.

He found her staring up into one of the larger trees. "What do you think?" she asked, gesturing.

Jack followed her pointing finger. Eight feet up the trunk was a spot about a foot and a half across where the bark had been almost completely torn off. "Looks like something was trying to carve its initials in the tree," he said.

"And kept making mistakes and having to erase," Alison agreed. "You can see claw marks there at the edge."

Jack nodded. They looked very similar, in fact, to the marks made by K'da claws.

Except that these scratch marks were much farther apart, which meant this animal had much larger paws. And they *were* eight feet off the ground. "I don't think we want to run into this guy," he said.

Alison snorted. "I don't think I'd even want to see him in a *zoo*," she said darkly. "I don't know if he'd bother a Phooka, let alone a whole group of them. But the Erassvas would be like dumplings on the hoof to something this size."

"Assuming he's a carnivore."

"It would be criminally stupid to assume anything else at the moment," Alison said. "Any thoughts?"

Jack chewed at his lip. "Seems to me our best bet would be to group all the Erassvas together in the middle where we can protect them."

" 'We'?" Alison said pointedly.

"Fine; where *you* can protect them," Jack said. "Whatever.

Then we let the Phookas roam around the outside, while you and I stay near the Erassvas."

"That's pretty much what I was thinking," she agreed. "Unless, of course, you're ready to give up on this caravan and send them back home."

"Not with those mercs still on our tail," Jack said firmly. "They'd slaughter the whole bunch of them."

"Why?" she demanded. "That's the part I don't get. Why would the Malison Ring waste perfectly good ammunition on any of them?"

Jack sighed. "I already said I can't explain. Trust me; we have to stick together."

Alison sighed. "Fine," she said in resignation. "In that case, we'd better start looking for a good place to turn west. We're going to need those foothill caves more than ever now. In fact, we're going to need a whole apartment complex worth of them."

"We're not going to the hills," Jack said. "I've been thinking, and I'm not sure anymore that the *Essenay* was destroyed like Frost thinks. I'm thinking maybe it just hid in the river and is making its way down toward us."

"Really," Alison said, her dark eyes probing his face. "You have any evidence for this? Other than wishful thinking?"

"Not really," Jack had to admit. "But the computer is pretty resourceful."

"The computer?" Alison asked pointedly. "Or your uncle?"

Jack frowned. "What are you talking about?"

"Don't play cute," she growled. "I heard that other voice, just before that last explosion. It didn't sound like any P/S computer system *I've* ever seen. Where was he hiding, anyway?"

Jack suppressed a grimace. He'd been hoping she hadn't caught Uncle Virge's change in tone there at the end. "I'm sorry. I really can't talk about that."

There was a long, uncomfortable silence. "You know, Jack, it can be fun to have secrets," she said. "But sometimes those secrets can turn around and bite you on the butt."

"Don't treat me like a child," Jack snapped. "I can't talk about it. Period."

Her lips tightened briefly. "Fine," she said. "Have it your way. I just hope you'll find it in your heart to loosen up a little before something I don't know kills me. So you want to tell Hren about our new marching order? Or should I do it?"

"I'll tell him," Jack said. He nodded at the claw marks. "And given *that,* I think that if I'm on point I should carry the Corvine."

"You ever fired one before?"

Jack gave her a lopsided grin. "I had ten whole days of training back at the Whinyard's Edge, remember?"

"That's what I thought," Alison said. "Tell you what. I'll keep the Corvine, and *I'll* take point."

"Whatever," Jack said, trying to keep the satisfaction out of his voice. Perfect. "You corral Greenie, and I'll go find Hren."

They'd been traveling in their new formation for nearly an hour when Draycos finally reappeared, slipping into sight through the undergrowth. "About time," Jack said as the dragon put a paw on his outstretched palm and vanished up his sleeve. "Any problems?"

"None," Draycos said. "The animals I smelled were plant-eaters, though with quite formidable-looking horns. I was able to drive them on their way with little difficulty."

"And this took you a whole hour?"

"No, of course not," Draycos said. "I scouted ahead for other potential threats, then circled back to see if I could learn what the mercenaries were doing."

"And?"

Jack felt a whisper of movement across the back of his right leg as the dragon twitched his tail. "I found no signs of pursuit," the other said. "Either they are still pondering their next move or else they have already decided on a different tactic."

"Probably the latter," Jack said. "I just hope it doesn't involve bringing the Kapstan over the forest and strafing randomly until they hit something."

"They wish to capture you alive," Draycos reminded him.

"They wanted Uncle Virgil alive," Jack countered. "I'm not so sure how badly they want me by myself."

"We shall see," Draycos said. "At least the heavy foliage will prevent them from using the transport's infrared detectors to easily locate you. And of course, they still do not know how K'da appear on such detectors."

"Don't be so sure," Jack warned. "Remember, Frost and Neverlin are working with the Valahgua. If I were Neverlin, as soon as I knew a K'da had survived I'd have screamed for all the data they've got on your people. Including how you show up on IR detectors."

"That data would not do them any good," Draycos said. "Valahguan sensors work differently from yours."

"Maybe," Jack said. "But don't forget that the Malison Ring had four of the Valahgua's nasty little Death weapons when they attacked your advance party. If the Valahgua were willing to hand those over, I don't think they'd be too hard to talk out of a couple sets of sensors, too."

"Perhaps," Draycos conceded reluctantly. "Odd. The Valahgua have always been very protective of their technology. But you're right—the Malison Ring certainly did have Death weapons."

"Which we'd better hope are a long way from here," Jack said as that thought suddenly struck him. "They could just sweep it across the forest and be done with it."

"It does not work that way," Draycos said. "Even in the vacuum of space the Death is a fairly short-range weapon. On a planet's surface, its range is much less."

"How much less?"

"Considerably," Draycos said. "In a forest like this, with life all around, no more than two to three feet."

"Thank heaven for small favors," Jack said.

"Yes," Draycos said. "Were there any problems while I was gone?"

Jack shrugged. "Alison's mad at me for keeping secrets, and there's something out here that likes to rip off tree bark eight feet off the ground. Aside from that, not much."

"Yes, I saw similar claw marks up ahead," Draycos said.

"But they appeared to be several days old. Perhaps the creature has moved on."

"I hope so," Jack said. "Because if he hasn't, we're probably going to lose a Phooka or two down the rabbit hole."

"Meaning?"

"Meaning that with the Erassvas together in the center this way, the Phookas have a bad habit of ranging away from the main group," Jack told him. "Far enough out, in fact, that they—blast." He pointed to the left, where a pale burgundy K'da was walking briskly away. "Come on. Let me show you how *my* day's been going."

The maverick K'da had worked his way around a stand of bushes by the time Jack reached him. Completely out of sight of the main group, digging industriously at a small insect mound, he would probably never have noticed if he'd been left behind. "Come on," Jack said, getting a grip on his crest and tugging on it. "Come on, big fella."

Reluctantly, the K'da allowed himself to be pulled away from his snack. Jack eased him around the bushes and started working his way back toward the edge of the group. "And it hasn't stopped, either," he continued to Draycos. "No matter what the Malison Ring has in mind, once it gets dark we absolutely have to quit for the day. If we don't, we'll probably lose half of them by morning."

"Perhaps I can help," Draycos offered. "I can patrol the outer edge of the group and watch for stragglers."

"Kind of like a sheepdog?"

"Not precisely the way I would have phrased it," Draycos said stiffly. "But essentially correct."

"What if Alison sees you?"

"What if she does?" Draycos countered. "What would one more K'da be among so many others?"

"I don't know," Jack said doubtfully. "She's pretty sharp, and there aren't any other gold ones. But you're right, I can't keep them all together myself. Let's give it a shot."

Draycos bounded from Jack's collar onto the ground. "You return this one to the herd and then cross over to the right flank," he instructed. "I will stay on this flank, and also keep watch to the rear."

"Where you'll be handy if the Malison Ring makes another move?"

"Not *if*," Draycos corrected him grimly. *"When."*

CHAPTER 11

His offer to watch the Phookas, Draycos quickly discovered, was easier to make than to fulfill.

For starters, the creatures were every bit as irresponsible and simple minded as Jack had warned. With the Erassvas mostly out of their sight, it took nothing more than an interesting log or bush or rock to lure many of them off the proper path. No sooner had Draycos gotten one back on-course than someone else would wander away.

It was a constant job just keeping track of them all. From the sounds of rapid footsteps he could hear on the other side of the traveling formation, he could tell that Jack wasn't having any easier a time of it.

What was far worse than the physical activity, though, was the constant pain of seeing his people reduced to animals.

If that *was* indeed what had happened to them. Because there was another, far worse possibility.

The possibility that *this* was in fact the natural state of the K'da. That it was only through their long relationship with the Shontine that Draycos's people had been lifted to the level of civilized beings.

It was a terrifying thought. If it was true, it would mean that the legends about their early relationship with the long-lost Dhghem were false. It would mean that stories of how the kidnapped K'da had planned and executed an escape from the Cark slavers were completely made up.

It would mean their entire history was a lie.

To his surprise and shame, he found that he couldn't face such a possibility. He, Draycos, poet-warrior of the K'da, had finally found something he was frightened to face.

So instead, he threw himself into his work, focusing his full attention on keeping his half of the herd in line. Perhaps later, when things were quiet, he would be able to take the time to think about who and what he and his people truly were.

It was just as well that he chose to ignore such questions and turn his full attention on the duties of the present. It was on one of his wider-ranging herding swings that he discovered the Malison Ring's trap.

It came as a distant but familiar whiff of scent as he was corralling a particularly stubborn K'da. Somewhere to their left, he recognized, a group of humans had gathered.

For a few seconds he stood still, his tail hooked firmly in the errant K'da's crest, trying to decide what to do. The humans weren't very close, probably at least a mile away. If he left immediately, he should be able to see what they were up to and get back before Jack and the others got too close.

But if he left right now, this particular K'da would almost certainly wander off again.

The greatest good for the greatest number. It was one of the basic rules of life and warfare, a rule he'd been taught in childhood. From some of the comments Uncle Virge had made over the past three months, he knew it to be a human saying as well.

And yet he also knew that a warrior could focus so much attention on the greater number that the needs of the individual became lost in the mist.

So where *did* his responsibilities lie here?

From behind him came a soft snuffle, and he turned his head to look. The gray-scaled K'da, the one he'd dubbed Taneem, was watching him, a mildly puzzled expression on her face.

Draycos cursed beneath his breath. He didn't have time for this.

And was instantly ashamed of himself. *The needs of the individual . . .*

A sudden idea struck him. If Draycos's people had indeed been raised up from the level of animals, maybe that potential lay deep within these K'da, too.

And if Taneem could learn, perhaps he could kill two lizards with one slash. "You," he called softly to her. "Gray K'da."

She cocked her head slightly to the side, her puzzlement deepening. "Yes, you," Draycos confirmed. "You—Taneem. Your name is Taneem now. Come here, Taneem."

Still looking uncertain, she nevertheless came to his side. "Take your friend," Draycos ordered her, unhooking his tail from the rogue K'da's crest. "Go ahead—wrap your tail around his crest and lead him back to the others. Can you do that?"

For a few seconds it seemed that he would have done as

well to talk to one of the shrubs. Taneem stared unblinkingly at him, apparently trying hard to sort it all out. Then, to Draycos's mild surprise, she stepped to the other K'da's side and tentatively looped her tail around his crest. "That's right," Draycos said encouragingly. "Perfect. Now take him back to the others and stay there with him. I'll be back soon."

Again, it seemed to take her some time to work it through. Then, with a flick of her tongue she turned back toward the group, the other K'da in tow. With one final lingering look at Draycos over her shoulder, she disappeared around a clump of tall ferns.

Draycos didn't wait to see any more. If they made it, they made it. Turning to his left, he headed toward the distant human scent.

The telltale odor increased steadily as he traveled, but as near as he could tell the intruders were stationary. He kept going until he'd reached a spot perhaps a hundred feet away from them, then shifted to stalking mode. He covered the last bit of distance as silently and carefully as he could manage.

It was just as well that he did.

The primary line consisted of Malison Ring soldiers spaced about a hundred feet apart. All were dressed in camouflage outfits, all of them hidden inside patches of reeds or ferns where they were all but invisible. Sitting silently in concealment, they were waiting for Jack and Alison to walk right into their arms.

Under normal circumstances, Draycos would have had no trouble dealing with them. He would have simply climbed into the treetops, worked his way behind the line, and taken out the soldiers one by one.

But as Jack had warned, Colonel Frost knew what he and his men were up against. This time, they'd come up with a new twist.

Just behind the main picket line a second line had been set up in various tree branches twenty feet off the ground. If Draycos had carelessly gone with the standard approach, he would have ended up squarely in their line of fire.

And as an extra added touch, the upper line consisted of nonhumans of species Draycos hadn't yet encountered in his travels with Jack. Frost had probably hoped their unfamiliar scent would help conceal them.

Slowly, carefully, Draycos backed away, watching for any other surprises the enemy might have planned. But the double picket line appeared to be the full extent of their cleverness. At least for the moment.

He took the long way back to Jack and the others, paralleling the picket line at a cautious distance. After a quarter mile the double line ended, replaced by a single line of soldiers spaced much farther apart.

Apparently, Frost had followed Alison's same line of reasoning regarding the caves to the west. He was expecting the fugitives to head in that direction, and had arranged his forces with that in mind.

Still, even a thin picket line could be trouble, especially to a crowd of unstealthy Erassvas and Phookas. Draycos and Jack would have to find a way to slip the group past the sentries without being detected.

Draycos had worried a little that Alison might have made too much progress toward the hidden enemy in his absence. To his relief, he found everyone sitting or lying comfortably on the ground not far from where he'd left them.

Jack was walking the perimeter, his tangler ready in his hand. Draycos waited until he was looking in his direction, then lifted a paw into view. Jack changed direction, and half a minute later Draycos was once again pressed against his host's skin.

"You okay?" Jack murmured as he resumed his patrol.

"Yes," Draycos said. "Why have we stopped? Is it the bell-wether's turn for a host?"

"No, not yet," Jack said. "I saw Taneem come back leading one of the other Phookas and figured you'd spotted trouble. I thought it might be a good idea to go to ground for a while, so I called a rest break."

"It was well that you did," Draycos said. "We have a problem."

Jack listened in silence as Draycos laid out the situation. "And you don't think we can slip past them even if we keep going north?" the boy asked when he'd finished.

"You, I, and Alison could," Draycos said. "But the others could not."

"So what we need is for all the soldiers to go away."

"Yes," Draycos said. For all the danger they were in, he felt a trickle of encouragement that the thought of abandoning the Erassvas and K'da had apparently not even crossed Jack's mind. The me-first attitude that Uncle Virgil had spent all those years hammering into the boy was fading away with gratifying speed. "Perhaps I can arrange a diversion."

Jack shook his head. "A K'da diversion is the first thing they'll expect," he said, chewing thoughtfully at his lip. "I wonder how clever they think we are. *And* how stupid."

"What do you mean?" Draycos asked.

"This." Reaching to his collar, Jack removed his comm clip. "I don't know if I ever mentioned it, but there's a way to gimmick comm clips so that they can be made to work as transmission scanners."

"With the ability to search for enemy transmissions?"

"Exactly," Jack said. "You usually can't actually eavesdrop on anyone, since most comm clips operate with full encryption. But if we had a clip like that we could estimate the strength of the mercs' own comm clip signals and get an idea of how close they were."

"*Do* we have such a device?" Draycos asked.

Jack shook his head. "There are a couple on the *Essenay,* but neither of the two I have with me can do that. But Frost has to know about the technique. If he thinks I'm clever enough, and if my comm clip suddenly goes on without me talking to anyone, he may think that's what I'm doing."

"But as Alison said earlier, turning it on may also give them the ability to locate *us,*" Draycos warned.

"Right," Jack said, grinning tightly. "And *that's* the how-stupid-am-I part. How far away did you say you drove that herd of horn-headed plant-eaters?"

Draycos cracked his jaws open in a smile of his own. "Not far," he said. "How shall I attach it?"

"Use this," Jack said. He glanced toward Alison, then surreptitiously slid one of the cartridges out of his tangler. "If you pop off this cap, the netting will just slide free instead of blasting out."

Draycos lifted his head slightly from Jack's shoulder for a closer look. The technique seemed straightforward enough. "What about the electrical shock?" he asked.

"Good point," Jack said, frowning. "I'd better take out the capacitor."

"Or you could simply adjust its strength," Draycos suggested. "We don't wish to put the animal to sleep, but a small jolt may encourage him to leave his grazing and move away from the area more quickly."

Jack cocked his head in salute. "Good point number two," he said. "Let's see what I can do."

Three minutes later, the cartridge was ready. "Remember, just attach it and then get back here," Jack said. "And don't get him moving too fast. We don't want Frost wondering why Uncle Virgil trained me to be a thief instead of an Olympic distance runner."

"I know what to do," Draycos assured him. "Don't leave this place until I return."

"We won't," Jack promised. "Good luck."

CHAPTER 12

Silently, the dragon headed off into the woods. Jack gave him a thirty-count to make sure he was out of sight, then headed back to the resting herd.

Alison was sitting with her back against a tree, her gun in her lap. "All quiet on the western front?" she asked.

"Seems that way," he confirmed, carefully filtering the annoyance out of his voice. Alison had gotten into the habit of peppering her conversation with these obscure comments, obviously references to things he'd never heard of.

It was irritating, but he wasn't about to give her the satisfaction of letting her know that. He certainly wasn't going to ask what in blazes she was talking about.

"Good," she said. "Does that mean you're over your twitchies?"

"Being cautious in enemy territory is *not* being twitchy," Jack insisted stiffly. "And, no, I think we ought to stay here a little longer."

Alison peered up at the sky. "If we do, we may be here all night," she warned. "We don't have much daylight left."

"I think it's worth it," Jack said firmly. "*I'm* staying, anyway."

"Fine," Alison said, resettling herself against the tree. "You're in charge of this expedition. So how about telling me a story?"

Jack frowned. "What kind of story?"

"Colonel Frost called you Jack Morgan," she said. "Two months ago, when we were raw recruits sweating through basic in the Whinyard's Edge mercenaries, they all thought your name was Jack Montana. Was it you or them who got your name wrong?"

Jack hid a grimace. "Them," he said. "Probably a clerical error."

"Yeah, right," she said. "Come on, Jack. Like it or not, we're stuck here together. I need to know that I can trust you."

"Fine," Jack said. "In that case, you can go first."

Alison lifted her eyebrows. "Go first where?"

"You weren't any raw recruit," he reminded her, sitting down facing her with his back to another tree. "You could start by telling me what you were up to that made Sergeant Grisko ready to kill both of us."

She sighed, lowering her eyes. "It was all Dad's idea," she said reluctantly. "He had this crazy notion that merc groups who took teenagers probably didn't keep very good records on them. He figured he could keep indenturing me to one after another, collect the money and then help me get out, and they'd never catch on."

"Cute," Jack said. "More stupid than cute, actually. But no

crazier than some of the scams my uncle and I pulled over the years."

"So you *are* a con artist?" she asked. "That's sort of what I figured."

"Reformed con artist," Jack corrected. "Trying to reform, anyway. So what were you doing in the Whinyard's Edge HQ that night?"

"I wanted to get a peek at their records on me," Alison said. "Just in case Dad's plan hadn't been as clever as he thought. I guess I should have waited until we were on Sunright."

"Or skipped it completely."

She made a face. "Dad wouldn't have liked that," she said. "He's—well, let's not go into that."

"Bad childhood?" Jack suggested.

Alison shrugged. "Mom and Dad and I never stayed in one place very long, if that's what you mean. Other than that . . . I don't know. I don't really have anything to compare it to."

"I know the feeling," Jack said ruefully, thinking back over his own life with Uncle Virge. "What kind of work do your parents do?"

"Whatever they can find," she said. "Dad's always chasing the Big One, as he calls it. The job that'll finally bring him fame and fortune and success."

"I gather he hasn't made it?"

She shrugged again. "There's been some success, I suppose. There hasn't been any fame. There *certainly* hasn't been any fortune."

Jack nodded. She was being evasive, but he could read between the lines as well as the next guy. Her father was a criminal like Uncle Virgil, though apparently not nearly as successful.

Which was ironic, considering that it was Uncle Virgil's spectacular career that had caught the attention of Arthur Neverlin in the first place, which was what had dragged Jack, and now Alison, into this mess. "Where are your parents now?" he asked. "Are they the ones you're expecting to pick you up?"

She shook her head. "These are some friends of theirs. Actually, I really don't know where Mom and Dad are. Like I say, they move around a lot. What's a K'da?"

With a supreme effort, Jack managed to keep his face expressionless. "A what?"

"A K'da," she repeated. "Frost said he didn't want you and your K'da to suffer the same fate as your uncle. Come on—I've told you about me. It's your turn."

"I have no idea what he meant by that," Jack said, feeling sweat break out on the back of his neck. He'd completely forgotten that last comment of Frost's just before he'd shut down his comm clip. This girl was way too observant for his taste. "Some slang term, I suppose."

She stared hard at him with those dark eyes. Jack held her gaze without flinching, and after a moment her lip twitched. "Fine," she said. "Don't tell me. Can I at least get your real name?"

"Jack Morgan," he said. "Raised by my uncle, Virgil Morgan."

"Virgil Morgan," Alison said thoughtfully. "I've heard that

name. One of the great con men and safecrackers of our age, isn't he?"

"Certainly in his own mind," Jack said, feeling a ghostly echo of pain and loss. Even more than a year after Uncle Virgil's death, it still hurt sometimes. "No, that's not fair."

"Not if even half the stories are true," Alison agreed, an odd glint in her eye. "So you're Virgil Morgan's nephew."

"Yes, we've established that," Jack said, eyeing her suspiciously. Was there a hint of actual admiration in her voice? Or was it just more sarcasm? Whatever it was, he didn't like it. "And I'm reformed, remember?"

"Sure," she said, the faint admiration turning to equally faint amusement. He liked that even less. "Well. That was fun, but we really ought to try to get a little more distance before sundown."

Ten yards behind her, Jack caught a glimpse of gold dragon scales. "If you insist," he said, wincing as he pushed himself up off the ground. Even during the brief rest break, his leg muscles had stiffened up considerably. "You still want to handle point?"

"I'm still the one with the gun," she said. "By the way, have you noticed that these Phookas can change color?"

Jack's first reaction was to wonder which of these animals could possibly have gotten riled up enough to go into K'da combat mode. He'd seen that effect a couple of times with Draycos, where some of the poet-warrior's heightened blood flow seeped into his gold scales and turned them black.

But a second later he realized what she was actually talking

about. As one K'da left his Erassva host and a differently colored one took his place, Alison would naturally interpret that as
the original Phooka changing colors. "No, I hadn't," he said.
"Interesting."

"You should pay better attention to your surroundings,"
Alison said reprovingly as she got to her feet. If she was feeling
stiff, it didn't show. "And try to keep them quiet. I'm guessing
the Malison Ring will make some move before nightfall."

However Draycos had worked his end of the scheme, he'd
clearly done a terrific job of it. The group reached the area
he'd described as the site of the Malison Ring picket line to
find it completely deserted.

Jack had gone perhaps twenty yards past the picket line
when, from somewhere ahead and to the right, came a sudden
crashing of branches and a distant howl of pain.

Ducking around trees and bushes, he ran toward the sound.
Rounding one last stand of reeds, he nearly ran full tilt into Alison as she stood at the edge of another of the sharp drop-offs.
"Watch it—watch it," she said, putting a hand out across his
chest. "This whole ridge is crumbly."

"What happened?" Jack asked.

"We've lost one," she said grimly, nodding down the cliff.
"Take a look. But be careful."

Holding on to a nearby tree branch, Jack eased up to the
edge. Thirty feet down a steep slope, a dusky red Phooka was
lying on his side, two of his legs thrashing weakly as he strug-

gled to free himself from a tangle of vines. "Did you see what happened?"

"About what you'd expect," she growled. "Stupid thing wasn't watching where he was going and walked off the edge of the cliff. Question is, what do we do about it?"

Jack took a step back and looked around. Draycos was nowhere to be seen, probably still playing shepherd off to the left. "Let's start by asking Hren," he said. "Hren? Hren!"

"Yes, young Jack?" the Erassva's voice called from behind him.

"Come here a minute, will you?" Jack called back. "We've got an injured Phooka on our hands."

The fat alien appeared and stepped to the edge of the drop-off with what seemed to Jack to be a complete lack of caution. "How sad," he said as he peered down. "How very sad."

"Never mind the sadness," Jack said. "How do we help him?"

"Help him?" Hren seemed puzzled. "There is no help for him, young Jack. Not down there. A few hours and he will be gone." He turned to go.

"Wait a second," Jack said, grabbing his arm as he looked down at the injured Phooka. The creature's eyes were half-closed, but even in the fading light Jack could swear he was looking directly at him. "We've got some rope in these packs."

"We'd need more than just rope," Alison said. "These things are heavy, and we'd be dragging him against all that veg-etation. At the very least we'd need a block and tackle."

"But we can't just leave him there to die," Jack protested.

Alison shrugged. "I'm open to suggestions."

Jack clenched his hands into fists. There *had* to be a way to do this. "How about if I go down to him?" he suggested.

"And do what?" Alison asked. "Hold his paw while he dies?"

"I was thinking more about carrying him to safety," Jack growled, pointing past the drop-off. "That cut goes around that low hill over there. If I can get through it, I should be able to get around the hill and meet you a little ways northwest of here."

"And what if you *can't* get through?" Alison countered. "It wouldn't be safe to leave the rope tied here—we might as well put up a sign telling the Malison Ring which way we've gone. If you can't get through, you'll be trapped."

"I'll get through," Jack said stubbornly, pulling off his backpack. "Just get me down there and take the herd around that hill. I'll do the rest."

"Jack—"

"And we're wasting time and light," Jack cut her off. "Give me a hand with this rope."

Alison hissed between her teeth. "Fine. It's your funeral."

The sky had darkened considerably by the time they were ready. "Just relax and walk your feet down the slope," Alison said, looping the rope around a thick tree trunk and pulling it taut. "I'll ease you down."

"Right," Jack said, doing one last check of the makeshift harness she'd created for him. "Here goes."

Jack had done plenty of climbing in his lifetime, mostly up

and down small buildings he was in the process of robbing. But going down this way, at the end of a rope he wasn't controlling, was a brand-new experience.

And definitely not a pleasant one. Muttering under his breath, he waded backward through the vines, trying hard not to get his feet tangled. It seemed like forever before he finally came to a halt beside the injured Phooka. "Easy, fella," Jack soothed the creature as he climbed awkwardly out of his harness.

The soothing tone wasn't necessary. The Phooka had abandoned even his weak attempts at freeing himself, and was lying motionlessly on his side. His eyes were still on Jack, his heaving flanks the only sign of life.

"Jack?" Alison's voice drifted down toward him.

Jack looked up. In the fading light she wasn't much more than a silhouette against the gray sky above her. "I'm here," he called back. "Get going. I'll see you around the other side."

Alison made as if to say something, then seemed to give a reluctant nod. "Be careful." She pulled up the rope, then disappeared away from the cliff.

Jack took a deep breath. *When you have a K'da, you're never really alone,* he told himself. "Draycos?" he called softly.

"I'm here," the familiar voice came. With a rustle of ferns, the dragon appeared from concealment. "I am not certain this was a wise move, though."

"Yeah, well, rescuing wayward K'da seems to have become my hobby," Jack growled. "Get over here and tell me what's wrong with him."

Draycos's examination was quick but thorough. "His left

foreleg is injured," he reported. "It might be broken, but I think it is merely sprained. The left hind leg also seems hurt, but not as badly."

"What are his chances for recovery?"

"Very good," Draycos assured him. "I received a similar sprain during the *Havenseeker*'s crash landing. I needed no treatment to recover."

"Good." Jack held out a hand to the injured Phooka. "Okay, big fella. Come aboard."

The Phooka didn't move. "Well, come on," Jack said, this time reaching down and grasping the uninjured foreleg paw. "You want to stay here all night?"

His only reaction was to try to pull out of Jack's grip. "I don't think he understands what you want," Draycos said.

"Oh, come *on*," Jack insisted. "He *has* to understand hosts."

"Yes, but you're not a host," Draycos countered. "At least, not the kind he has always known."

Jack let his breath out in a huff. He should have guessed it wouldn't be this easy. "So what now? We carry him?"

"Or we leave him here to die," Draycos said.

"I was afraid of that," Jack said disgustedly, measuring the fallen Phooka with his eyes. He looked a lot bigger, and a lot heavier, than he had from thirty feet up. "Let's get to it, then."

"Yes," Draycos said, prodding at the Phooka's side with his muzzle. "Can you help me get him onto my back?"

"Sorry, pal," Jack said, pushing at the side of Draycos's long neck. "My job."

"I'm stronger than you are."

"Absolutely," Jack agreed. "You're also the only one who can scout ahead and clear obstacles out of our way." He lifted his eyebrows. "Unless you *really* want to try cutting vine meshes with him balanced across your back."

Draycos's tail curved unhappily. But he was too smart not to see that Jack was right. "Very well," he said reluctantly. "I will assist you."

"That's okay." Crouching down, Jack got a grip on the Phooka's two uninjured legs. Then, bracing himself, he hauled the creature up and swung him onto his shoulders. "Geez," he muttered as he settled his load into place. "Why couldn't we have found a colony of baby K'da?"

"In a K'da colony, each generation is conceived and delivered together, within a two-year period," Draycos said. "This colony must be in the middle of that cycle."

"I was being rhetorical," Jack said with a sigh. "Don't just stand there. Find me a path."

CHAPTER 13

By now it was completely dark. Briefly, Jack wondered how Alison was doing with the rest of the herd, then put her from his mind. She could take care of herself, and he was likely to have enough troubles of his own without borrowing any of hers.

In the dusk, from thirty feet up, the footing along the cut had looked pretty tricky. In full dark, and up close and personal, it was even worse. Everything around him seemed to be twisted vines, stiff reeds, and thorny plants that grabbed at his clothing and shoes. Even with Draycos moving ahead and cutting the worst of it from his path, it was pretty slow going.

The limp Phooka balanced across his shoulders didn't make it any easier.

"At least we don't have anyone sniping at us," Jack puffed after fighting his way through a particularly unsociable row of reeds. "That's something, anyway."

"True," Draycos said. "And I find that fact ominous. The comm clip trick should not have fooled them nearly this long."

"Not unless they're *really* stupid," Jack admitted. "Maybe they decided to call it quits for the night."

"I don't know why they would," Draycos said. "They must certainly have equipment for seeing in the darkness. The disadvantage would be ours."

"Mine and Alison's, maybe, but not yours," Jack pointed out. "You do a lot better in the dark than we do. And personally, if I were them, I'd be a little leery about going up against a K'da poet-warrior at night."

"Perhaps," Draycos said, slashing through yet another stand of reeds. "We shall see when we rejoin the . . ." He trailed off.

"The herd?" Jack suggested quietly.

There was a sharp swishing noise through the reeds as Draycos twitched his tail. "I thought I could become used to the idea," the dragon said, a deep sadness in his voice. "But I cannot. I'm sorry."

"Nothing to be sorry for," Jack assured him. "I've never run into any primitive humans myself, but there are supposed to be a few tribes of them still scattered through Earth's denser jungles. I'd probably be just as weirded out if I ran into one of them."

There was a moment of silence, and Jack winced to himself. The situations weren't really the same, and they both knew it. "At any rate, I appreciate all you are doing for them," Draycos said. "Taking their burden upon yourself. Quite literally, in this case."

"No problem," Jack said. "Besides, I was herded around pretty much the same way back in the Whinyard's Edge. About time I got to see how the other side lives."

"I trust it is to your liking?"

Jack hunched forward and got a fresh grip on his passenger.

"Just great," he said, straightening up again and flinching as the leaves of a low-hanging branch brushed against his forehead. "I could do this all night."

"Let us hope you won't have to."

They continued on in silence. The ground didn't get any easier to navigate, but as his night vision slowly improved Jack began to get the knack of seeing and deciphering the various shades of gray around him. Draycos's gold scales appeared almost luminous in the faint starlight, providing him with a fairly clear view of the path the dragon was carving out.

Jack's improved vision undoubtedly saved him from a few stumbles over the next hour of travel. Unfortunately, it didn't do anything to help with the weight slowly crushing his shoulders.

But there was something else about his passenger, a growing feeling that Jack couldn't quite put his finger on. A kind of restlessness, along with an almost twitching that he couldn't exactly feel but somehow knew was there.

At first he assumed it had to do with the Phooka's double leg sprain. But adjusting his grip and trying to walk more smoothly didn't seem to affect the restlessness. The more he tried to ease the Phooka's ride, in fact, the more twitchy he became.

Jack had just decided it was time to ask Draycos about it when the Phooka's weight suddenly vanished. "Yowp!" Jack gasped.

"What?" Draycos demanded, twisting around.

"Sorry, sorry—I was just startled," Jack hastened to assure him, squirming a little as his former passenger twisted himself into place around Jack's chest, back, and legs. "I guess he decided he could use me as a host, after all."

"He is on you?" With a noisy bound, Draycos landed at Jack's side, his forepaws slipping into the gap in Jack's shirt. "Are you all right?"

"I'm fine," Jack said, pushing the probing forepaws away. "Cut it out, will you? That tickles."

"I was merely concerned," Draycos said, reluctantly pulling back.

"I'm fine," Jack repeated, straightening his shirt collar. "And this is our chance to make some decent time. Let's get moving."

And with the injured animal now riding Jack's skin like a good K'da should, the trip did indeed become easier. There were still a few patches of dense vegetation that Draycos had to cut through, but everywhere else Jack was able to plow his way through on his own.

It took them another half hour to get around the hill Jack had pointed out to Alison. On the far side was a much gentler slope, and twenty minutes later they were back to the level they'd been on when the Phooka had fallen off the ridge. "There we go," Jack murmured, breathing hard. "Piece of cake."

"You will someday have to cook for me this cake you often speak of," Draycos said dryly. "Come—we must find Alison and the others."

"Go ahead," Jack said, pushing aside the reeds at the base of a thick tree and sitting down against the trunk. "I'll wait here."

"That may be dangerous," Draycos warned. "There are

many night creatures around. Some are undoubtedly predators."

"I've got my tangler," Jack reminded him, pulling out the weapon and setting it on his lap. "I just need to rest for a few minutes."

"Then I will wait with you," Draycos said. "When you're ready, we'll go together."

"Look, just go, all right?" Jack said, starting to feel annoyed. "If you want to know the truth, I'm more worried about Alison than I am about me. Anyway, they can't be *that* far ahead of us. Just find them, then come back and get me."

"But—"

Abruptly, Draycos broke off, and in the darkness Jack saw his tongue flicking rapidly in and out of his mouth. "What is it?" he whispered.

"Movement," Draycos murmured back, putting his snout right up against Jack's ear. "The Malison Ring soldiers have arrived."

Jack's heart seemed to freeze in his chest. "Where?" he breathed.

"To the south," Draycos said, his tongue flicking out twice more. "Twenty of them at least, including nonhumans. They are traveling north in a sweep-line, fifty to one hundred yards back from our position."

Reflexively, Jack pressed his back harder against the tree. By pure blind luck he'd sat himself down on the north side of a tree that was wide enough to shield him from the view of the approaching soldiers. But that would only protect him until they passed and someone decided to take a look to the side.

"And," Draycos added, "there are three to five more already past us to the north."

Jack frowned. Two separate waves? Could Colonel Frost have figured out that he and Alison had split up?

"The lead group will be scouts," Draycos said, answering his unspoken question. "The larger group is the main fighting force."

So Frost *didn't* know he and Alison had been separated. Jack started breathing a little easier again. "Can you tell where Alison and the others are?" he asked Draycos.

Again, the tongue flicked out. "No, but the lack of activity implies they have not yet been attacked. Possibly not even spotted."

And in the meantime, Jack and Draycos were sitting between two enemy waves, both of which were completely unaware of their presence. There ought to be some seriously interesting ways to take advantage of that. "Any idea how the bad guys are traveling?"

"Most likely in a similar formation to that which they used earlier," Draycos said. "They will be in small groups of two to five soldiers. All the members of a group will be in sight of each other, but they will be spaced far enough apart to keep me from stopping all of them before they can sound an alarm."

Jack grimaced. "Any ideas?"

"They will be expecting a K'da warrior," Draycos said, lowering his voice even further. "But they will *not* be expecting a K'da warrior with a tangler."

"Ok-a-a-ay," Jack said slowly, frowning as he handed over the weapon. "And this is going to help us how?"

"You will see," Draycos said, taking the tangler and tucking it under his left foreleg. "How many shots are left?"

"Eleven."

"Good," Draycos said. "Stay here and remain still. The tree and its surrounding reeds should protect you from—"

And suddenly, without even a whisper of warning, Jack's head and shoulders were shoved hard into the tree trunk behind him as the red Phooka riding his skin suddenly leaped from the front of his shirt.

Reflexively, Jack opened his mouth to shout a warning, strangled it down just in time. *Move!* he thought urgently toward the Phooka, wiggling his fingers toward the creature as violently as he dared. The soldiers could arrive at any second. *Get out of here!*

But the red dragon ignored him. He shook himself once, like a dog just in out of the rain, and twisted his long neck around once to look at Jack. Then, turning around again, he jabbed his tongue out a few times and started casually loping northward.

He'd gotten perhaps ten paces when the forest exploded with the brilliant light and the shattering noise of gunfire from behind him.

"No!" Jack howled, the sound of his voice swallowed up by the stuttering thunderclaps.

But it was too late. Before the red Phooka could even react, his scales were already bursting apart with multiple hits. He writhed once in surprise and agony, collapsing to the ground.

An instant later he was gone.

Jack stared at the spot where the Phooka had been, his stomach wanting to be sick. Draycos had told him how K'da simply vanished when they died, going two-dimensional and fading away.

But to watch it happen right before his eyes was as eerie as it was horrifying.

And still the gunfire continued to rake the area. Jack pressed his hands tightly to his ears, trying to block out the noise hammering his skull and wondering what in blazes the soldiers were doing. Did they really think that poor, stupid animal could have escaped their attack?

And then, suddenly, he understood. Of course no mere animal could have lived through that. But they weren't hunting animals. In fact, odds were they didn't even know the Phooka herd existed.

They were hunting Draycos, poet-warrior of the K'da.

And they probably thought they had just killed him.

Jack looked around, squinting in the flickering light as he searched for his partner. He finally spotted him, clinging upside down to the tree trunk among the branches five feet above Jack's head. The dragon's scales had gone black in K'da combat mode, and there was a glint in his glowing green eyes that sent a fresh shiver down Jack's spine.

With a final lingering burst, the gunfire ceased. Cautiously, Jack eased his hands away from his throbbing ears.

Only to find there was an echo of the same sound coming from somewhere in the distance in front of him.

Alison and the others were under attack.

"Draycos!" he whispered urgently.

"I know," the dragon whispered back, his voice deathly calm. "Stay here. I will return for you."

CHAPTER 14

There was no need for stealth now, not with the chattering gunfire in the distance drowning out all other sounds. Draycos leaped upward through the branches, ignoring the swishing leaves that otherwise would have been a dead giveaway of his position.

But then, why would the mercenaries below him even care about noises overhead? As far as they were concerned, he was dead. They had just killed him.

He could feel a snarl of fury building within him. Ruthlessly, he forced it back. Right now, the combat situation required his complete attention. There would be time later to mourn the innocent Phooka the mercenaries had slaughtered.

To mourn him, and perhaps bring him justice.

Fifteen feet above the ground, a particularly thick branch angled out to the right. Changing direction, Draycos headed along it until it began to bend beneath his weight. There, he crouched down, bringing Jack's tangler out from carrying position and settling it into his paw.

He was just in time. With the battle begun, and the K'da poet-warrior finally disposed of, the mercenaries had also abandoned their efforts at stealth and were hurrying northward toward the distant gunfire as quickly as the terrain and vegetation would allow. A group of four passed almost directly beneath him, their guns held ready.

Smiling tightly to himself, Draycos fired.

Four shots. Four invisible bursts of thread instantly entangling their victims. Four nearly invisible flickers of light as the capacitors delivered a powerful electric jolt through the threads.

Four muffled thuds as unconscious soldiers hit the ground.

The next foursome was moving through the woods twenty feet farther along the right flank. Tucking the tangler back under his foreleg, Draycos dug his claws into the branch for traction and threw himself toward them.

There was no convenient branch or tree trunk waiting at the far end of his leap. But again, subtlety was no longer required. He landed six feet behind the hurrying mercenaries, half-crushing a—fortunately—thornless bush. Four more shots, and four more of the enemy were out of action.

The tangler still had three shots left. With a little luck on his part and a little carelessness on his enemies', Draycos knew he could probably take out another foursome before the weapon ran dry.

But he didn't dare take the time. The gunfight ahead was growing more intense by the minute, and if Alison wasn't already in serious trouble she soon would be.

Meanwhile, Jack should be all right, provided he stayed put as he'd been told. Tucking the tangler back under his foreleg, Draycos leaped into the trees and headed north.

He had covered roughly half the distance when he spotted the flickering light of the gunshots. He had covered nearly half of what was left before the sound separated itself enough for him to realize that there were, in fact, three distinct types of weapons involved.

Two were standard projectile weapons: the mercenaries' rapid-fire machine guns and Alison's Corvine pistol. The third, from the soft *chuffing* noise it made, seemed to be a higher-powered version of Jack's own tangler. Apparently, Colonel Frost really *was* serious about taking Jack alive.

The light flashes were becoming more distinct, and Draycos could now see where each group was coming from. He made one final leap to a tree right on the edge of the battle and paused there to study the situation.

And as he did so, he found himself raising his estimation of Alison's warrior training, wherever that training had come from. Taken by surprise, and at the low end of five-to-one odds, she was nevertheless holding her own with remarkable skill.

Starting with her choice of combat position. She had taken refuge behind a large tree, which had apparently survived some long-ago flood that had washed away a good deal of the soil at its base. The result was a shallow hollow in the ground filled with an exposed tangle of thick roots. Lurking within the resulting cage, Alison could shoot at her attackers all she wanted, while they in turn had little chance of getting through with a tangler cartridge. Even as Draycos watched, yet another spattering of white threads burst harmlessly against the roots.

But that didn't mean she was safe. From the pattern of fire, it was clear the mercenaries were using their machine guns to pin her in place while they waited for the main force to sweep in on both sides and surround her. Once that happened, all they had to do was work someone in close enough to get a clear shot, and the battle would be over.

Or worse, they might realize it wasn't Jack in there and decide they didn't need her alive. The tree roots might block tangler cartridges, but they wouldn't protect her from the mercenaries' machine guns. Draycos had to take them out before what was left of the main force arrived.

Problem was, there were five soldiers pinning Alison down, and he had only three shots left in his tangler.

Which meant he would have to do this the hard way. Maneuvering around the side of the tree, he picked out the soldier farthest back from the others. If he took out that one first, then did the same to the next in line, he could use his remaining tangler cartridges on the other three.

He was bracing himself to leap when, without warning, a line of shots tore into the tree just below him.

He twisted back around the other side, barely making it before the slugs shattered the spot where he'd been crouching. Tucking his legs in close to his body, he pressed himself against the trunk, wincing as the edges of the tree disintegrated around him. The soldiers below had spotted him.

And unless he did something fast, he was going to die.

"Stay here," Draycos whispered, his voice barely audible over the distant gunfire. "I will return for you."

And with that, he was gone. Jack pressed his back against his tree, watching as the K'da's shadowy form headed upward and then disappeared to the right. A minute later, from that same direction, Jack thought he saw the flicker of a tangler charge. A few seconds after that, he caught a glimpse of another flicker a little farther away.

There was a whisper of movement to his left, and Jack turned just as more shadowy figures hurried past. He pressed harder into his tree, but as far as he could tell, none of the mercenaries even turned around.

And then they were gone.

Jack took a deep breath, feeling his heart pounding in his ears. *Stay here,* the dragon had said. Stay here where it was safe, while he and Alison dealt with the attack.

Like heck he would.

He found the first group of four soldiers barely ten feet away, sprawled unconscious on the ground. Draycos had nearly missed one of them, he noted: the tangler webbing only covered him from shoulders to hips.

That could prove useful. Unstrapping the soldier's helmet, Jack lifted it off and put it on.

"—not moving, and there's no response from any of them," Colonel Frost's voice came tartly from the helmet's comm. "Morgan must have gotten them."

"Copy," another clipped voice said. "What about the girl?"

"Caprizini has her pinned," Frost said. "We can take her any time we want. The important thing is to find Morgan."

"Copy," the other said. "Circling back now."

"Make sure he's in the bag before you move," Frost

warned. "And remember: tanglers only. I want him alive *and* unharmed."

"Copy."

Jack grimaced. So they knew he was back here, and they were on their way to get him. Meanwhile, Draycos had scampered off with his only weapon.

But that was okay. It was time to trade up anyway.

The soldier had a small pistol belted at his right and a pair of concussion grenades ready at his left. His main weapon, still cradled in his slack grip, was a compact over/under weapon with a machine gun on top and a long-barreled tangler underneath.

It took Jack a few seconds to dig the gun out from under the tangler mesh. Folding its collapsible metal shoulder stock out of his way, he headed back toward the tree where Draycos had left him.

He was halfway there when the background chatter on his helmet comm abruptly changed tone. "Dumbarton, looks like Morgan's got Hammerstein's gun," Frost said sharply. "We've got movement on it—heading west."

Jack looked down at the weapon in his hands, his stomach suddenly knotting. So there were trackers in the guns. Frost had been trickier than he'd expected.

But if Frost had been clever enough to put in trackers, maybe he'd been clever enough for something else, too.

Experimentally, Jack swung the weapon in a horizontal arc. As he did so, a small red light just below the sight winked on and then off. He'd guessed right: along with the trackers, Frost had also included a friend/foe system to warn his soldiers if they were pointing their weapons at one another.

On the surface, the arrangement made a lot of sense. Even with night-sight goggles, vision in the middle of a forest was pretty limited. And with these lopsided odds, Jack and Alison could shoot at pretty much anything that moved, while their opponents had to be careful not to shoot one another in the confusion of battle.

The downside to the system was that once Jack had one of their guns, as he did now, all he had to do was find a line of fire that gave him a red dot and pull the trigger.

Problem was, the tangler didn't have nearly enough range to poke its way through all the undergrowth. That just left him the machine gun, and that would mean killing them.

His stomach twisted into a fresh knot. He'd never in his life killed anyone, and he didn't really want to start now. At some point it might become necessary, but that wasn't a decision he was ready to make on his own.

Fortunately, if he did this right, he wouldn't have to.

He swept the gun in a complete circle, noting where the lights went on. The Malison Ring soldiers didn't yet have him surrounded, though they were definitely working on it. From what Frost had said, they would probably wait until they had a complete circle before moving in.

That should give him just enough time.

He set the gun down beside the tree where Draycos had left him. Returning to the half-webbed soldier, he dragged the man over to the tree and rolled him into concealment beneath the reeds. He wrapped the other's limp hands around the gun, propping the weapon up on a couple of sticks. On an infrared viewer, the whole thing ought to look like someone lying quietly in ambush. Digging one last time beneath the tangler threads, Jack helped himself to the soldier's two concussion grenades. Then, taking a moment to heap a few handfuls of dead leaves over the soldier's legs for extra concealment, he returned to where the other three soldiers were sprawled.

Even with the limitations of night-vision systems, Jack's clothing would never pass as a Malison Ring uniform, and there wasn't enough time for him to switch outfits with someone else. But there were other ways. Lying down on the ground beside one of the soldiers, Jack rolled the unconscious man up onto him, leaving only his helmeted head showing.

Again, it wasn't something that would hold up to close examination. But Jack had no intention of giving Dumbarton's soldiers that much time. Turning his head to face the tree where the fake ambush was waiting, he pulled the pin from one of the grenades and lay still.

The soldiers were good, all right. Even with the darkness and distant noise, Jack had expected he would spot *some* sign of their arrival. But his first warning was the sudden flurry of tangler shots spattering the decoy's position from all directions. "Done," Dumbarton's voice came in Jack's ear.

"You got him?" Frost asked.

"We got him and a half," Dumbarton reported, a note of satisfaction in his voice.

"Watch it," Frost warned. "This kid's clever—"

"Colonel!" a new voice cut in. "I think I just spotted the K'da!"

"Where?" Frost snapped.

"Up on a tree near the girl."

"Hammerstein said they already nailed him," Dumbarton objected.

"I guess Hammerstein was wrong," Frost said icily. "What's *your* excuse, Caprizini?"

There was a sputter of gunfire. "Can't get him from here," Caprizini said. "The trunk's too thick."

"Is he close enough to the ground to use a grenade?"

"He's too close to the girl," Caprizini said.

"Then just keep him pinned," Frost said. "As soon as Dumbarton's got Morgan, he can get over there and flank him."

"Do we still need the girl?" someone put in. "I thought we mostly wanted Morgan."

"Let's make sure we actually have Morgan first," Frost said. "Dumbarton, move in. Slow and careful."

"Copy."

There was a rustling in the bushes. Jack eased his head up a bit and saw a circle of shadowy figures closing in on the decoy's position. Something moved at the corner of his eye, and he flinched slightly as one of the soldiers took a long step over him and the man he was hiding beneath. The circle closed to within three yards of the tree.

And with a flip of his wrist, Jack lobbed the grenade right into the center.

He had expected a mild concussion blast like the ones created by the grenades he'd worked with back with the Whinyard's Edge. They were small, civilized things that would knock down everyone for three yards and leave them stunned and confused for a few minutes.

Unfortunately for Dumbarton and his buddies, the Malison Ring used much more powerful grenades.

The blast was deafening, the sound slamming into Jack like a runaway truck. The shock wave was even worse, lifting the unconscious soldier on top of him a couple of inches into the air and shoving him right off onto the ground.

Carefully, struggling to keep his balance, Jack pulled himself upright. He was shaking all over, half his body numb, and *he'd* been lying flat on the ground when the grenade went off. The soldiers who'd been moving toward the blast would be lucky if they were out of bed in a week.

There were voices coming from the helmet comm, but it was impossible to make out the words through the ringing in his ears. Pulling off the helmet, he tucked it under his arm and gave his ears a careful rub. His hearing was starting to come back, fortunately. Still rubbing at his ears, he turned toward the north.

And sprawled flat on his back as a pair of glowing silver eyes appeared squarely in front of him.

"*Blast* it," he muttered, scrambling back to his feet. It was the gray female Phooka, of course, the one Draycos had dubbed Taneem. "Don't *do* that."

Taneem cocked her head quizzically to the side and started to back up. "Wait a second," Jack said, stepping toward her as an idea started to sift through his still-dazed brain. The soldiers near Alison's position had said they had Draycos pinned up a tree.

But if they now saw Draycos on the ground running away . . .

"I need you to do something for me, Taneem," he said, gingerly cupping his hand under the Phooka's triangular jaw. She twitched a little at his touch but didn't try to pull away. "I need you to run north—that way"—he pointed—"until you find your other people and the Erassvas. Can you do that?"

She cocked her head again, her glowing eyes steady on him. Then, abruptly, she turned and bounded off through the trees.

"Right," Jack muttered under his breath. Whether she'd understood any of that or not, at least she *was* headed north. Now if she would just keep going past the Malison Ring soldiers and not get distracted by a pretty butterfly, this might work.

He could only hope she would also run past the soldiers fast enough to keep herself from getting shot.

But there was nothing he could do about that now. Settling the helmet back onto his head, trying to listen to the chatter through his still-ringing ears, he headed after her.

There was a flat *crack,* and even at his distance Draycos felt a ripple of the shock wave roll over his scales. From the sound and the lack of flame, he guessed it had come from a concussion-type grenade.

And it seemed to have come from near the spot where he'd left Jack.

Had the boy been captured?

He hissed in frustration. But whatever had happened to Jack, there wasn't anything Draycos could do about it right now. The soldiers below continued to plaster his tree with gunfire, the machine-gun rounds slowly but steadily chipping away at the edges of the trunk.

So far, Alison's own gunfire was keeping them from leaving their positions and coming around to where they could get a better shot. But sooner or later her weapon would run dry, or reinforcements would arrive, or the hail of metal would simply chew away enough of the tree for them to get to him.

They were making considerable progress toward that last goal, in fact. Already a couple of inches on each side of the trunk had been splintered away, forcing him to tuck his legs more tightly against his body to stay clear. Other rounds were hammering against the back of the tree, and he could only imagine how much more damage was being done back there. Two to three more minutes, if they didn't run out of ammunition, and they would start hitting him.

Unless . . .

He twisted his head around to look upward along the trunk. It was tall enough, he decided, and in the faint and sputtering light of the gunfire it looked like the top section was leaning the right way.

There was one way to find out for sure. Turning to face downward again, he made sure he had a solid grip on the trunk with his hind paws. Then, extending his forepaw claws, he began digging into the trunk in front of him.

By the time the flying splinters began jabbing against his scales, he'd carved a groove perhaps two inches deep into the wood. That might not be deep enough; but whether it was or not, he'd run out of time. Digging his foreleg claws into the tree beneath the groove, he leaned forward, pushing as hard as he could against the upper part of the tree with his hind legs.

Nothing happened. Setting his jaw, he pushed again. Still nothing. Even with the tree as badly damaged as it was, he simply didn't have the leverage to break the top section free.

And then, as he tried to think of something else to try, there was a startled shout from below him. The gunfire faltered; and then, to his surprise, it started up again at full force.

But this volley wasn't directed at him and his tree. Instead, it seemed to be concentrated on something at ground level.

Jack? Hissing helplessly between his teeth, Draycos forced himself to look.

But it wasn't the boy he spotted running at full speed through the trees. It was, instead, one of the Phookas.

How the creature had ended up here in the middle of the battle he couldn't guess. But for the moment, that didn't matter. What mattered was that with the mercenaries' attention distracted, he finally had a chance to move.

He twisted around on the tree, half-expecting to get shot in the process. But the soldiers' full attention was apparently on the sprinting Phooka below. Digging his claws into the wood, he headed up, climbing onto the thinner sections of trunk where there was little protection from gunfire from below.

But again, the mercenaries were apparently not watching. He reached a main branch extending outward in the direction of the soldiers and leaped onto it, running as far along it as he could.

The branch seemed to dip beneath his weight. Then, from below and behind him, he heard the sharp crack of fracturing wood. He stopped and turned back around.

And as he did so, the tree finally broke. Slowly, almost majestically, the top bowed over and began to topple toward the soldiers below. Holding tightly to his branch, Draycos rode it down.

The treetop didn't make it all the way to the ground, of course—the forest was far too dense for that. Instead, it tore its way noisily through the surrounding trees, ripping off its own branches and twigs as well as theirs, before getting caught up in larger branches and stopping a dozen feet above the ground.

But that was all Draycos needed. Caught in the rain of debris, with the spectacle of a tree falling toward them, the mercenaries had reacted exactly as he'd expected. Abandoning their positions, they were scrambling madly to get out of the way.

And as the treetop settled reluctantly to a halt, Draycos attacked.

It was no contest. Between Draycos's earlier tangler attack, the incident with the concussion grenade—whatever exactly had happened with that—and now the falling treetop, the soldiers had had one confusing distraction too many.

He caught the first two completely off-guard, knocking

them out with blows to the sides of their necks before they even knew he was there. The third was able to turn nearly all the way around before Draycos sent him to join the other two. The fourth and fifth managed to get all the way around, and the fifth was even able to get off a wild shot.

And with that, it was over.

Or at least, Draycos hoped it was over. Crouching low to the ground, his senses alert, he scanned the area to the south. If Frost had sent in reinforcements, they could be arriving at any time.

Across the way, a figure wearing a Malison Ring helmet emerged from between a pair of trees. Draycos tensed but then relaxed as a hint of the newcomer's scent touched his nostrils and tongue. It was Jack, alive and apparently well.

There hadn't been any fire from Alison's position since the treetop had come down. Still, Draycos doubted she had lost any of her watchfulness. Keeping a wary eye in that direction, he headed toward the distant figure.

Jack had taken off the helmet by the time he arrived. "You've been a busy little dragon, haven't you?" he commented as he surveyed the area.

"And the busyness is going to continue," Draycos said. "We must leave before reinforcements arrive."

Jack shook his head. "Don't worry about it," he said. "Frost has another wave on the way, but I'm guessing they're just coming to retrieve this first bunch." He grinned tightly. "He wants them back before you hamstring them like you did those first two."

Draycos looked back toward where he'd left his latest batch

of unconscious soldiers. Now that Jack mentioned it, it really *wouldn't* take very long to deal that same injury to them. And it would certainly put them out of the fight.

"Jack?" Alison's voice called cautiously.

Draycos grimaced. It wouldn't take long, but he certainly didn't want to do it with Alison watching. "We should be on our way," he said.

"No argument here," Jack agreed, putting out his hand.

Draycos laid his paw on the palm and slipped up the sleeve, settling into his accustomed place across the boy's back. A surge of warmth and strength flowed into the K'da as he did so—he hadn't realized just how long it had been since he'd been connected to his host. "I'm ready."

He sensed Jack taking a deep breath. "It's me, Alison," the boy called, starting forward. "Don't shoot."

CHAPTER 15

"I figured Frost was overdue to pull something cute," Alison said as they made their way through the forest. "So when we hit the stream up here, I decided to send everyone else ahead while I went back and waited for trouble to show up." She waved a hand at Jack. "And for you to show up, too, of course. Speaking of which, shouldn't you have a red Phooka with you?"

"I did," Jack said, grimacing. "The soldiers got him."

"Oh." Alison seemed taken aback. "I'm sorry. I just assumed that was the one who went tearing by just before they cleverly brought the top of that tree down on top of themselves."

"No, that was the gray one," Jack told her. "She must have gotten lost from the rest of the herd."

Alison snorted. "Wandered away on purpose, more like. That one's been trouble since we started. So the red Phooka . . . ?"

"He was the first set of gunfire you heard," Jack said. "I was hiding by a tree and he just took off."

"Odd," Alison said. "Did he attack them or something?"

"No, he was just wandering away," Jack said. "Not that odd, really. He'd probably picked up the herd's trail and was trying to get back to them."

"I was talking about the mercs' reaction," Alison said. "They shouldn't be spooking nearly this soon. That's a bad sign."

"What do you mean, spooking?"

"Shooting at something that's not a threat when they're supposed to be sneaking up on someone," she explained. "I wonder if they know something about Phookas that we don't."

"I don't know," Jack lied. Of course the soldiers would have orders to shoot at anything even vaguely K'da-shaped on sight. But Alison had no way of knowing that. "Maybe they've run into whatever it is that clawed the bark off that tree we saw," he suggested. "That would sure spook *me*."

"Maybe," she said. "Might explain why they were burning so much ammo shooting up that tree, too. But if there was something up there, I never saw it. I don't suppose you thought to grab one of their guns or anything."

"Actually, that would have been a bad idea," Jack told her. "They've got trackers in the guns. I don't know where."

"Probably the shoulder stock," Alison said. "That's where they usually put things like that. Keeps them clear of the moving parts that way. Here we are."

The stream was, to Jack's mind, more like a small river than the little babbling brook he'd expected. It was at least five yards across, moving swiftly but quietly. "Where are they?" he asked, peering across at the other side.

"If they're where I told Hren to stay, they're fifty yards upriver and twenty yards north on the far side," Alison said. "Afraid you're going to get your feet wet. Hey, what do you know? There she is."

Jack followed her pointing finger to see Taneem emerge from behind a row of reeds at the water's edge. "Oh, good," he said, a wave of relief rolling through him. He already had the red Phooka's death on his conscience. He didn't particularly want Taneem's there, too. "Right where I told her to go, too. Good little Phooka."

"You *told* her to come here?"

"Well, I told her to find the rest of the herd," Jack corrected. "This is close enough for jazz."

"No, I'm still working on the *told her* part," Alison said. "Since when do you talk to Phookas? Or maybe I should say, since when do they *listen*?"

"You should try it sometime," Jack said blandly, taking a step toward Taneem and holding out his hand. With only a slight hesitation, and clearly to Alison's amazement, the gray Phooka walked right up to him.

And to Jack's own surprise she laid her muzzle across his palm.

"Careful," Alison muttered. "Lots of sharp teeth in there."

"It's all right," Jack said, gazing down into Taneem's silver eyes. So she remembered him holding her muzzle this way earlier. Interesting. "So where are we going, again?" he asked, letting go of Taneem's muzzle and taking a step backward.

"Upriver," Alison said. She was still staring at the two of them, an unreadable expression on her face. "If you and your new pet would follow me?"

Jack gestured. "Lead the way."

They stepped into the water and turned upstream. As the icy water flowed around his shins, Jack winced, wondering how deep it was going to get.

Wondering, too, why Draycos was suddenly so tense.

They found the rest of the group exactly where Alison had said they would be. The Erassvas were huddled together beneath a tall outcropping of rock, looking altogether miserable. The Phookas were scattered around them, lying quietly in ones and twos around their hosts' feet.

"Cheerful-looking bunch, aren't they?" Jack murmured as he and Alison approached.

"Hren's not very happy with me," she said. "I think he's finally grasped the fact that the people back there want to hurt us."

Jack grimaced. If he only knew how badly. "He can't give up on us now," Jack warned. "Frost's mood hasn't had anywhere to go lately but down. Who knows what he'd do if they tried to go back?"

"I'd just as soon not find out," Alison agreed. "Well, maybe passing out some ration bars will help."

"You go ahead," Jack said. "I want to take a stroll around the perimeter."

"Your tangler have any ammo left?"

"I've got three shots," Jack said. "But I don't think I'll have to use any more of them tonight."

Alison grunted. "I hope you're right. Watch yourself."

She headed toward the huddled Erassvas, while Jack angled off toward the eastern edge of their encampment. "You should have taken some of the mercenaries' tangler rounds," Draycos murmured from his shoulder.

"Couldn't," Jack murmured back. "They're using military-caliber ammo. Too big for my civilian version."

"Then you should have taken one of their weapons," Draycos countered, an edge to his voice.

"Their weapons include handy little trackers, remember?" Jack said, frowning down into his shirt. This wasn't the calm, patient K'da poet-warrior he was used to. "In fact, they probably hoped we *would* help ourselves to one."

"Alison has told you where the tracker is."

"Sure, *now* I know," Jack said. "At the time, I didn't. What have I done wrong *this* time?"

"You deliberately sent a civilian into danger," Draycos bit out. He lifted his head from Jack's shoulder to glare into the boy's eyes. "Or do you deny that was your intent when you ordered Taneem to find the herd?"

"No, that was exactly what I had in mind," Jack said, struggling to hold on to his own temper. Draycos was being completely unreasonable. "I don't know if you were aware of it, buddy, but you'd been spotted. I figured you could use a diversion."

"I did not need a *civilian* to be that diversion," Draycos snapped.

"Hey, *I* didn't ask her to wander into a war zone," Jack shot back. "She got there all by herself. What was I supposed to do? Walk away and leave her?"

There was a long silence from inside his shirt. Then, to Jack's surprise, Draycos gave a long, tired sigh. "I cannot protect you anymore, Jack," the dragon said quietly. "Not now that they know I survived the Iota Klestis attack. There are simply too many of them."

Jack grimaced. He should have known there was something like that behind the dragon's anger. "Okay, so things have changed," he said. "But things *always* change. The trick is to figure out how they're changing and adapt."

"I understand that," Draycos said. "The difficulty is that I can no longer think of how to do that."

"Then we'll just have to figure it out together," Jack said firmly. "And before you get too depressed, let me point out that you've now repulsed two separate attacks and decoyed a third, all in one day. That's a pretty good record."

"I could not have done so without your help."

"Which is how it's supposed to be," Jack reminded him. "We're partners, remember?"

"I suppose—" Abruptly, the dragon broke off. "Listen."

Jack stopped in midstep, holding his breath as he strained his ears. In the distance, he could hear a low rumble. "Sounds like the transport firing up its main drive," he said. "Geez. I hope Frost hasn't decided to carpet bomb the forest after all."

But the sound didn't seem to be approaching. It rose once in volume as the pilot fed power to the drive, then faded steadily away until it was lost in the background forest noises.

"Now, *that's* interesting," Jack said, frowning into the darkness. "You don't suppose they've given up, do you?"

"More likely Colonel Frost has decided to speak to Neverlin," Draycos said.

"Probably," Jack said, nodding. "Do a little ranting and ask for further instructions."

"Or for more troops," Draycos said darkly.

"No, I don't think so," Jack said, scratching his cheek as he gazed into the darkness. "Seems to me they have to be running a shoestring operation here. Reinforcements may not be available."

"Explain."

"Basically, I figure there are only so many Malison Ring soldiers Frost and Neverlin can trust with the whole story," Jack said. "Pulling in new troops from outside their little conspiracy would mean more chances for something to leak out."

"And they cannot afford for StarForce or the Internos government to hear of this," Draycos said. "I see."

"Especially with only two and a half months to go before the refugees arrive," Jack agreed. "So what you see is pretty much what you get."

"You may be right," Draycos said. "Certainly the presence of the soldier Dumbarton at both the Iota Klestis ambush and the Chookoock family slave auction supports that theory."

"Not to mention right here on Rho Scorvi," Jack said.

Draycos's head lifted from his shoulder again. "He is *here*?"

"He was the guy in charge of the group I clobbered with that concussion grenade," Jack said, frowning at the sky as a sudden thought struck him. "Now that I think about it, between you, me, and Alison, a *lot* of Frost's men got clobbered back there."

"Far too many for him to have collected and taken back aboard his transport so quickly," Draycos agreed thoughtfully. "Especially as there were no likely spots nearby for a vehicle that size to land."

"So did he just abandon them?" Jack asked. "That doesn't seem likely."

"I agree," Draycos said. "More likely he brought the transport to the area on lifters and dropped or rappelled more of his troops in to care for the casualties."

Jack grimaced. "So Frost may be gone, but we still have his hyenas to deal with?"

"Most likely," Draycos said. "Perhaps they will have orders to take no action until he returns."

"Maybe," Jack said doubtfully. "Still, at the very least, they'll probably want to avoid further combat until tonight's attack force has recovered."

"Indeed," Draycos agreed. "We should have at least a day or two of breathing space."

"I'll take it," Jack said. "Let's go back and run all this past Alison."

Alison listened thoughtfully as Jack explained the line of reasoning he and Draycos had come up with. "Sounds good to me," she said when he had finished. "I wonder how close the nearest InterWorld transmitter is."

"It's got to be at least a few hours away," Jack said. "Add in whatever time Frost and Neverlin will need to figure out a new strategy and we're probably talking at least a day. Maybe more if Neverlin is in transit somewhere and Frost can't get hold of him right away."

"I doubt Neverlin's anywhere except hanging around his own InterWorld transmitter waiting for the joyous news of our capture," Alison said sourly. "And he probably doesn't need to rappel his men down, by the way. A Kapstan usually carries a short-range floater plus one or two ground-hugger armored cars. If Frost left the floater behind, they could shuttle troops all over the forest if they wanted to."

"Oh, that's encouraging," Jack said with a grimace. "How come you know so much about Kapstans, anyway?"

"Same way I know they can carry up to thirty troops," she said. "Mercenaries and mercenary equipment are my job." She cocked her head to the side, the posture somehow reminding Jack of Taneem. "You ready to tell me what exactly they want with you?"

Jack lifted his hands, palms upward. "I know Neverlin is extremely annoyed with me, for a couple of different reasons," he said. "But if all he wanted was to kill me, a few well-placed missiles would have taken care of the problem."

"And they wouldn't have bothered with tanglers back there, either," Alison agreed. "They definitely want you alive."

"For which we should both be grateful," Jack said, shivering. "*Why* they want me alive, though, I haven't a clue. Really."

For a moment Alison was silent. "Well, work on it," she said at last. "Just in case your ship *didn't* survive its high-dive belly flop."

She leaned back to look at the small section of stars visible through the trees. "Too bad we haven't run into any decent-sized clearings. With the transport gone, you could whistle up the *Essenay* and we could be out of here before they knew what was happening."

"Wouldn't work," Jack said. "Uncle Virge will have the comm off, along with every other system he can do without. He won't turn it back on until he's well inside the forest and ready to start listening. Any idea how much farther we've got to go?"

"I'd guess we did eight miles today, as the gooney bird flies," Alison said. "Maybe a little more. Barring any serious trouble, four to five more days ought to do it."

Four to five days, with the Malison Ring on their tails the whole way. But there wasn't much they could do about that. "Let's make it four," he said. "You want me to take the first watch?"

"I think we can safely skip that for tonight," Alison said. "Like you said, the mercs aren't likely to come looking for more trouble right away. And both of us can use as much rest as we can get."

"Sounds good to me," Jack said. Suddenly, his eyelids were drooping with fatigue. It had indeed been a full and rich day. "Pleasant dreams."

Besides, even if he and Alison both slept through the night, the camp wouldn't be left unguarded. Not if Jack knew Draycos.

CHAPTER 16

There was no trouble that night, from the mercenaries or anything else. Alison got everyone up at dawn, then sat around in obvious irritation for another hour and a half while Hren and the other Erassvas insisted on picking themselves a breakfast of berries and watching the Phookas perform their ritual morning dance. After that, the group finally got under way.

The day turned out to be a much calmer version of the previous one. Once the morning mists burned off, the air began to warm up, though it never got above chilly in the perpetual twilight beneath the trees. Still, the cool made for good travel weather. Moreover, the night's sleep had worked wonders with the Erassvas' mood, and though the aliens walked mostly in silence, they no longer seemed angry or resentful.

As before, Alison and the green Phooka led the way. Jack brought up the rear, moving back and forth to either side as he watched for Phooka strays. Draycos, for his part, traveled in a wide-ranging circle around the rest of them, alert for signs of enemy activity.

But for this day, at least, the Malison Ring seemed uninterested in starting any fresh trouble. The result was a quiet, uneventful, almost pleasant journey.

And it gave Jack the chance to make some unexpected discoveries.

All through his childhood, he'd tried numerous times to talk Uncle Virgil into letting him have a pet. But the other had always turned him down, insisting he didn't want any animals underfoot on his ship. As a result, Jack's only contact with pets had been with those of other people, usually during the course of some scam.

Most of those contacts had been very brief, with Jack unable to spare much time or attention from the job at hand. He'd thus come away with the vague impression that, aside from superficial things like color of fur or feathers, all animals were pretty much the same.

Now, to his mild surprise, he discovered that nothing could be further from the truth. Though yesterday's travels had hinted at it, it was only during this second day that he began to realize just how different the Phookas were from one another.

They had markedly different personalities, for one thing. Some were very obedient, even docile, while others were stubbornly independent. Some seemed to plod along with little interest in their surroundings, while others could be distracted by the slightest hint of something new or interesting.

The curious ones, he found, were relatively easy to bring back to the main group. All he had to do was let them get their fill of the latest plant or bug, at which point they could be led back to the fold. The fiercely independent ones, the ones who wandered off simply because they felt like it, required a firmer hand or a more diplomatic approach if Jack didn't want to get a warning snap of tooth-filled jaws for his trouble.

Fortunately, none of them actually bit him. With a little trial and error, he eventually worked out ways to handle even the most stubborn ones.

Jack had grown up among the thieves and con artists and killers of the Orion Arm's criminal underworld. His adventures with Draycos over the past three and a half months had added soldiers and slaves to that list of acquaintances. The laid-back Erassvas and their Phooka companions made for a welcome change of pace.

"I could get used to this," he commented to Alison during one of their brief rest breaks. "Maybe when this is all over I'll buy a flock or herd of something and go into business for myself."

She snorted. "You'd last two weeks," she said. "After that, it would drive you crazy. You're not the herdsman type."

"You might be surprised," Jack said, annoyed in spite of himself that she would dismiss the idea so quickly.

"Oh, I'm surprised all the time," she countered calmly. "But not about something like this. Trust me."

The day continued uneventfully, and as the forest's twilight began to darken Alison found a slightly protected hollow for them to camp in for the night. Again Jack volunteered to check the perimeter; and as he did so, he related his earlier conversation with Alison to Draycos.

"She's right," Draycos said when he'd finished. "There are people who have the skill and patience to spend their lives taking care of animals. But you are not one of them."

"Yeah, but I'm good at it," Jack insisted. "You've seen me. I could do this."

The K'da lifted his head slightly from Jack's shoulder. "I do not understand your attitude," he said. "Are you saying you *would* want this sort of job?"

Jack hesitated. "Well . . . no, probably not," he had to admit. "I just don't like everyone taking for granted that I *couldn't* do it."

"Of course you *could* handle the job, at least for a short time," Draycos said. "Indeed, as you just pointed out, you *are* doing it. The average intelligent being can perform an amazingly wide range of activities when it is necessary. What I meant—and I presume what Alison meant, as well—was that a herdsman's job is not what you are best suited for."

"No, I'm best suited to be a thief and con man," Jack said, grimacing. "That's what Uncle Virgil always told me, anyway."

"Uncle Virgil had his own reasons for saying such things," Draycos said. "You have many talents, Jack. When the time comes, you will find the job that best fits you."

Jack sighed. "Maybe."

"There is no 'maybe' about it," Draycos said firmly. "Why do you doubt?"

"Because I'm already fourteen years old and I still haven't figured it out," Jack said. "I'll bet *you* knew you were a poet long before that."

"There were some indications, yes," Draycos conceded. "Even before I could compose poems of my own, I very much loved the poetry of others."

"See, that's the thing," Jack said. "I like poetry, too, especially stuff like yours that actually rhymes. But I still couldn't write a poem to save my life."

"Have you ever tried?"

"Once, back when I was ten," Jack said. "It was pathetic. Nothing like yours or the songs my mother used to sing to me."

Draycos lifted his head from Jack's shoulder. "Your mother used to write songs?"

"I don't know whether she wrote them or just sang them," Jack said. "And I can't sing, either."

"I would like to hear one of them," Draycos said. "Do you remember any?"

Jack pursed his lips. He hadn't counted on having to give a recital. "There's one I remember pretty well," he said. "I'm not a hundred percent sure of the tune, but here are the words:

> "We stand before; we stand behind;
> We seek the *drue* with heart and mind.
> From sun to sun the dross refined,
> Lest any soul be cast adrift.

> "We are the few who stand between
> The darkness and the noontime sheen.
> Our eyes and vision clear and keen:
> To find the *drue,* we seek and sift.

> "We toil alone, we bear the cost,
> To soothe all those in turmoil tossed,
> And give back hope, where hope was lost:
> Our lives, for them, shall be our gift."

Jack stopped, his eyes unexpectedly filling with tears. "There were a lot of other songs," he said. "That's the only one I really remember."

"It's beautiful," Draycos said quietly. "Tell me, what is *drue*?"

"I asked Uncle Virgil once, and he said it was a valuable mineral," Jack said. "I've never been able to find it in any dictionary, though. It must have been the local slang name for something."

"Yes, I remember you telling me your parents had been miners," Draycos said. "Odd, though. The tone of that song seemed more noble and dignified than I would expect from miners. It is certainly unlike anything I have heard from K'da and Shontine miners."

"Maybe it's from one of the nonhuman races," Jack said. "There are a couple out there who get lofty and dignified about pretty much *everything*. No sense of humor at all."

"Perhaps," Draycos said. "At any rate, thank you for sharing it with me. I will ponder its meaning. Perhaps I will even try to translate it into my language."

"Whatever you want," Jack said. "Me, I think I'll just have a ration bar and get some sleep."

"Of course," Draycos said. His head rose briefly from Jack's shoulder, and then with a surge of weight he leaped out of the boy's shirt. "While you do, I will make a perimeter check."

"Okay," Jack said, fastening his shirt all the way up. It wouldn't do for Alison to notice that his full-body dragon tattoo had suddenly disappeared. "Watch yourself."

"I will." Silently, Draycos moved off into the growing gloom.

With a sigh, Jack headed back to where Alison had settled the Erassvas and Phookas. Bringing up that old poem had stirred up feelings of pain and loss and loneliness that he'd thought he'd buried long ago.

But at least he'd accomplished the goal he'd set for himself tonight. He'd given Draycos something to think about besides whether or not he was doing an adequate job of protecting his host. There was enough danger and trouble out here without the dragon having to deal with those kinds of doubts.

It had been easy. But then, distracting people with words or thoughts or ideas was what Jack had always been best at.

It was, after all, what being a con man was all about.

Frost's men again made no trouble during the night, and after the usual morning ritual they were off.

Once again Jack found himself settling easily into his role as herdsman. By now he could almost anticipate how each of the various Phookas would behave, and several times that morning was able to head off one of the strays almost before he got going.

It was working in the other direction, too. Not only were the Phookas becoming accustomed to his presence, but they also seemed to be learning to recognize his voice. He found himself talking to them as the troop traveled, and not just to give them orders or warnings. While it was clear they didn't really understand his words, they did seem to pick up on his tone of voice and respond accordingly.

It brought to mind one of the sayings Uncle Virgil had often quoted to him: *My sheep hear my voice, and they follow me.*

What the saying actually meant Jack didn't really know. Uncle Virgil had used it to illustrate that if he and Jack could con the leader of some group, the rest of his people would usually follow blindly along with him.

Still, somehow it seemed to apply here as well. Perhaps even more accurately.

They continued on, making their way steadily toward the distant river. If Alison was right, they would be at or even past the halfway point by nightfall. If the *Essenay* had survived, they might pull this off yet.

It was just after noon when the whole thing suddenly fell apart.

"There," Alison said, pointing down a low ridge toward a wide patch of yellow-orange plants. "See all that orange stuff?"

"I see it," Jack said. "And?"

"And I think we'd better give it a wide berth," Alison said. "The last time we passed plants that color they were surrounded by some very large and very nasty-looking insects."

Jack pursed his lips. He couldn't remember even seeing any such plants before, let alone any insects around them. But then, he'd probably been chasing down a Phooka at the time. "Did you ask Hren about them?"

"He thinks they're pretty," she said. "About the insects, he has no clue. I get the feeling his expertise ends about a quarter mile in from the edge of the forest. But *I* sure didn't like the look of the bugs."

"Then let's go with that," Jack agreed, casually opening the front of his shirt a little. Beneath his clothing, he felt Draycos shift around to get a better look. "You want to veer east, or west?"

"East, I think," she said. "The terrain looks a little easier that direction."

"Fine by me," Jack said. Up to now Alison had proved herself a competent leader, and he saw no reason to start questioning her instincts. "We'll get Greenie—"

And then, from behind them came a terrified scream.

"Hren!" Jack shouted, spinning around and fumbling for his tangler.

"Out of the way," Alison snapped, elbowing him in the ribs as she darted past, her Corvine already in her hand. She disappeared around a stand of tall reeds as another scream sliced through the air. Cursing under his breath, Jack dashed after her.

He came around the reeds to a horrifying sight. A huge brown-and-gray creature the size and general shape of a Kodiak bear was lumbering through the group of Erassvas, his huge forepaws flailing away at the fat aliens as they tried desperately to get out of his way. Two of them were already sprawled unconscious on the ground behind him.

The Phookas, far nimbler than their hosts, so far seemed to have avoided the beast's claws. But for all their extra maneuverability, they seemed equally bewildered and helpless before the fury of the attack.

Alison skidded to a halt in the mat of dead leaves and raised her gun. "Don't shoot," Jack snapped. "You'll hit one of the Erassvas."

"We have to risk it," she snapped back.

"No, we don't," Jack said, grabbing her gun arm and pulling it down. "Draycos—*go*!"

And with the banshee wail of a K'da battle cry, Draycos leaped from beneath Jack's shirt.

Even over the rest of the noise Jack heard Alison's strangled yelp. Draycos's leap landed him against the side of a tree; grabbing the trunk with all four paws, he shoved off it, hurling himself like a self-guided missile at the attacker.

The Kodiak paused in his rush, lifting his head toward this new threat. But it was already too late. Draycos's forelegs caught the beast solidly in the throat, the claws digging into the thick fur. The rest of the K'da's body whipped around that pivot point, and a split second later Draycos was dug in on the creature's back.

The Kodiak roared, a deep throbbing that seemed to cut straight through Jack's stomach. The beast reared up on his hind legs to tower above the Erassvas and Phookas, his huge forepaws reaching back over his shoulders to try to dislodge this insolent Phooka that had dared to fight back.

But while he might have tangled with an occasional Phooka, he had never before faced a K'da. Draycos dodged the long claws with ease, ducking or slipping sideways on the creature's broad back. Twice Draycos met the incoming paw with a counterslash of his own claws, eliciting more of the low-pitched bellows. Through it all his sharp teeth continued to dig

178   Timothy Zahn

into the creature's back, and his tail whipped with stinging force against the Kodiak's sides and the back of his hind legs. The beast continued to roar, but to Jack's ears the bellows seemed to be taking on an edge of desperation.

And then, suddenly, it was over. Rearing up one final time, the Kodiak swiveled on his hind legs and dropped to the ground. On all fours again, he loped back the way he had come.

Draycos stayed with the Kodiak for perhaps twenty feet, apparently making sure he was really serious about leaving. Then, with a powerful four-footed spring, Draycos shoved off backward from his grip on the Kodiak's fur, looking for all the world like a fighter pilot ejecting from a damaged aircraft. He landed on the ground and paused, watching and listening until the crashes of the creature's exit were lost in the forest murmurs.

Only then did Draycos turn around and walk back to the group.

"Mother of God," Alison murmured, her voice as tight as Jack had ever heard it.

Jack looked at her profile, suddenly aware that he was still holding her gun arm. "It's all right," he said. "He's a friend."

With a clear effort, Alison dragged her gaze away from Draycos. For a moment her eyes held Jack's; then they dropped to his open shirt. "Yes, he was riding my skin," Jack confirmed, a sinking feeling in his stomach. Now, with the danger past, the full implications of revealing Draycos's secret to this girl were starting to hit him.

"What—?" She swallowed hard, looking back at Draycos. "What *is* it?"

"You asked me once what a K'da was." Jack nodded to Draycos. "This is Draycos, poet-warrior of the K'da."

Alison took a deep breath. "I see," she said. To Jack's mild surprise, her voice was almost back to normal. "Well."

Reaching down, she pried his hand off her arm. With only a slight hesitation, she dropped the Corvine back into its holster. "Well," she said again. "We'd better check the Erassvas. See who needs patching up."

She turned a cool gaze onto Jack. "And after that," she added, "we're going to sit down and have a *long* talk."

CHAPTER 17

Fortunately, the Erassvas were more shaken up than actually hurt. Apparently, the Kodiak's attack strategy was to stun his victims and then go back and finish off whichever one he chose as the meal of the day. Jack and Alison got them settled under the trees, applied a few bandages where claws had cut through skin, and left them to rest and recover.

Afterward, as promised, Alison walked Jack over to a different tree—one within sight of the Erassvas—and sat him down.

And with Draycos standing mostly silently at Jack's side, he told her the whole story.

"I'll be fraggled," Alison murmured when he'd finished. "You two have *definitely* been through the meat grinder on this one."

"And it's not over yet," Jack said, studying her face. But she was every bit as good at masking her thoughts and feelings as he was. Her face said exactly what she wanted it to, which in this case was basically nothing.

"So why haven't you taken this to the Internos government?" she asked. "The Malison Ring's a pretty big group, but StarForce could eat them for breakfast."

"That would be great," Jack agreed. "*If* we could trust them. If *I* were Neverlin, I'd have made sure I got to a few of the top people in StarForce, the Internos Police, and maybe even the government itself before I started this whole thing. Nothing big or fancy or obvious, but enough to cover my back."

Alison made a face. "You may be right," she admitted. "Though if it makes you feel any better, I doubt the whole Malison Ring is involved. Frost is only—let's see; only the fifth or possibly fourth in the chain of command. General Aram Davi is the man in charge, and I haven't heard his name even mentioned. Best guess is that Frost is pulling this underneath Davi's nose."

"Rather like Neverlin was doing," Jack said, nodding. "It would certainly be nice if that was the case. Might limit his manpower even more."

"Not to mention his resources," Alison agreed. "What *I* don't get is this business of cozying up to the Valahgua. Aren't they worried these guys will turn around and bite them once the K'da and Shontine are out of the way?"

Jack shrugged. "Maybe Neverlin thinks he can handle them."

"Or perhaps he does not truly understand the threat," Draycos added. "I have met Neverlin only twice, but he does not seem to plan sufficiently far ahead."

"More likely you've just managed to catch him by surprise," Alison said. "Normally, Neverlin's the type who plans everything out to the last detail, with contingency plans already prepped for anything that might go wrong."

"And you know all this how?" Jack asked.

"My dad did a scam once on one of the Braxton Universis board members," she explained. "I remember him saying at the time that Neverlin was the one he was going to really have to keep an eye on."

"Then we're back to him thinking he can handle the Valahgua," Jack concluded. "He must have one beaut of a trick up his sleeve. Especially since he's seen their Death weapons in action and knows what they can do."

"Which brings us to the other really big question mark," Alison said. "Namely, what the blazes are the Valahgua doing in the Orion Arm in the first place?"

"They wish to destroy us, of course," Draycos said, his tail lashing the air restlessly.

"I'm sure they do," Alison said. "But way out *here,* this far from their main stomping grounds? What did you *do* to these guys, anyway?"

"We did nothing," Draycos insisted, his voice dropping ominously. "They attacked *us.*"

"Easy, Draycos," Jack soothed. "I'm sure she didn't mean anything by that."

"Or maybe she did," Alison retorted. "Round-trip, we're talking about a four-year mission here. Nobody does that unless they have a *very* good reason for it."

"Maybe they just don't like leaving loose ends," Jack said, keeping a wary eye on Draycos. The dragon still looked offended, but he had his annoyance under control again. Three and a half months of dealing with Uncle Virge's snide comments had apparently done a good job of thickening his skin.

"Or maybe they think the K'da and Shontine are planning to regroup here and come back after them."

"If so, they are wrong," Draycos said. "We have left our homes forever. Here is now where we shall live, or where we shall die."

"Still seems like overkill to me," Alison said. "But I suppose that's not something we need to worry about right now."

"No, what *we* need to worry about is getting off this rock alive," Jack agreed. "Do you really have people coming for you? Or was that just some scam?"

Alison's lip twitched. "Oh, they're coming," she said sourly. "Problem is, they could get here anywhere from now to two weeks from now."

"Terrific," Jack growled. "And you were planning to mention this when?"

"I wasn't, because it wasn't any of your business," Alison said. "I was expecting you to just drop me and take off."

Jack made a face. But in all fairness, she *had* told him he didn't have to stay with her. "Yeah, whatever. So bottom line is that they probably won't get here until it's all over."

"Basically," she conceded. "Which means it's up to you and me and Draycos."

"And Uncle Virge," Jack reminded her.

"Assuming the ship survived," Alison agreed. "Incidentally, not that it matters right now, but I don't think Uncle Virgil could have pulled off a personality imprint like that with a P/S/8. That's got to be at least a ten or eleven in there."

Jack shrugged. "He upgraded everything else on the *Essenay*. Why not the computer system, too?"

"Point," she said. "So if the *Essenay doesn't* come for us, we'll need to think about a place to hole up for a couple of weeks."

"You speak of the rocky area at the western end of the forest?" Draycos asked.

"Unless you saw something better as we were coming in, I'd say that's our best bet," Alison said. "The problem is that we have a lot of bodies to hide. *And* a lot of associated mouths to feed."

She looked over at the Erassvas huddled together around their trees. "Unless you're ready to cut them loose."

"No," Jack said firmly.

"It would be easier for us," Alison persisted. "And in all honesty, it might be better for them."

"What, getting abandoned in the woods with a lot of predators they've probably never even seen before?" Jack growled. "How does *that* qualify as good for them?"

"Because it would get them out of the sights of the predators with guns," Alison said bluntly. "Once we aren't with them anymore, what reason would Frost's men have to bother them?"

"Because they're K'da," Jack said.

Alison raised her eyebrows. "Are they?"

"Of course they are," Jack said. But even as he said it he could feel the sand sliding out from under his argument. After all, Draycos himself had called them animals. Did the physical form matter when the mind wasn't there?

He set his jaw. No. Whether they were as alive and intelligent as Draycos or not, the Phookas still deserved to be treated with dignity. "They are," he repeated firmly. "Besides, we've also dragged the Erassvas out here. We just going to abandon them, too?"

"Well, there's definitely no reason the Malison Ring would care about *them*," Alison pointed out, looking at Draycos. "You're the local expert, Draycos. *Are* these K'da, or aren't they?"

Draycos turned to look at the Phookas as they dug for grubs. "They have the form," he said, his tail lashing again. "But for the rest . . . I do not know what could have happened to make them this way."

"Something in the food, probably," Jack said. "It's the same biomass the Erassvas eat from, after all, and they're nearly as oblivious as the Phookas are."

"Though that predator—what did you call it again?" Alison asked.

"A Kodiak," Jack said. "I think it's a kind of bear."

"I notice that Kodiak didn't seem especially lethargic," she said, her voice suddenly thoughtful. "And he's eating from the same biomass. Draycos, you called your relationship with Jack a symbiosis. Does that mean you take nutrients from him?"

"No," Draycos said, his eyes still on the Phookas. "There is no chemical transfer. I take merely a place to rest, and give only companionship and protection in return."

"And advice," Jack added, trying to lighten the tone a little. He couldn't afford to let Draycos slip back into one of these black moods of his. "He gives a lot of advice, too."

"And I'll bet it's sorely needed," Alison said dryly. "No, I was just wondering if there might be more to it than just the Phookas' food."

"Like what?" Jack asked.

"I'm just guessing here," Alison said slowly. "But remember, I saw you playing soldier in the Whinyard's Edge a couple of months ago. You're a lot more confident and capable now than you were then. A *lot* more."

Jack shrugged. "Maybe I'm just a late bloomer."

"Maybe," Alison said. "But maybe you and Draycos are doing some trading in something besides nutrients. Something like attitudes and skills, maybe."

Jack opened his mouth . . . closed it again. Some of the decisions he'd made back at the slave camp had been suspiciously like those of a certain K'da poet-warrior of his acquaintance. "Draycos?" he invited.

"I do not know," the dragon said. His agitated tail swishing had settled down to the slow circular tip movements that showed he was thinking hard. "No one has ever suggested that such a transfer takes place between K'da and host."

"Maybe the Shontine are already so much like you that no one's ever noticed," Alison suggested. "I'm thinking it might be worth a little experiment."

"What kind of experiment?" Draycos asked, his voice suddenly suspicious.

"A very simple one," Alison said. "I take one of the Phookas."

"No," Jack said, the word coming out reflexively.

"Why not?" Alison asked. "You've got a K'da. Why shouldn't I have one, too?"

"What do you think this is, some kind of style statement?" Jack growled. "These are living, thinking beings."

"Fine—call it an adoption if you want," Alison said patiently. "But it's the simplest way to see if it's the environment that's doing this to them, either the food or their current hosts."

It made sense, Jack had to admit. That was the most irritating part. But still . . . "I don't know," he said hesitantly. "Draycos?"

"I also do not know," the dragon said, his tail back to its earlier restless lashing. "It seems wrong to experiment this way with living beings."

"What are you afraid of?" Alison asked, an edge of challenge in her voice. "That you'll find out that your particular group of K'da is the exception? That *this*—" she gestured toward the Phookas—"is how K'da usually are?"

Draycos seemed to stiffen, and for a moment Jack thought he could see a little black edging into the gold scales. Was that really what the dragon was thinking? "That's ridiculous," he jumped in before the dragon could respond. "Draycos and his people helped plan and stage a revolt against slavers back when—"

"Yes, Alison," Draycos said quietly. "That is indeed what I fear."

For a long minute no one spoke. "I'm sorry," Alison said at last. And she really *did* look sorry, Jack thought. "If it helps, I don't really believe that."

"Yet the universe is what it is," Draycos said. "What we believe or do not believe does not affect that reality."

"Then let's settle it," Jack said, his mind suddenly made up. "Uncle Virgil always used to say that no fact was as scary as uncertainty. Let's grab a Phooka, stick him on Alison's back, and see what happens."

"You have such a way with words," Alison murmured.

"Shut up," Jack advised her, his eyes on Draycos. "Draycos?"

There was a shuffling sound behind him, and Jack turned to see Hren waddling toward them. "We are thirsty, young Jack," the Erassva said.

"There should be some water ahead," Jack told him, getting to his feet. "If you'll collect the others, we'll get moving."

"Yes, young Jack." Hren headed back toward the other Erassvas.

Jack turned back to Draycos. "We need a decision here, buddy," Jack said. "Do you want to pick one of the Phookas, or should Alison and I do it?"

For another moment Draycos was silent. "Who would you choose?"

"No contest," Jack said. "Has to be Taneem."

"Taneem?" Alison asked.

"The gray one with the silver eyes," Jack told her. "She seems to have a lot more understanding than the rest of her friends. Not to mention a lot more curiosity about what's going on."

"Sounds like a good candidate," Alison said, looking around. "You see her anywhere?"

A bit of gray beside a squat bush caught Jack's eye. "Over there," he said, pointing. "I'll go get her."

"Hold it," Alison said. "Let me try something. Taneem? Taneem, come here."

The gray head appeared around the side of the bush, and Jack could almost imagine a quizzical look on her triangular face. "Come here, Taneem," Alison repeated.

And with that, the Phooka came the rest of the way around the bush and trotted over to them.

"You're right," Alison said to Jack as the Phooka came to a halt at her side. "So. How exactly do I do this?"

Jack glanced at Draycos, but the dragon remained silent. "Hold out your hand to her, palm upward," he suggested. "That's how they usually get aboard the Erassvas."

"Like this?" Alison asked, holding out her hand tentatively toward Taneem as instructed. Now that the moment had arrived, the girl seemed to be having a few second thoughts. "I don't need to take hold of her head or muzzle or anything?"

"No," Jack said. "Okay, Taneem. Go ahead. Go onto Alison."

Taneem looked at Jack, then Alison, then Draycos, and back to Alison. Then, looking almost as hesitant about it as Alison, she lifted one of her forelegs and set the paw on Alison's palm.

And with a flicker of gray scales, she vanished up Alison's sleeve.

Alison jerked like she'd touched a live wire. "Good—" She broke off with a strangled gasp, her whole body twitching violently. "Good God in heaven," she breathed, settling down a little. "Whoa. That's . . . that's really intense."

"It'll get easier," Jack said, watching her closely. So far she looked all right. "How do you feel?"

"Weird," Alison said. She started to rub her stomach, then paused. "Is it safe to touch her? I mean, I'm not going to accidentally scratch her off, am I?"

"No, no," Jack assured her. "She's solid and strong and she isn't going anywhere. At least, not until she decides to get off."

Alison lifted her shirt a little, peering down at her shoulders and chest. "This is incredible," she said. "I'd never have dreamed . . . I can't even think of anything to say."

"Well, that's a first," Jack said. "Meanwhile, the Erassvas are thirsty. You feel up to taking point, or do you want me to do it?"

Alison gave her new companion a last look, then lifted her eyes resolutely away. "I can do it," she said, all brisk business again. "Let's go find Greenie and get out of here."

CHAPTER 18

They gathered their traveling companions together, and with Alison and Greenie in the lead they once again headed north toward the river.

Jack had hoped to stay close to Alison during the march, or at least to find time here and there to check on her. But with the Kodiak's attack now in the—for them—distant past, the Phookas and Erassvas had settled back into their old, careless ways. The Phookas again wandered freely, rushing off to grab a quick bite or see something interesting, and Jack again found himself being run off his feet trying to keep the herd together.

The Erassvas, for their part, began complaining about their thirst in increasingly loud voices. If the mercenaries were anywhere nearby, Jack thought sourly, they'd be able to find their quarry with their eyes closed.

Fortunately, after only about twenty minutes the travelers found a stream. Everyone drank their fill, and with the Erassvas now at least quieter they continued on.

The forest's water supply seemed to be getting more abundant, Jack noticed as he jogged back and forth keeping the Phookas in line. They were crossing more and more streams now, most of them reasonably narrow, but a few wide enough to make the travelers get their feet wet as they crossed.

Possibly as a partial result of the increased water supply, new plants and trees began to make their appearance. One of them was a purplish, knee-high shrub with two-inch thorns that reminded Jack of the hedge wall back on the Chookoock family estate on Brum-a-dum. The thorns didn't seem to bother the Phookas any, but after nearly impaling his shin on a pair of the shrubs Jack learned to watch for them and keep his distance.

Another newcomer was a tall, spindly, and rather rubbery tree that liked to grow in widely spaced groups of five to twelve. Unfortunately, they also seemed to come associated with a thin but strong pale green vine that grew at all angles between the various members of a given group. Together they formed a netlike structure that had a bad tendency to block off the best routes through the forest.

The vines were too tough for Jack's and Alison's knives to get through easily, especially since the springy trees they were attached to didn't provide a solid foundation for cutting. That meant that whenever the travelers couldn't go around a group they had to call in Draycos to slash open a path. Jack tried several times to get the other Phookas to help out, but the concept of using their claws to cut vines that weren't concealing food seemed to be completely foreign to them.

Fortunately, not all the new flora was determined to make their lives more complicated. There was also a yellow-leaved bush with bright red berries that was greeted with great enthusiasm by the Erassvas. As near as Jack could gather from Hren's explanation, mumbled around a mouthful of the berries, it was a plant that grew near the river and was one of the highlights of their continuous journey around the forest's edge. The first group of bushes they ran into generated a half-hour delay as Erassva and Phooka alike happily stood around stuffing their faces.

Alison wasn't happy with the delay, and wasn't shy about saying so. But Jack knew that after the scare they'd had earlier a treat like this would help boost the Erassvas' morale. Sure enough, when they finally hit the trail again, the uneasy grumbling was gone.

They didn't see any more Kodiaks that afternoon, but near sundown they did run into another herd of the horn-headed plant-eaters Draycos had told Jack about. The creatures themselves were about the size of large elk, with roundish bodies and rather mouselike faces. Each had two sets of horns: one that looked like extra-long wild boar tusks set into the sides of their heads just behind their mouths, plus a second set farther back that reminded Jack of the flat fan shapes of moose antlers. Nonpredators or not, Alison made sure to give them a wide berth.

With the day's delays clearly on her mind, she kept them going until the blue had faded from the sky overhead before finally calling a halt. With Draycos's help Jack got the Erassvas and Phookas settled amid a grove of the rubbery trees, situating them where the vine mesh would give them protection from predators from at least that direction. Then, leaving Draycos on guard, he went to find Alison.

He found her kneeling beside a stream twenty yards farther

along their path, filling her canteen. "How are you feeling?" he asked.

"Fine," she said. "Never better. Why?"

"Why do you think?" Jack growled, studying her profile as he crouched down beside her. She certainly looked okay. "Taneem been giving you any trouble?"

"Not really," Alison said. "There was a time a couple of hours ago when she felt kind of itchy, and back when we were crossing that extra-wide creek she was moving around or something and tickling me."

"Probably bringing her claws a little ways into their 3-D form and scratching your skin," Jack said. "Draycos does that sometimes in his sleep. Never tickles, though."

"You're probably not as ticklish as I am," she said, pulling her canteen from the creek and recapping it. "Do I need to get her off me for a while or anything?"

Jack shook his head. "The only limit is how long they can stay *off* you," he said. "Draycos once had to stay on me for three days straight, and it didn't seem to bother him any."

"Except probably drove him a little stir-crazy," Alison said, getting back to her feet. "Do we want to bring them in shifts for some water, or just move the whole camp here for the night?"

"Let's do the shift thing," Jack suggested. "If the mercs decide to come hunting, they'll probably expect us to park by water."

"Good point," she said. "Okay. If you and Draycos want to start shuttling them over, I'll go take guard duty with the main group."

"Right," Jack said. "By the way, how many rounds does your Corvine have left?"

"Eleven," Alison said. "We'd never make it through another firefight like the one we had two nights ago."

"I'll keep that in mind."

The stars were starting to appear through the treetops by the time they finally finished getting everyone to the stream and back. Only then, as they settled in for the night, did Jack and Draycos finally have a chance to talk.

"What do you think?" Jack asked quietly as they sat together.

"I see no signs of trouble," Draycos said. "Though I am a little concerned by the fact that Taneem stayed with her the entire day instead of coming off to eat."

"It sounded like she was sleeping a lot of that time, too," Jack said, frowning across at Alison. She was little more than a dark silhouette against the fading light, sitting against the vine netting, her head slumped forward onto her chest. "Is that abnormal?"

"Not necessarily," Draycos said. "It sometimes takes a while to adjust to a new host, especially when the K'da is young. Of course, Taneem *is* an adult."

"On the other hand, this is a radically different host than the one she's used to," Jack reminded him.

"True," Draycos said, clearly still not convinced. Or else he was simply afraid to let himself hope that anything would come from the experiment. "She may simply come off Alison very well rested."

"No, there's more going on here," Jack said, scratching his cheek. "Remember the red Phooka who fell down that cliff? He didn't want anything to do with me, and in fact resisted the whole idea until it was either that or run off the end of his time limit. And even then he got off me just as soon as he could."

"I'm certain he found the change confusing."

"Confusing and uncomfortable both," Jack agreed. "Taneem, on the other hand, seems to have taken to Alison like a cat to nip."

For a moment Draycos was silent. "We will have to wait and see, I suppose," he said at last. "On another more serious subject, did you hear the air vehicle passing back and forth over the forest for much of the afternoon?"

"No, I didn't," Jack said, frowning. "How come you didn't say something earlier?"

"Because you and Alison were busy," the K'da said. "Also, there was little that either of you could do about it."

"We could have gotten ourselves ready for an ambush," Jack countered.

Draycos twitched his tail in a negative. "There was no indication that the vehicle was landing nearby. It was also not flying directly overhead, but instead along a course a kilometer or more to the east of our path."

"So either they were out looking for us," Jack said slowly, "or else they already knew where we are and were setting up another picket line in front of us."

"The latter would be my guess," Draycos said. "I thought that once it's full night I would scout ahead."

"Sounds good," Jack said. "Only this time you're going to have company."

"Jack—"

"No argument," Jack said firmly. "I need to know what's going on out there. Anyway, you'll be there with me. What can go wrong?"

The dragon sighed. "Very well. Do you wish to tell Alison, or shall I?"

Jack looked across at Alison. "Let's let her sleep," he decided. "But you'd better make a pass around the area before we go. Make sure no one's close enough to sneak up on the camp."

The forest was alive with the same nocturnal creatures Draycos had seen on their two previous nights. Fortunately, there were no hunting mercenaries among them.

Nor did he see or smell any of the creatures Jack had dubbed Kodiaks, or the horn-headed plant-eaters whose presence might attract such predators. The only even mildly dangerous creatures were small predators similar in size to the heenas he and Jack had encountered at the Vagran Colony spaceport soon after they met.

Unlike the heenas, though, these animals hunted alone instead of in packs, and seemed to concentrate their efforts on small rodentlike creatures. The likelihood that they would take on a group of Phookas, Draycos decided, was small enough to safely ignore.

He returned to the encampment to find Jack ready. "I

thought we'd take about a hundred feet of rope, my tangler, and my knife," the boy said. "You think of anything else we need?"

"I believe that's most everything we have, actually," Draycos pointed out. "The area appears to be secure. Let us go."

They set off through the woods. Only a little of the starlight overhead made it through the forest canopy, but that was enough for Draycos to find his way without difficulty. Jack, for his part, held on to Draycos's tail and let the K'da guide him.

They'd been hiking for perhaps forty minutes when they reached the mercenaries.

"I don't see anything," Jack whispered as they lay side by side behind a wide tree trunk.

"They are there," Draycos assured him, flicking out his tongue as he tasted the air. "There is a hidden ground line of seven men, approximately fifty feet apart, stretched directly across our path."

"I hear running water," Jack said. "Another creek?"

"A fairly wide one, yes," Draycos confirmed. "The soldiers are hidden on the far side."

"So we come strolling up to get a drink, and they pop us," Jack said. "There's probably a gap in the trees right over the stream, too, so you can't use the skyway and jump them from behind."

"Yes, there is a gap," Draycos confirmed. "But even if there weren't, I could not easily use such a frontal attack. A few yards behind each man is a second soldier, hidden off the ground in one of the trees."

"Sounds like the same setup you ran into our first day out of the box," Jack said, a frown in his voice. "Don't these people learn?"

"Of course they learn," Draycos said. "But they have no way of knowing that I've seen this particular ambush strategy."

"Ah—right," Jack said, nodding. "That group was waiting northwest of us, while we were heading north. We never even got near it."

"And so they try again," Draycos concluded, tasting the air a few more times just to be sure. But there were no other surprises waiting for them.

At least none that could be detected by K'da senses. If there were more subtle booby traps around, it would be up to Jack to find and disarm them.

"So what do we do?" Jack asked.

Carefully, Draycos lifted his head for a better view. There were, he saw, bushes and stands of reeds all along their side of the stream. Plenty of cover for a hunting K'da to creep in close. The stream itself was fairly wide, and seemed to be flowing reasonably slowly. From the calmness of the surface, he guessed the stream was at least a couple of feet deep.

He lowered himself back down. "Come," he said, gesturing behind them. "I have a plan."

Together, he and Jack backed away from the ambush line. "We will need a dummy," Draycos said when it was safe to talk. "Can you construct something from branches and vines?"

"Probably," Jack said. "You want human or K'da?"

"Human will do," Draycos said. "Give me the rope. I'll be back soon."

With the rope coiled beneath his left foreleg, he headed a few yards farther back from the enemy until he found one of the slender, rubbery trees that had begun cropping up during the day's travels. Near its base another tree's roots had looped their way up into the air before disappearing back underground. Picking the thickest of the roots, he tied one end of his rope to it. With the other end clenched between his teeth, he started up the rubbery tree.

He was no more than fifteen feet up when he felt the trunk starting to bend under his weight. He kept going, digging his claws into the soft bark to keep from being dumped off, until the tree was bending over so far that he was climbing nearly horizontally. Tying the other end of rope there, he headed down.

Once back on the ground, he spent a few minutes pulling the rope through the root loop, bending the treetop back down again. It was a tricky job, requiring all his strength to keep the rope from being yanked out of his muzzle and paws as the tree bowed over and the tension on the rope increased.

Finally, he judged he'd pulled enough of it through. Holding the rope tightly between his teeth, bracing his hind legs against the root loop, he slipped a section of the rope through another nearby tree root and secured it with a quick-release knot. Then, carefully, he eased off his grip.

There was a sharp jerk as the bent tree readjusted itself, startling a group of birds who had been picking seeds or insects out of the topmost branches. They all flew off madly together in a tight cluster, sending the treetop swaying in the opposite direction and putting a twitch of extra tension on the rope and knot.

But the knot held, and the branches settled down. Now, one good tug on the loose end of the rope would release the knot and let the tree straighten up again, pulling the rope through the looped root as it did so.

Back on the planet Sunright, he'd pulled a version of this trick on one of the Whinyard's Edge soldiers. This time, though, he wasn't looking for a prisoner for interrogation.

This time, it was going to be a prelude to combat.

Gathering the rest of the rope into a loose coil, he returned to where he'd left Jack. "Mortimer's all ready," the boy said, holding up the Jack-sized stick figure he'd made from branches wrapped and held together with vines. "What do you think?"

"It looks just like you," Draycos said.

"Thanks," Jack said dryly. "You can probably find a reed down by the creek to use as a breathing tube."

Draycos frowned at him. "How did you know I was going to send the decoy down the stream?"

"Didn't you—?" Jack broke off. "No, I guess you didn't tell me. Huh. That's weird."

"Great minds thinking alike, no doubt," Draycos said. "Though you have no doubt already deduced it, let me tell you the rest of the plan."

It took only a minute for him to fill Jack in. "Yeah, that's more or less what I was expecting," the boy said. "We're starting to think alike, all right. Not sure whether that's good or bad."

"For the moment, let us assume it's good," Draycos said. "Now help me get—what did you call it? Mortimer?—help me get Mortimer on my back. Then carefully—*carefully*—move up into position."

"Don't worry about me," Jack said. "You just watch yourself, okay? *I'm* the one they don't want to kill."

"That thought had occurred to me," Draycos agreed grimly. "I shall be back as quickly as I can."

CHAPTER 19

Draycos headed off, moving silently through the shadows, the dummy wedged firmly onto his crest.

Jack waited until he was out of sight. Then, tucking the end of the rope securely into his belt, he drew his tangler and started back toward the creek.

He wasn't nearly as quiet as Draycos, or at least it didn't sound like it in his own ears. Still, he managed to reach a spot where he could see the creek without having drawn any obvious attention from the hidden soldiers. The rippling noise from the water and the general background of insect chirps and animal rustlings probably helped cover the sound of his approach. And, of course, the soldiers were almost certainly not expecting anyone to show up until morning.

The minutes dragged by. Jack peered into the gloom, trying to spot the enemy positions. But the soldiers were too well camouflaged. He just hoped they hadn't spotted him and were even now creeping stealthily toward him.

Something moved at the corner of his eye. He jerked, trying to bring up his tangler—

"Shh," Draycos warned, catching Jack's gun hand with his paw.

Sternly, Jack ordered his heart back to normal. "Don't *do* that," he whispered.

"My apologies," the dragon said. "Give me the rope."

Jack unlooped the rope from his belt. "I made a lasso with a slipknot in the end for you," he said, handing it over.

"Thank you," Draycos said. "Stand ready."

With the lasso end gripped between his teeth, the K'da slipped toward the creek. Jack gave him a few seconds, then carefully stood up into a crouch behind one of the trees, making sure he had a solid grip on the rope. Draycos was in combat mode, his gold scales turned to black, and even knowing he was there Jack couldn't see him.

Of course, the waiting soldiers would undoubtedly have infrared and starlight vision enhancers. Jack hoped the dragon was being especially careful.

More minutes went by. Jack kept his eyes on the stream, wondering if this was actually going to work. The dummy seemed to be taking way too much time getting down here, and he wondered uneasily if it might have gotten snagged on something at the bottom of the creek.

And then, there it was: a reed poking out of the water, making its slow way downstream. And as Jack listened, he could hear the stealthy hiss of someone breathing through it.

He frowned. *Breathing?*

But even as the question arose, so did the obvious answer. Draycos, hidden in the bushes beside the stream, was making the breathing noises, trying to attract the soldiers' attention without being too obvious about it.

For a minute Jack wondered if maybe the dragon was being a little *too* subtle. The reed was still moving, drifting its way downstream, and still there was no reaction from the other side.

And then, one of the shadows across the creek seemed to shiver. A second later, it had resolved itself into the figure of a soldier. Holding his machine gun ready, he stepped warily to the water's edge and leaned over the creek, peering down at the dummy beneath the surface.

And as a warbling K'da battle cry shattered the nighttime quiet, Draycos leaped across the stream.

The soldier jerked back, trying to bring his gun to bear on the dragon who had suddenly appeared. But Jack's tangler shot got there first. In the darkness he couldn't see the threads as they wrapped themselves around the soldier, but the flash of the cartridge's capacitor was all he needed to know the shot had been squarely on-target. The man teetered and started to fall.

But before he could do so, Draycos reached him. Sailing over his shoulder, the dragon dropped the loop of his lasso neatly over the other's shoulders as he passed. "Now!" he shouted as he hit the ground and spun around. He leaped up onto the soldier's back, his claws digging into the other's battle vest. Jack gave a sharp tug on the rope—

And as the quick-release knot came free and the tree snapped back toward vertical, the lassoed soldier was yanked off his feet and dragged into and across the stream. He shot through the reeds at the edge, plowing his way through bushes and drifts of dead leaves as he was pulled across the ground. He and Draycos shot past, and Jack ducked away from his tree and sprinted after them.

Sounds of sudden commotion could be heard from the far side of the stream as he reached the unconscious soldier and braked to a halt. "Here," Draycos said, lifting the other's over/under machine-gun/tangler combination. "Hold out the stock."

Jack unfolded the metal shoulder stock and held it out. Draycos's claws slashed once, and the stock with its hidden tracker was no longer attached to the weapon. "Ready," Jack said, dropping the severed metal onto the ground and looping the gun's strap over his shoulder.

Draycos bent down and slid his paws beneath Jack's shoes, and a second later Jack found himself flying high into the air straight up into the branches of one of the bushier trees.

He caught a branch with each hand, the gun banging against his back as he got his balance. "Clear," he called down softly as he worked his way quickly over to the trunk, wincing as the tangle of branches grabbed his sleeves and scratched his face. "Watch yourself."

His only answer was the sound of splashing from the direction of the creek as the other soldiers charged to their comrade's rescue. Peering down, Jack found that Draycos had vanished. "And happy hunting," he murmured to himself. Lifting the gun, making sure it was on its tangler setting, he waited.

They came in pairs, the first two soldiers moving swiftly but quietly through the trees, their guns swinging back and forth and up and down as they searched for their quarry. Twice one of them looked up into Jack's tree, his gun lifting as he did so to point in the same direction. But Jack had moved to the far side of the trunk, and there apparently wasn't enough of him showing through the branches for them to spot.

The two soldiers headed toward the man Draycos had captured. As they did so, Jack saw two more pairs coming in behind them and to either side, staying back and watching for trouble.

Unfortunately for them, trouble was already watching them. Smiling tightly, he lined up the muzzle of his borrowed tangler on the first of the closest pair and squeezed the trigger.

The mercenaries were good, all right. Even before the cartridge hit, both men reacted to the sound of the shot, swinging their guns upward and firing in unison. But the branches that had hidden Jack from their sight now also protected him from their fire. As his shot hit its target and dropped the soldier to the ground, their own cartridges exploded into a snarled mess in the branches.

But only one of the soldiers was down, and the other now knew exactly where Jack was. With a hoarse shout to his comrades, he opened fire, plastering the tree with tangler threads. Still shooting, he began to circle, trying to get a clear shot. Two of the other soldiers rushed up to join him, and now there were three tanglers firing at Jack instead of just one. The last pair stayed well back, where they could cover the rest of the group.

And with nowhere to run, Jack was now the proverbial sitting duck.

"Come on, dragon, move it," he muttered, wincing back from the soldiers' shots as he tried to fire back. But the one clear shot he'd had was long gone, and all he succeeded in doing was plastering the nearest branches with tangler threads of his own.

Which might not be such a bad thing, he realized suddenly. If he could make himself a nice little cage of tangler threads, he would be more or less safe. At least until they gave up on taking him alive and switched to machine-gun mode.

He fired a few more rounds into the branches around him, shifting his aim to keep up with the circling soldiers. Between his shots and theirs, it was getting increasingly difficult to see what was going on down there. He could only hope that Draycos would spot the two soldiers standing distant guard, their eyes on the trees and ground-hugging bushes.

And with Jack's own thoughts and attention on those same trees and bushes, he and the soldiers were all looking in the wrong direction when the K'da made his move.

He appeared behind the three soldiers still shooting into Jack's tree, boiling up without warning from a drift of dead leaves that had hidden him from both eyes and infrared detectors. Before they could even react, his forepaws took out two of them, slapping against the sides of their heads hard enough to send them cartwheeling in opposite directions.

The third was faster than the others. He swung around and dropped to one knee, trying to swing his gun around to this new threat. But Draycos was already in motion, leaping over the soldier's gun and past his shoulder. The dragon's tail whipped around the man's neck as he passed, gagging him as it slapped across his windpipe and yanked him backward off-balance. The action also brought Draycos's own momentum to a sudden halt, dropping him to the ground behind the man.

Draycos had just hit the matted leaves when the two remaining soldiers opened fire with their tanglers. The first shot, aimed where Draycos would have been if he'd continued his arcing leap, missed completely, zipping past to explode its netting over one of the distant bushes.

The second shot, instead of missing, clipped the corner of the kneeling soldier's arm. Some of the threads whipped around his face and chest, Draycos managing to snatch his tail out of the way just in time. The rest of the threads spread out harmlessly though the air over the K'da's head.

Not enough of the threads were wrapped around the soldier for the shock capacitor to knock him out. But it didn't matter. Draycos had already twisted around, slapping the side of the man's neck with one paw as he snatched the tangler from his hands with the other. As the stunned soldier toppled over, Draycos dived to the side, staying behind him so as to use his body as a shield against the two remaining gunners. Flipping the barrel of the tangler up over the other's ribs, Draycos fired.

But the two soldiers weren't there anymore. They had ducked to either side, taking cover behind nearby bushes as Draycos's shots went harmlessly past.

They were fiddling with their weapons, probably switching to machine-gun mode, when Jack maneuvered the barrel of his own weapon through the mass of tangler threads around him and nailed them both.

. . .

It took a while for Jack to work his way through the masses of tangler threads and get back down the tree. Long enough, in fact, for Draycos to go examine the two more distant soldiers and then return to the four he and Jack had first taken out. "That was fun," Jack puffed as he unslung his gun again and peered in the direction of the creek. "Where are the ones who were up in the trees?"

Draycos twisted his neck back toward the creek. "They don't appear to be approaching," he said. "I do not understand why not."

"Maybe we can find out," Jack suggested. Crouching down, he unfastened the nearest soldier's helmet and slipped it over his own head.

"—not move," a familiar voice growled. Familiar, yet unexpected.

It was Colonel Frost. The man they thought they'd heard leaving the planet.

"The others aren't responding," another voice protested.

"And you think getting yourselves waxed along with them will do them any good?" Frost shot back.

Jack cleared his throat. "Oh, come on, Frost, be a sport," he said into the helmet's microphone. "Let them try their luck. We don't mind. Besides, it's got to be pretty uncomfortable sitting up there in those trees."

There was a brief silence. "Very good, Morgan," Frost said, his voice three shades darker than the night around them. "You and the K'da both. I don't suppose you sustained any injuries?"

"Nothing worth mentioning," Jack assured him. "A few more of your men are a little worse for wear, though. I thought you'd left us."

"I'm not going anywhere," Frost promised coldly. "This K'da of yours is tougher than I expected. Certainly tougher than I was told. I'm beginning to understand why the Valahgua want them wiped out."

"You're probably also beginning to understand why they're sitting behind the lines and letting you and Neverlin and the Chookoock family do all the work and take all the risks," Jack said. "Not to mention absorbing all the damage. You've got to be asking yourself right now whether or not it's really worth it."

Frost gave a soft chuckle. "Believe me, boy, it's worth it," he said. "New technology is the golden ring these days, especially when you have a company like Braxton Universis standing ready to market it."

"Only you haven't *got* Braxton Universis," Jack reminded him.

"We will," Frost said confidently. "And from what I saw on those Shontine advance ships, we all stand to make a very tidy profit on this operation."

"Your soldiers here on the ground might have a different opinion."

"Soldiers are expendable," Frost said bluntly. "That's their job. Besides, most of them will recover just fine. Your K'da doesn't seem to have the stomach for killing."

Jack looked at Draycos. The dragon's tail was swishing almost gently through the air, but there was a look in his eyes that sent a shiver down Jack's back. "I wouldn't count on that if I were you," he warned Frost.

"Maybe," the colonel said offhandedly. "All I know is that people who hide in the middle of civilians and herd animals are cowards."

Jack grinned tightly. So Frost had completely missed the point of why they'd brought the Erassvas and Phookas along. "Look who's talking," he countered. "You want to come out here personally so we can have this out man-to-man?"

"Don't be absurd," Frost scoffed. "Duels went out with flintlock pistols, and they were never anything but stupid to begin with. But let's talk about you. Aren't you tired yet of running and living off ration bars?"

"Oh no, I love forests," Jack assured him. "More than that, I love taking out mercenaries. You must be running pretty low on them by now. Is that where your ship went? To scare up a few replacements?"

"You'll see," Frost promised. "But I'll grant you that this is taking far more of my time and energy than I'd planned. So what exactly do you want? Maybe we can come to some agreement."

"What I *want* is to be left alone," Jack said. "But for now, I'll settle for you clearing your tree-sitters out of our way. They can come collect this bunch, and you can fly them back to your base camp to get patched up."

"As I said, no stomach for killing," Frost said contemptuously.

"As *I* said, don't count on Draycos's kind heart," Jack said, putting some darkness of his own into his voice. "We're getting tired of playing tag out here, and we now have a couple of nicely lethal weapons of our own. So get your men out of our way, and keep them out."

"Or you'll commit cold-blooded murder?"

"I'll commit cold-blooded self-defense," Jack countered. "And don't forget, Neverlin wants me alive."

"For now," Frost said icily. "But that may change. Either way, I certainly don't need to keep those Erassvas or their herd animals alive. Or that girl you have with you, either. Who is she, by the way?"

"Just a hitchhiker," Jack said. "Speaking of hitchhikers, how did you get that tracking transmitter into my ship?"

"What makes you think there was a transmitter aboard?" Frost countered blandly.

"I gather it worked off the ECHO drive," Jack continued. "What did it do, use the drop-power to boost out some kind of signal as soon as we popped back into normal space?"

"Actually, the gadget sends a sort of ripple across hyperspace itself," Frost said. "A nearby ship with the right equipment can pick it up and follow you straight in."

"Cute," Jack said. "Cutting-edge technology, no doubt."

"Not even on the market yet," Frost said smugly. "And when it is, it'll go exclusively to StarForce and the Internos Police. Had I mentioned the advantages of having Braxton Universis in your pocket?"

"Maybe once or twice," Jack said. "So are you going to send someone to pick up your trash? Or are Draycos and I going to have to start clearing the table ourselves?"

"We'll get them," Frost said quietly. "And then we'll get out of your way. For now."

"Good enough," Jack said, an unpleasant sensation at the back of his neck. There'd been something in Frost's voice just then, something he didn't like at all. "And tell Neverlin that the next time he wants to talk, he should just drop me a message on the net."

"The next time Mr. Neverlin speaks to you, it'll be face-to-face," Frost promised darkly. "Good night, Jack."

There was a click, and the comm went dead. "What do you think?" he asked, pulling off the helmet.

Draycos flicked his tongue out a few times. "They don't appear to be coming closer," he said. "I believe he means to do as he says."

"Which should definitely worry us," Jack said, grimacing. "Someone like Frost only pulls back when he's got something else already planned."

"Any idea what that could be?"

"Not a clue," Jack admitted. "Maybe we'll find out tomorrow morning when we try to get through here."

"I was thinking we might want to veer a little ways east or west of this particular spot," Draycos suggested.

"Oh, definitely," Jack agreed. "I didn't mean we'd go through *here*." He shook his head. "I just wish I knew what he sent the transport to get. More men or more equipment, probably. Either way, we're not going to like it."

"Sufficient unto the day, Jack," Draycos said. "Is that correct?"

"'Sufficient unto the day is the evil thereof,' yeah," Jack confirmed. "Uncle Virgil used to quote that one a lot. Usually when he'd messed up on a job and needed some time to figure out what to do next."

"Interesting how many truthful sayings he seemed to adapt to his own purposes," Draycos said. "Perhaps he had more education than he let on."

"Or he just picked it up as he went," Jack said, resettling the strap of the machine gun more comfortably over his shoulder. "Let me grab a couple spare tangler clips for this thing, and then we'd better get back. I just hope Frost didn't hit the camp while we were out here playing soldier."

The camp, to Draycos's quiet relief, was just as they'd left it. The Erassvas were sleeping soundly, with the Phookas either dozing, searching for food, or waiting their turn to spend an hour on their blubbery hosts. If Frost's men had been there, they hadn't left any traces behind, not even any scent.

Draycos was mildly surprised to find Alison still sound asleep as well. Up to now the girl had slept lightly, ready to snap awake at the slightest hint of trouble. Perhaps the long days of travel and tension had finally caught up with her. Certainly after tonight's activities Jack was also asleep practically before he hit the ground.

But with Alison, Draycos wondered if it might be more than simple fatigue. Perhaps Taneem's presence on her body was doing something to her.

He gazed down at the sleeping girl, his tail lashing with

frustration and concern. When they'd begun this experiment, they'd all assumed it was the Erassvas' sluggishness that was affecting the Phookas. Could it be that it was actually the other way around?

But there was nothing he could do about it right now. Whatever was going on, everyone still desperately needed their rest. Including Draycos himself.

So he would give the perimeter one final sweep, and then he would settle down to rest as best he could. Tomorrow should be soon enough to try to find out what was happening with Alison.

Sufficient unto the day, the thought whispered again through his mind, *is the evil thereof.*

CHAPTER 20

Jack had hit the ground exhausted, almost too tired to even care that the mercenaries hadn't attacked the camp. He was therefore not particularly surprised when he woke to find sunlight already filtering through the trees and the Phookas in the middle of their morning dance.

Stifling a groan, he worked his way up into a sitting position against a tree, glancing down into his shirt as he did so. Pure reflex; he already knew from the feel of his skin that Draycos was gone. Running the perimeter, no doubt, and Jack grimaced at the thought. No matter how much he tried to help out, the heaviest burden always seemed to fall squarely on the K'da's shoulders.

But he could only do what he could do. Taking a few deep breaths, working the kinks out of his muscles, he watched the Phookas with half an eye while he pulled a ration bar from his pack. Alison had thoughtfully included a variety of flavors, but after three days he was starting to get roundly sick of them. Still, it was better than starving.

He was halfway through his breakfast when he spotted Draycos through the trees, working his way around the dancing

Phookas. A minute later, he was at Jack's side. "Good morning, Jack," the K'da said. "I trust you slept well?"

"The sleep of the dead," Jack agreed, peeling back the wrapping of another ration bar and holding it out. "How about you? You get any sleep at all?"

"I had enough," Draycos assured him. Taking the ration bar delicately between his teeth, he flipped his head sharply, and the food disappeared into his jaws. A half-dozen quick chews and it was gone. "I have been around the perimeter," he went on. "There's no scent of the mercenaries anywhere nearby."

"Unless they're sneaking up from downwind," Jack warned, blinking a little as the light westwardly breeze drifted across his eyes.

"No." Draycos was quietly positive. "It would take a much stronger wind than this to keep their scent from me."

"We'll just have to watch out for windstorms, then," Jack said. "Is it my imagination, or are you getting better at sniffing out these guys?"

"It is not your imagination," Draycos confirmed. "In fact, all my senses appear to be growing sharper."

"Good." Jack paused, eyeing the other. There'd been something in the K'da's voice just then. "It *is* good, isn't it?"

"I don't know," Draycos said. "There is . . . but that is certainly only a myth."

"What is?"

"It's nothing," Draycos said firmly. "I should not even have mentioned it."

"Well, you did," Jack said. "And you're sure not going to back out of it now. Come on, symby, give."

Abruptly, Draycos's neck arched, his crest stiffening. "What did you call me?" he demanded.

"Uh . . ." Jack found himself pressing his back hard against his tree. What had he said? "Just . . . symby. Kind of a short-hand for symbiont. I'm sorry—shouldn't I have called you that?"

"No, not at all," Draycos said, his body relaxing again, a troubled look in his eyes. "It was just that Polphir, my last Shontine host, used to call me that. Had I ever mentioned that to you?"

"Not that I remember," Jack said, frowning now himself. "It just sort of popped into my head."

"I see," Draycos said, his tail tip making slow, thoughtful circles. "At any rate, I apologize greatly for my reaction."

"That's okay," Jack said. "My heart needed a little restart anyway. So tell me about this myth."

Draycos turned his head to look at the Phookas as they finished their dance. "There's an ancient legend that suggests that a K'da approaching death sometimes experiences heightened senses."

Jack felt his stomach tighten around his breakfast. He'd already been wondering if his body might be rejecting Draycos. "Uh-oh."

"But as I say, it is only a myth," Draycos hastened to add. "Recall that back aboard the *Havenseeker* I was very near death. Yet I experienced nothing like that."

"But in the last month you've taken to falling off my back straight through walls," Jack reminded him. "That's definitely not normal K'da behavior."

"Yet I also feel better than I have in years," Draycos countered. "Whatever is happening, I do not believe I am dying."

"I hope not," Jack said. "I wonder what that might mean for . . ."

He trailed off, looking around as a thought suddenly struck him. Every other morning during this trek Alison had been the first one up and ready to go. Usually she'd been right in his face when he opened his eyes, in fact, nagging him to get his butt in gear.

But this morning, she hadn't yet even made an appearance. "Have you seen Alison?" he asked, getting to his feet.

"She was over there," Draycos said, flicking his tongue toward some of the red-berry bushes where Hren and the other Erassvas were chowing down. "Just past the Erassvas."

"Come on," Jack said, picking up his borrowed machine gun/tangler and looping its strap over his shoulder.

They found Alison lying on the ground on her back, her head partially propped up on a thick tree root. Her eyes were closed, but Jack could see her chest rising and falling rhythmically with her breathing. At least she wasn't dead. "Alison?" he called as he and Draycos approached.

There was no response. "Alison?" he repeated, crouching down beside her and shaking her shoulder. "Come on, girl. Time to wake up."

To his relief, she opened her eyes. But only halfway. "Jack?" she croaked.

"I'm here," Jack said. "What's wrong?"

"Nothing's wrong," she said, closing her eyes again. "Just sleeping."

"We can see that," Jack said, easing her open collar back a couple of inches. There was no sign of the gray dragon on her neck or shoulder. "Where's Taneem? Alison, where's Taneem?"

"Over there," Alison said, lifting her hand from her lap and pointing vaguely around her. "Hungry. Went for breakfast."

"I'll find her," Draycos said. Turning away, he ducked around the milling Erassvas and disappeared.

"Are you feeling all right?" Jack asked, looking down at Alison again.

"I'm fine," she said. But there was no particular life in her voice, and the words were noticeably slurred. "Just tired. Already told you." With obvious effort, she opened her eyes again. "Anything wrong?"

"Aside from you, no, everything seems fine," Jack said. "Draycos has been around the camp, and says no one's sniffing around."

"Good," Alison said, closing her eyes again. "Maybe we scared them off."

"Hardly," Jack growled. Even in the middle of a conversation she was starting to slip away again. What had Taneem done to her, anyway? "No, they've just switched tactics. Alison?"

"Good," she muttered. "Sure you and Draycos can figure it out."

"Alison?" Jack shook her shoulder again. "Alison!"

But she was asleep again. This time, no amount of shaking would rouse her.

"Blast," Jack bit out, getting back to his feet and looking

around for Draycos. The K'da was nowhere to be seen. "Draycos?" he called. *"Draycos!"*

A couple of the Erassvas looked up, then returned to their berry picking. "Come on, dragon," Jack muttered, looking around. His gaze fell on one of the matted vine meshes— "You," he said, stepping over to the nearest Phooka. "Yes, you," he said as the animal looked up. "Come here."

He hooked a pair of fingers behind its crest and pulled it over to the vine mesh. "Here—cut this," he ordered, pointing to the vines at the edge of the mesh. "Right here. Understand?"

The Phooka looked quizzically up at him. "Cut," Jack repeated, lifting one of the Phooka's forepaws and making slashing motions across the vines. "Cut. Come on, you stupid—"

"I can do that," Draycos's voice put in from behind him.

Jack looked over as the dragon loped up to him. "There you are," he said accusingly. "Where have you been?"

"Looking for Taneem," Draycos said. "I can smell her, but I don't see her anywhere. She must have gone farther away than usual."

"That's Taneem for you," Jack gritted. "Come on, get this cut, will you? We need something to carry Alison with."

"Can you tell what is wrong with her?" Draycos asked, slashing his claws through the vines at the points Jack had indicated.

"All I know is that I can't get her to stay awake," Jack said. "We're going to need the *Essenay*'s medical diagnostics to get anything more than that."

"You intend to use this vine mesh to carry her?"

"The mesh, and a couple of Phookas," Jack said. "We'll tie it between them with pieces of rope and lay her on it."

"That should work," Draycos said. "Shall I select the Phookas?"

"I'll do that," Jack said. "You go get the rope from my pack."

"Are you certain you are up to the task?" Draycos asked.

"What, picking out a couple of stretcher carriers?" Jack scoffed. "I could do it in my sleep." He looked down at Alison. "No offense," he added sarcastically.

"I meant, are you certain you wish to deal with the Phookas?" Draycos said. "You seem less patient with them this morning."

Jack curled a hand into a fist, a flood of anger and disgust rising chokingly into his throat. Sternly, he forced it back down. "I'm frustrated, that's all," he said.

"With the Phookas?"

"With everything." Jack eyed Draycos. "Well, not with you," he amended. "But with everything else."

"I'm sorry," Draycos said, ducking his head in apology.

"No, *I'm* the one who should be sorry," Jack said, grimacing. "Everyone's doing the best they can. Even the Erassvas and Phookas. I'm just . . . we've got a whole platoon of K'da here, or we should. Only they aren't good for anything."

"They still have life," Draycos reminded him. "A few days ago that was enough for you to consider them worth saving, even at the risk of your own."

"Maybe I've changed my mind."

"Have you?" Draycos countered. "Or have your thoughts merely been colored by fatigue and fear?"

Jack sighed. "Uncle Virge would have a field day with that one," he said. "But I'm too tired to argue. Which probably proves your point."

"I make no point," Draycos said. "I merely caution against making decisions when one is tired or fearful or angry."

"I know," Jack said. "I just forget sometimes." He took a deep breath. "And things aren't going all that badly right now, anyway, are they?"

"No, they are not," Draycos agreed cautiously. "But at the same time, they are perhaps going less well than you think. While searching for Taneem, I heard the Malison Ring floater moving around somewhere to the west."

Taking up guard position between them and the cave area? Probably. "That's fine," Jack said. "We were planning to change course today anyway. I guess this means we're angling east instead of west. Go get the rope, will you? I'll grab a couple of stretcher carriers."

"Very well." Turning, Draycos trotted back toward where Jack had left his pack.

Jack headed toward the nearest group of Phookas, studying them as he walked. Though all of them had a tendency to wander away from the herd, he knew which ones were the steadier and more obedient of the group. He spotted two of the latter digging at the base of a bush near Hren, and changed direction toward them.

"What now, young Jack?" Hren asked as Jack walked up. Hren's lips and chin were stained with berry juice, but there was nothing comical about his expression. It was about as stiff and angry as Jack had ever seen it. "Do you bring us to yet more danger?"

"There may possibly be more danger, yes," Jack had to admit. "But we'll do everything we can to keep you as safe as possible."

"*You* will keep us safe?" Hren countered. "You, who brought us into these dangers, now say you will keep us safe?"

"I'm sorry, Hren," Jack said. "If I'd known the bad men behind us would be so persistent . . . look, if we'd left you behind, all the Phookas would be dead. The bad men would have killed them. This was the only way I knew to save them."

"Yet out here they may die anyway."

"But at least now they have a chance," Jack said. "You *do* care what happens to them, don't you?"

"*We* care, yes," Hren said. "Do *you*?"

Jack grimaced. Stupid, useless, pain-in-the-neck animals . . . but Draycos was right. A few days ago, in a better state of mind than he was in right now, he'd considered them worth saving.

More to the point, Draycos considered them worth saving right now. "Yes," he told Hren. "I do."

Hren was silent for a moment. "Then we will continue on," he said. "Even if you have brought us here to die, far from our people and the berries we most love."

"You're not going to die," Jack assured him, wishing he really believed that. "We're not going to abandon you."

"It would seem young Alison has already done so," Hren

countered. "Yet hear me: We will not give up our lives easily. Not for any creature."

"I know you won't," Jack said. "You're a strong people, Hren, despite your casual ways. As for Alison, she hasn't abandoned anyone. She's just tired. We'll let her sleep, and she'll be fine." He looked back over toward her.

And as he did so, a flicker of gray caught his eye. Taneem was back from her hunt, strolling casually toward the rest of the group. "There she is," he said with relief. "Taneem! Taneem, come here!"

The gray Phooka didn't answer but kept padding her way through the milling crowd. Jack opened his mouth to call her again.

And stiffened. She wasn't just coming to rejoin the herd.

She was heading straight toward Alison.

"Taneem!" Jack called again, dashing toward her. Whatever the Phooka was doing to Alison, she had to be doing it while she was on the girl's skin. If she got back on—"Taneem! Draycos!"

To his left, he caught a flash of gold scales through the trees as Draycos bounded toward the girl and the gray dragon.

But they were both too late. Taneem got to Alison first and set her paw almost delicately on the side of Alison's neck. An instant later, the Phooka was gone, sliding beneath the collar.

"Blast!" Jack snarled as he braked to a halt at Alison's side. "Can you get her off?"

"No," Draycos said, his voice grim as he peered down into Alison's collar. "Not without Taneem's permission. I am sorry. I should not have left her."

"Don't blame yourself," Jack growled. "I'm the one who sent you away in the first place." He took a deep breath. "Whatever's happening, we'll just have to see it through. Let's get this stretcher rigged and get out of here."

They gathered the Erassvas and Phookas together, and with Alison nestled into her vine hammock between the green bellwether and a dark blue-green Phooka, they headed off.

Draycos didn't have many opportunities to see how things were going at the front. With Jack now having to lead, he had to cover both flanks of the group, watching for trouble as well as keeping the Phookas from wandering too far away.

But even with the bulk of his attention outward, it was quickly apparent that there was less herding necessary than there had been on previous days. On his third great circle around the travelers he made a point of moving in close enough to see what exactly was going on.

And was greeted by an extraordinary sight. The ten Erassvas were all walking closely together just behind Jack and Greenie, playing follow-the-leader as they'd been doing since Alison first set up this particular marching order. What was new was the fact that the Phookas, too, were mostly staying close to both the Erassvas and Jack himself.

Draycos wondered about it as he returned to his outward sweep. Were the Phookas still leery about predators after the previous day's Kodiak attack? That might explain why they were staying close to the boy carrying the guns.

But it hadn't been anyone with a gun who had chased the

Kodiak away. Draycos had done that. Yet there was no indication that the Phookas had even registered that fact, let alone were acting on it. It wasn't because of the bellwether, either, the one Jack called Greenie. While the Phookas had always followed him, they had never shown any particular interest in staying close by as they did so.

No, there could be only one reason the Phookas were staying so close to Jack. Somehow, in their dim and undeveloped minds, they had latched onto him as their leader. Their guide.

Their herdsman.

Jack might not think he had the patience to be a herdsman. He might not particularly like the task. But there was no denying that he had a talent for it.

You have many talents, Jack, Draycos had assured the boy earlier. *When the time comes, you will find the job that best fits you.*

It would be Draycos's job to make sure the boy lived until that time came.

CHAPTER 21

They'd been traveling about two hours when they hit the edge of the bog.

Hit it quite literally, in fact. Jack didn't even spot the silent, algae-covered water until he'd taken his first knee-deep step into it.

"How's it look?" Jack asked as Draycos reemerged from between a pair of droopy-leaved trees, picking his way carefully across a narrow land bridge.

"Like most such places," the K'da replied. "A great deal of water, much of it nearly impossible to see until one is already in it."

"Could you tell how big it is?"

"I estimate it is at least a few miles across," Draycos said. "It will take the rest of the morning to get around it. Possibly longer."

Jack chewed his lower lip, an idea beginning to play at the edge of his mind. "What if we go *through* it?"

Draycos arched his neck. "You must be joking. Didn't you hear what I just said? Bogs and swamps, particularly unfamiliar ones, are among the worst places possible for a soldier to make a stand against an enemy."

"Normally, sure," Jack agreed. "But this isn't a normal military situation. Frost wants me alive. He wouldn't dare attack around this much water, even with just tanglers. Maybe even *especially* with tanglers."

Draycos twitched his tail. "Yet if he *should* decide to take that risk, we would find ourselves with little maneuvering room."

"Yeah, but his men would be in the same boat," Jack pointed out. "And since you K'da seem to fight as well from trees as you do from solid ground, you'd run rings around them."

Draycos twitched the end of his tail. "I still do not like it."

"Neither do I," Jack conceded. "But Alison's in no shape to fight right now, and I *really* don't want us to have to face down Frost's men without her. Seems to me that every hour we can keep him off our backs is an extra hour for her to try to snap out of whatever's gotten its grip on her."

He nodded toward the bog. "The only question is whether we can get all the way through without losing anyone. *And* whether there's more than one way out the other side. Be kind of counterproductive if we went all the way through and then came out to find an ambush all set up and waiting for us."

"As to the latter, I expect there will be multiple exits," Draycos said. "As to the former . . . we will find out soon enough."

· · ·

The bog was humid, full of buzzing insects, and disgustingly smelly. But aside from that, it wasn't nearly as bad as Jack had expected.

The Erassvas, for all their bulk, turned out to be surprisingly nimble when it came to maneuvering along narrow land bridges. Even when they strayed off the path, they tended to float high enough in the water that it was easy for them to pull themselves back to safety. The insects and odors didn't seem to bother them at all.

Even better, Jack quickly discovered that Greenie had a knack for finding a path through the pools and stands of reeds. After the first mile, in fact, Jack was confident enough of the Phooka's abilities to send Draycos back to the rear of the party to watch for stragglers.

Through it all, Alison and Taneem dozed peacefully.

A little before noon they reached a sort of island amid the stagnant water and Jack called a halt. With Hren's help he got Alison and her vine hammock off the two Phookas and onto the ground.

He was sitting under a tree, munching on a ration bar, when Draycos arrived from the rear. "How are things going back there?" he asked the K'da.

"The mercenaries appear to be behaving themselves," Draycos told him, stretching out on the ground. He looked as tired as Jack felt. "The Phookas are a different story entirely."

"Keeping you busy, are they?" Jack asked, feeling a little guilty. While he'd been plodding more or less straight through the swamp, the K'da had been putting in a lot more miles, much of it probably leaping back and forth between trees.

"In truth, it is not as bad as it could be," Draycos conceded. "They still seem to prefer to stay as close to you as possible. But in this terrain, they are often unable to see you. It is at those times when they have a tendency to wander off."

"Maybe I should try to put myself somewhere in the middle of the group," Jack suggested. "Greenie seems capable enough of finding his own way."

"But without you, I doubt he will continue at the necessary speed," Draycos pointed out. "No, this still remains our best marching order." He looked over at Alison. "Has there been any change in Alison's condition?"

"Not that I could see," Jack said. "She seems to sleep pretty soundly, except when she's dreaming or something. She does a lot of twitching and muttering then."

"Anything you could understand?"

Jack shrugged. "A few words here and there. Frost got mentioned a lot, and so did Neverlin. Braxton's name came up once or twice, too."

"Braxton the man or Braxton the corporation?"

"I couldn't tell," Jack said. "Most of the rest was verbal scribble."

"And Taneem has been with her the whole time?"

"Like a squatter in cheap housing," Jack said sourly. "I'm thinking that the next time she hops off to get a snack, we might want to make sure she stays off. At least for a while."

"I'm afraid you're right," Draycos said regretfully. "I do not understand what is happening between them. Certainly nothing like this ever happens between K'da and Shontine."

"But remember what Alison said," Jack reminded him.

"You and the Shontine may already be so much alike that you just connect naturally together—your basic square pegs in the square holes. Taneem's coming from a"—he glanced quickly around to make sure none of the Erassvas were in hearing distance—"from a lethargic slug of an Erassva to a vibrant, smart-mouthed human. Maybe it's taking them both a while to acclimate to the change."

"Perhaps," Draycos said. But he didn't sound entirely convinced. "We can only hope the stress will not damage either of them."

"Yeah." Jack popped the last bite of the ration bar into his mouth. "Let's get Alison back in her hammock and hit the road."

It was late afternoon when they finally reached the end of the bog. "Nice to be on solid footing again," Jack commented as he and Draycos maneuvered Alison out of her hammock onto the ground. "Any sign of the bad guys?"

"I smell no one," Draycos said, his tongue flicking rapidly in and out of his snout. "Perhaps they have lost our trail."

"More likely they just decided they might as well take the rest of the day off," Jack said. "They'll probably be back full strength bright and early tomorrow morning."

"I hope for their sakes—" Abruptly, Draycos broke off, his head twisting to the east.

"What?" Jack asked, his hand going automatically to the machine gun slung over his shoulder.

"A predator approaches," Draycos said, turning to face that direction. "Another of the species we fought yesterday."

"Where?" Jack demanded, scrambling to his feet. One brush with the Kodiaks had been more than enough for him. Glancing down at his weapon, he switched it over to machine-gun mode. It would be risky to use the noisier setting, but he had no intention of trying to restrain such a beast with tangler cords.

"There," Draycos said, his tongue darting out.

"Got it." Lifting the gun, pointing it in the direction Draycos was facing, Jack braced himself.

"What's going on?" Alison murmured.

Startled, Jack looked down at her. Her eyes were half-closed, but she was definitely awake. "Predator on the way," he told her, feeling a flicker of relief. Bringing a comatose girl back to civilization hadn't been something he'd really been looking forward to. "Another of our friendly Kodiaks, Draycos says."

"Got it," she said, fumbling in her holster for her Corvine. The fingers paused, her eyes widening as she suddenly noticed the machine gun in Jack's hands. "What in the—? Where'd you get *that*?"

Before Jack could answer, there was a rustling in a group of bushes on the far side of the clearing, and a Kodiak lumbered into view.

Jack raised his gun a little higher, setting his teeth together as he aimed at the animal's massive torso. Beside him, he sensed Draycos lowering himself into a crouch, claws digging into the ground as he prepared to spring. "Easy," Alison murmured. "Let him get closer."

Jack nodded silently. The Kodiak took a couple of steps forward, then paused, his head moving back and forth as he surveyed the silent Erassvas and Phookas frozen in place watching him.

And then, to Jack's amazement, the beast turned and clumped back into the trees.

"Well, *that* was interesting," Alison said, pushing herself to her feet. She swayed a bit, and Jack caught her arm to steady her. "I'm okay," she said as she regained her balance. "What in the world did you say to him?"

"I threatened his family, of course," Jack said, peering through the trees where the Kodiak had disappeared. There was no sign of the creature. "What do you mean, what did I say? I didn't say or do anything." He nodded toward Draycos. "Maybe the other Kodiak has been spreading the word about Draycos."

"No," Draycos said, straightening out of his crouch, his tail tip making thoughtful circles in the air. "I believe he was more concerned about the Erassvas."

"You're kidding," Jack said, frowning at the bulky beings. They didn't look any more threatening than they usually did.

"Not at all," Draycos said. "Their odor has changed since last night. I noticed it this morning but assumed it was due to the change in their diet."

Just about the time Hren was warning Jack that the Erassvas wouldn't give up their lives easily, in fact. "You think they've finally gotten roused?"

"*Something* has certainly happened to them," Draycos said. "And many animals use scent cues to hunt. Perhaps their current odor is one which warns predators away."

"Actually, that makes sense," Alison murmured. "They're such obvious targets they ought to have gone the way of the dodo by now."

"Until something kicks in the adrenaline," Jack said. "Something like the first Kodiak attack yesterday."

"So the first predator gets a free shot at a given group, and everyone else after that has a fight on their hands," Alison concluded. "At least until the Erassvas' biochemistry switches back again. I guess this Kodiak must not have been hungry enough to risk it."

"Maybe," Jack said. "I somehow doubt the mercs will notice the changed attitude, though."

"Or will care even if they do," Alison agreed. "Let me see that gun, will you?"

"Don't worry; we dumped the tracker," Jack assured her, putting the safety back on and handing it over.

"Unless they got cute and threw in a backup." For a moment she turned the weapon over in her hands, poking and prying and peering at its various components. Then, with a grunt, she handed it back. "It's clean."

"Like I already said," Jack reminded her. "So what was this all-day nap of yours all about?"

"Fraggled if I know," she admitted. "But I *do* feel a whole lot better than I did yesterday. Maybe I was just tired."

"Join the club," Jack said with a sniff.

"I'm sorry—would you like to ride for a while?" Alison asked sweetly, gesturing to the vine hammock at her feet.

"What about Taneem?" Draycos asked before Jack could come up with a suitably sarcastic answer.

"She's fine," Alison assured him. "She's been sleeping most of the time, too, I think. But she's fine."

"This from your vast experience with K'da?" Jack put in.

Alison gave him a look of strained patience, then lifted her collar an inch and peered down into her shirt. "Taneem?" she called.

For a moment nothing happened. Then, the upper right side of Alison's shirt stirred and the top of a dark gray K'da crest pushed up against the cloth as it transformed into three-dimensional form. Alison opened her collar a little more, and the crest was joined by the top of Taneem's head and a single silver eye peering through the gap. "Yes?" a tentative voice asked.

Jack felt his mouth drop open a little. Taneem was actually *speaking*?

"This is Jack, Taneem," Alison said, pointing to him. If she was surprised by the Phooka's new verbal skills, she didn't show it. "And this is Draycos. Do you remember them?"

The single visible eye swiveled to look first at Jack and then at Draycos. "I think so," Taneem murmured.

"They're friends," Alison said, talking to the Phooka as if to a young child. "Do you understand?"

The eye swiveled to Jack, then back to Draycos. "I think so," she said again.

"Good," Alison said. "Then—" She broke off as the dragon crest abruptly flattened back down onto her skin. "Taneem?" she called. "Taneem?"

There was no response. "She's a little shy, I think," Alison said. "Still, it's progress."

"It is indeed," Draycos agreed, his tail making slow circles again.

"Aren't you glad now that we saved them?" Jack asked.

An instant later he wished he'd kept his mouth shut. Draycos spun to face him, his crest stiff, glowing green eyes glittering unpleasantly. "Sorry," Jack apologized hastily. "Sorry. I didn't mean it that way."

The crest relaxed a little. "I know," Draycos said, some of the fire going out of his eyes. "Yet you are right. To my shame, you are right. For a time I did not permit myself to hope."

"Just don't hope too high and too fast," Alison warned. "This whole thing is *very* new to her. She's not going to be operating at the level of a K'da poet-warrior any time soon."

"*I'm* just glad she's able to talk," Jack said. "And in English, yet. Is that what you were muttering in your sleep? English lessons?"

Alison frowned. "What are you talking about? I don't talk in my sleep."

"How would *you* know?" Jack countered.

"My parents told me," Alison retorted. "What was I saying?"

Frost, Neverlin, Braxton . . . "Just your basic nonsense muttering," Jack said. "Nothing I could make out. So you weren't teaching her English?"

"Not that I know," Alison said, still looking troubled. "I assume she picked it up the same time Hren and the other Erassvas did. So what's our current plan?"

"We've veered east from their last ambush attempt, so it's probably time to turn north again," Jack said. "If your guess a couple of days ago was right, we've still got two or three more days before we hit the river."

"Then we'd better move it," Alison said. "What was this about an ambush?"

"It didn't work," Jack said. "We can leave the details until it's too dark to travel."

"Fine," Alison said. "You can go back to your herding—I'll take point."

. . .

Heading north, as it turned out, was easier said than done.

The first obstacle was a line of crumbly-edged cliffs like the one the ill-fated red Phooka had fallen down on the evening of their first day in the forest. Alison found a way through, but it cost them time they didn't really have to spare.

The second obstacle was another bog, or perhaps an arm of the same one they'd spent the day slogging through. Alison was half-inclined to go on in, citing the same reason of enemy stalemate that Jack had given Draycos earlier in the day. She seemed surprised and even a bit embarrassed when she learned that the party had already done that once, and that Jack for one had no interest in a repeat performance.

The sun was dropping toward the horizon and a line of evening clouds was creeping across the sky when they finally finished circling the swampland and Alison called a halt. "What do you think?" she asked as Jack and Draycos joined her. "We've got maybe another hour of light left. Do we want to keep going north, or should we angle northeast and get back to the path we were on earlier?"

Jack peered through the trees, studying the terrain. Neither direction looked any better or worse than the other. "I vote for northeast," he said. "That'll put the bog at our backs, which means they probably won't be coming at us from that direction."

"And we'll have a place to retreat to if necessary," Alison agreed. "So we'll angle northeast until dark, then turn north again tomorrow?"

"That should work," Jack said. "Draycos?"

"I have no objections."

"Good." Alison craned her neck. "Anyone seen Taneem? She hopped off just before I called break."

"She is over there," Draycos said, flicking his tongue to the side.

"I see her," Alison said, nodding. "Taneem? Come on, girl. Time to go."

Obediently, Taneem trotted toward them. She eyed Jack and Draycos a little nervously as she approached, sidling gingerly past them as if afraid to touch either of them. She placed one of her forepaws on Alison's outstretched hand, and a second later had gone two-dimensional and slithered up the girl's arm. "At least she's not completely oblivious to the universe, like the other Phookas," Jack said.

"No," Draycos rumbled. "Instead, she has become excessively timid."

Jack had hoped the K'da wouldn't notice that. "Give her time," he urged quietly. "Like Alison said, she's new to this."

"I know," Draycos said. But Jack could still hear the disappointment in his voice. "Come—help me get the rest of the Phookas moving."

He padded away. Jack looked at Alison, lifted his eyebrows. "I don't know," she said, shrugging helplessly. "But he's right—let's get moving before we lose the daylight."

It was quickly clear that neither the Erassvas nor the Phookas were really interested in going any farther. As Draycos set off on his moving-sentry duty he could hear Hren complaining to

Alison, insisting they be allowed to settle down for the night. For her part, Alison responded by ignoring his protests and continuing to walk.

The Phookas, without the ability to complain, simply began dragging their feet. Draycos could hear Jack's running footsteps weaving in and out of the herd as the boy urged, cajoled, and occasionally ordered them to keep going.

Once or twice Draycos heard the sound of a light slap when none of the words would do the trick. More frequently, he heard a muttered curse that the boy had apparently borrowed from Uncle Virge's vast collection of such words. Clearly, Jack was as exhausted as the rest of them.

But one way or another, he kept the herd moving, and he kept it mostly together. Draycos kept an eye out for stragglers as he ran the perimeter, again finding himself impressed by Jack's ability at the task. There were very few stragglers that made it anywhere near Draycos, and even those Jack usually managed to snag before the K'da had to step in.

The sky overhead was darkening, and he was starting to look for a suitable place to camp for the night, when he heard the sound of the Malison Ring floater.

He froze in place, swiveling his head back and forth. It was coming up from behind them, from the south, he decided. And unlike earlier that day, this time it was headed straight for them.

The long-expected attack had begun.

CHAPTER 22

"Jack!" he called, turning inward toward the main group. "Alison! They are coming!"

"Where?" Alison called back.

"Above and to the south," Draycos told her as he leaped over the last line of bushes between them. Across the way, he saw Jack hurrying toward them, gripping his machine gun awkwardly across his chest.

"I hear it," Alison confirmed grimly, looking up at the dark canopy of leafy branches high overhead.

"Where are they?" Jack demanded as he ran up.

"Straight above us," Alison told him. "No place to land— must be planning a rappel drop."

Jack looked up. "No, that's too simple," he said darkly. "Frost has something else in mind."

Above them, the sound of the floater's lifters changed subtly. "Perhaps so, but this is certainly part of it," Draycos told him, looking around. Just to the side of the likely drop zone was a tall, thick tree. "Get the Erassvas and Phookas out of the way," he ordered, leaping into the tree's lower branches. "Then stand ready." He paused and looked down. "Tanglers only, please," he added.

"You got it," Jack said, thrusting his gun into Alison's hands. "Here—you're a better shot than I am. I'll get the others to cover."

Draycos turned back around and headed up the tree. Out of the corner of his eye he saw the familiar blood trickles flowing into his scales, turning them from gold to black. In the deepening gloom, it would be an effective camouflage.

He was sixty feet off the ground when, with a faint rustle of branches, six coils of rope dropped into view through the canopy, unrolling themselves to the ground. Draycos froze, pressing himself into the crook of a large branch. A second later, in perfect unison, six Malison Ring mercenaries in quick-drop harnesses crashed through the canopy, machine gun/tanglers at the ready, sliding swiftly down their ropes toward the ground.

They were lined up three by three, each soldier of a three-some separated by two or three feet, with about six feet separating the two different groups. Apparently, three of them were dropping from each side of the floater, which clearly wasn't a very big aircraft. The result was an attack group that was forced to bunch up more than they probably would have liked.

From Draycos's point of view, it was as good a setup as he could have hoped for. Bracing himself, he watched as the soldiers continued sliding toward the ground below.

And as they passed his position, he leaped.

His outstretched left paw caught the nearest rope just above the soldier's head, his momentum shoving the soldier back into his fellows as they all continued to slide down their ropes. With his grip on the rope as a pivot point, the K'da's leap changed abruptly into a sweeping, horizontal circle. His body caught the other two ropes of his group as he swung around them, squeezing all three closer together. His tail snapped out as he continued his circle, snaring the farthest rope of the other threesome, as his hind claws likewise caught the other two.

And with all six ropes now in his grip, he ignored the sudden flurry of shouts and activity from below and curled himself into a ball.

And as he pulled the ropes together, the six men suddenly found themselves clustered together like fruit on a vine. "Now!" Draycos shouted.

The word was barely out of his mouth when the first of Alison's tangler cartridges sizzled its way upward, catching the nearest soldier squarely across his chest. The white threads whipped out, entangling him and the two men beside him, as the shock capacitor sent a jolt of current through all three of them. Still firing, she moved sideways beneath the dropping men, methodically plastering the entire group. A couple of seconds later, the now-unconscious soldiers had been turned into something a giant spider might have wrapped up and tucked away for a future meal. "Is that it?" Alison called.

Draycos looked up, listening for the sounds that would indicate more soldiers were on the way. But he didn't hear any.

What he *did* hear was the faint noise of drumming hooves below him. Hooves that were rapidly coming closer.

He turned his head back toward the ground, trying to locate the sound. From the west, he decided. A moment later he spotted a small group of bodies racing toward them. "Alison!" he called again. "A group of horn-headed plant-eaters are coming toward you."

"I hear them," she called back, turning to face that direction. "Sounds like a stampede."

"Get everyone on the eastern sides of the trees where they'll be safer," Draycos ordered. He was catching more glimpses now through the branches as the animals approached. There seemed to be just five of them, running as if a demon was pursuing them.

A demon, or perhaps one of the Kodiak predators. Draycos shifted his attention to the trail of scattered leaves swirling behind them, searching for signs of pursuit.

And because he was looking in the wrong direction, he was caught completely by surprise when the five animals burst into view beneath him.

He'd been right the first time. They were indeed fleeing from demons.

Only the demons weren't behind them. They were riding them.

"They're on the animals!" Draycos barked. "Tangle the animals!"

But it was too late. The five Malison Ring soldiers had already leaped backward out of their makeshift saddles, hitting the ground running. As the hornheads sped mindlessly on, the soldiers trotted to a halt, swinging their weapons up into firing position.

One of them staggered and collapsed unconscious as Alison got him with a tangler round. But before she could get off a second shot she was forced to dive for cover as two of the others sent machine-gun bursts spattering through the bushes beside her. She made it behind a tree, pressing herself against the trunk as the two soldiers continued to fire. The other two looked straight up at Draycos, still clinging to his ropes.

And with the bitter sense of having been caught like a freshly trained recruit, Draycos realized he was trapped. There was no cover anywhere around him, nowhere he could leap to or climb to in time. Nowhere at all he could go.

Except down.

Bracing himself, he let go of the ropes.

The first burst of machine-gun fire sliced through the area he'd just left. He tucked his legs and tail close in toward his body as he dropped, trying to make the smallest possible target of himself. Below him, the tangler-webbed group was slowing as the sensors in their quick-drop harnesses spotted the ground approaching and put additional friction on the ropes. Another salvo of machine-gun fire shot past, closer this time, one of the rounds twitching across the tip of Draycos's left ear.

And as he reached the falling soldiers, he snapped his legs out and grabbed hold of the webbing on the far side, putting the webbed group between him and the two gunners.

But the gunners weren't going to be thwarted so easily. Both continued firing, sending short bursts past either side of the group, pinning Draycos in place while they waited for their moving target to stop moving.

A second later it did just that. The webbed soldiers hit the ground, toppling over in a confused tangle of torsos and legs and tangler thread. Draycos dropped flat behind them, pressing himself against the ground as he again used their bodies for cover.

But that cover wasn't going to last long. One of the two mercenaries continued to fire bursts across the left side of Draycos's shelter, blocking any escape in that direction, while the other began circling to Draycos's right. Unless the K'da did something, and fast, in another few seconds he would be directly in the second soldier's line of fire.

And he would die.

He risked a look around the mass of bodies, wondering if Alison might be in a position to counterattack. But she was pinned down the same way he was, with one of her pair of soldiers raking her tree with fire while the other circled to the side to try to get a clear shot.

And then, even as Draycos braced himself for a desperate and almost certainly fatal dash for safety, over the stutter of the machine guns he heard a war whoop.

He turned his head. Jack was charging across the battle zone toward him, firing his tangler wildly at the soldiers as he ran, screaming defiance at the top of his lungs.

It was probably the last thing the mercenaries expected from their young quarry. It was certainly the last thing Draycos expected, and his warrior's instincts winced as the boy deliberately threw himself into harm's way.

But if the soldiers wanted Draycos dead, they wanted Jack alive even more. For a second the machine-gun fire stopped as both soldiers switched over to their tangler settings.

It was all the opening Draycos needed. Bounding over the pile of webbed soldiers, digging his claws into the threads for extra traction, he threw himself at the nearer of his two at-tackers.

The other tried to swing his gun up, but he was too late. Draycos slammed into him, grabbing his combat vest with one paw as he slapped the side of his head with the other. The soldier's knees buckled as he blacked out, and Draycos turned toward the other gunner.

But before he could shove off the unconscious soldier something hard slammed into his side, and an explosion of white threads burst around the two of them. An instant later a jolt of current arced through him, turning his muscles to jelly and dropping him and the soldier together onto the ground.

Clenching his jaws, Draycos tried to force his body to respond. At least he wasn't unconscious; apparently with the charge split between two of them it had been low enough to leave him awake.

But it had been more than enough to also leave him helpless. It would be at least another few seconds, he estimated, before his muscles would be back under his control.

There was a sudden movement, and out of the corner of his eye he saw Jack drop to his knees beside him. "Draycos!" the boy gasped.

Get away! Draycos tried to snap. But his mouth couldn't even manage that.

Besides, it was already too late. A pair of boots stepped into Draycos's field of view, and with a startled squawk Jack was hauled to his feet. "Got him," the soldier called.

"This one, too," someone else called back.

With a supreme effort, Draycos turned his head. One of

the other soldiers had a grip on the back of Alison's shirt collar and was half-pulling, half-dragging her toward them.

"Do we even want her?" the third soldier retorted as he walked toward Jack, his gun pointed warily at Draycos. "I thought we just wanted Morgan."

"Hey, you want her popped, I'll be glad to do it," the soldier holding Alison offered, giving her a shake. "She's the one who waxed J'nauren."

"I wouldn't do that if I were you," Jack spoke up quickly. "Frost is going to want her alive."

"She something special to you?" the soldier demanded, shaking Alison again. "Huh?"

"Alive *and* unharmed," Jack added. "He's going to want the K'da alive, too."

The third soldier grunted. "Oh, absolutely," he said sarcastically. "We'll get him a nice box of scorpions, too."

The feeling was starting to come back into Draycos's muscles now. Carefully, he tried moving his forepaws. They twitched a little with the effort but otherwise were definitely recovering. If Jack could stall for another few seconds, Draycos would be ready for action.

Problem was, he was still tied up in the tangler webbing, his claws turned toward the unconscious soldier and away from the threads. He would have to turn his forepaws over to get to them, and he would have to do so without the soldiers noticing.

"We leave the K'da but take both kids," the soldier holding Jack ordered. "The colonel can sort 'em out back at camp. Give Rinks a call and have him fire up the winch."

"Right," the third soldier said. Shifting his gun to a one-handed grip, he reached toward a comm clip on his collar.

And with a shriek, a gray tornado erupted from the back of Alison's collar.

The soldier holding her never had a chance. Even as he jumped back, Taneem's claws slashed across his throat, nearly severing his head. The third soldier snarled something and grabbed his gun again in a two-handed grip, whipping it around as he tried to bring it to bear on this new and unexpected danger. Beside Draycos, Jack slammed hard onto the ground as his guard shoved him away and grabbed for his own weapon. Taneem hit the ground, spun around, and launched herself toward the two remaining soldiers.

And with their full attention on her, and none of it on him, Jack reached over and dug his fingers beneath the tangler mesh. His fingertips touched the end of Draycos's right forepaw—

In a fraction of a second Draycos had slid up the boy's sleeve onto his arm and from there onto his back. A fraction of a second more, and Draycos had launched himself out again through the back of Jack's collar.

But the K'da's muscles were still not entirely recovered from the tangler shock. His leap was awkward, his attempted blow against the nearest soldier's head weak and off-target.

But it didn't matter. As Taneem's sudden appearance had drawn their attention away from him and Jack, Draycos's own attack now drew their eyes away from Taneem.

And before they could recover she was there, claws and

teeth and tail slashing wildly and frantically. Five seconds later, it was all over.

Draycos took a deep breath. "Is everyone all right?" he asked.

"I think so," Alison said, her voice shaking as she came toward them. "Mother of God. That's . . ."

"Yeah, I know," Jack assured her. But he didn't sound all that steady himself. "Welcome to the club. Taneem? You okay?"

Taneem didn't answer. She was staring at the soldiers she'd just killed, her eyes wide with disbelief. Her back and tail were arched with a growing horror as the reality of what she'd just done began to sink in. "Taneem, are you hurt?" Draycos asked.

With an effort, she turned to look at him. "What?"

"We asked if you were hurt," Draycos repeated, walking over to her.

"No," she said, her voice distant. "No, I'm all right." She started to look back at the soldiers.

"Look at me," Draycos said. "Taneem, *look* at me!"

Taneem flinched, twitching her head back to him. "I'm sorry—"

"Now listen to me," Draycos cut her off, putting into his voice every bit of the weight from his years as a warrior. "What you did, you did to protect your host. If you hadn't acted, they would have killed her. Perhaps not now. But they *would* have killed her."

Taneem's breaths were coming quick and shallow. "But—" She started to turn back to the bodies.

"Do not look at them," Draycos ordered, flicking his tail up against the side of her muzzle and pressing her head firmly back to face him. "They are dead, you killed them, and it was necessary that you do so. That is the reality."

Out of the corner of his eye he saw Jack stir, and glanced a silent warning at the boy. Early in their relationship, Jack had made it very clear that killing wasn't acceptable here in human society, not even when K'da and Shontine law would have permitted him to dispense such justice. Draycos had accepted that, and had ever afterward tried to neutralize their opponents without permanent damage.

But this was hardly the same situation. Clearly, Taneem already understood that killing wasn't to be used except as a last resort. What she needed now was reassurance and comfort, not guilt or a legal opinion.

Fortunately, Jack got the message. He nodded fractionally at Draycos and kept quiet.

"He's right, Taneem," Alison said, coming up and stroking the side of Taneem's head. Her hand, Draycos noticed, was shaking a little, too. "You saved my life. As well as the lives of Hren and the rest of your friends."

"Speaking of which, can we put this discussion on hold until we're out of here?" Jack said, peering up at the sky. "Sooner or later they're going to start wondering what's holding up the show."

"Agreed," Draycos said, looking around. The Erassvas and Phookas were starting to come out of their hiding places now, with Hren and Greenie in the lead. "Alison, get the green

Phooka and start moving north," he ordered. "Jack, you will organize the herd and keep them together. Taneem, you go with Alison."

"Just a second," Alison said. Stooping down, she retrieved one of the dead soldiers' machine guns. "If you don't mind?" she asked, holding it out toward Draycos.

"My pleasure." He slashed his claws across the metal shoulder stock, cutting it and its embedded tracker away from the weapon.

"Thanks," Alison said, slinging the gun over her shoulder. "Come on, Greenie. Time to go, boy."

Obediently, the green Phooka lumbered over to her, glancing indifferently at the three dead soldiers as he passed. Alison hooked a finger behind his crest, and together they headed off. "Go on, Taneem," Draycos prompted. "Stay with her."

"All right." Taneem gave one last, lingering look at the soldiers. Then, arching her back once as if trying to shake away the memory, the Phooka turned and left.

Draycos watched her go, something stirring deep within him. No; not the Phooka. Not anymore.

Taneem was a K'da.

Jack stepped beside him. "Well," he murmured. "Suddenly this is getting very interesting."

"Indeed it is," Draycos agreed grimly. "Come. We must find a camping place before it becomes fully dark."

CHAPTER 23

They found a good place half an hour away beside a small creek. Jack and Alison got the Erassvas and Phookas settled; and then, at Alison's insistence, she and Taneem took the first watch.

Jack argued a little, but not very much. He was exhausted, and even though Draycos hadn't said anything, Jack knew the K'da was tired as well. And as Alison pointed out, she and Taneem *had* slept most of the day.

Still, desperately tired or not, Jack slept fitfully, waking every hour or so from a bad dream. Most of those dreams ended with a vision of the dead soldiers Taneem had killed.

Rather to his surprise, the mercenaries didn't launch another attack that night. Alison woke him up a little after dawn—Draycos was already up—and after a quick breakfast and the Phookas' morning dance they were off.

Jack did notice that Taneem didn't participate in the dance. She watched instead from Alison's side, her tail lashing restlessly.

They made good time that day. For once the terrain seemed to be working in their favor, with no cliffs or overly wide streams or large bogs in their way. There were still the stands of rubbery trees and their vine meshes to deal with, more of them with every mile they traveled. But with Taneem at the front of the group with Alison there were no more delays while they waited for Draycos to finish his rounds and cut through the vines.

As for the native animals, they seemed to be avoiding the travelers as well. Jack spotted only one herd of hornheads, and no Kodiaks at all. Draycos mentioned once that the Erassvas' new odor was even stronger than it had been on the previous day, but whether that was the cause or it was just the luck of the draw he couldn't say.

Just before noon Alison called a break, and as the Erassvas and Phookas foraged for food she and Jack sat together beside a pair of trees and compared notes.

"No, we haven't seen any Kodiaks all day," Alison said. "At least, not up front. I did spot a couple of small hornhead herds, but they kept their distance."

"How fast were they going?" Jack asked.

"Not *that* fast," Alison assured him. "At least we'll have some warning if the Malison Ring tries that one again."

Jack shook his head. "Frost doesn't seem the type to try the same trick twice. I wonder when that transport of his is due back."

"It already is," Alison said. "It came in last night, while you and Draycos were sleeping. Taneem and I heard it."

Jack stared at her. "And you didn't wake us up?"

"No, because there wasn't any reason to," Alison told him.

"It was coming in from the west and landed somewhere way to the south. It never got anywhere near us."

"And you didn't think to even mention it when we got up this morning?"

"I'm mentioning it now," Alison said, regarding him coolly. "What's the problem? We both know Frost isn't going to just throw something wildly at us. Whatever he's planning, it'll take him at least until evening to set it up."

"That's not the point," Jack growled. "You need to keep Draycos and me on top of everything that happens around here. *Especially* Draycos, who in case you've forgotten is our local military expert."

"My deepest and most profound apologies," Alison said, an edge of sarcastic anger in her tone. "It won't happen again."

"It had better not," Jack warned. Still, she *was* probably right about Frost's intentions. Anyway, this was no time to be fighting among themselves. "Because the next time it does, I'm patching you through to the *Essenay* and letting Uncle Virge give the lecture. Trust me; you won't like it."

For a moment Alison continued to glare at him. Then, her eyes softened and a reluctant smile twitched at her lips. "I can imagine," she said dryly. "In that case, it *definitely* won't happen again." Her lip twitched away the smile. "And you're right, I should have told you sooner. I'm sorry."

"That's okay," Jack said, feeling his own tension draining away. "You were right, too. Frost isn't going to just charge madly into anything."

"No." Alison's throat tightened. "Not after last night."

Jack looked around, but Taneem was nowhere to be seen. "You still freaked out about that?"

"Wouldn't you be?" she countered. "Well, no. I guess *you* wouldn't."

"Actually, I am," Jack admitted. "At least a little."

"Even after living with Draycos for almost four months?"

"Even so," Jack said. "Taneem's attack seemed different, somehow. I'm not quite sure why."

Alison shrugged. "No big mystery there," she said. "Draycos is a trained warrior who knows exactly what he's doing. Taneem's more like a child who's suddenly been thrown into an adult body without even an instruction book. It's all very new to her."

"I think you're right," Jack agreed. "She's probably never even killed anything bigger than a three-bite lizard."

"Or if she has, she's long since forgotten all about it."

Jack grimaced. "She won't forget this one."

"I doubt any of us will." Alison paused. "But it's gotten me thinking. You remember Draycos saying the Valahgua were the aggressors back wherever it is they came from?"

"Are you saying you don't believe him?" Jack demanded, letting his voice harden.

"I'm not saying anything at all," Alison said patiently. "I was just noticing that a K'da in full-bore host-protection mode could easily be seen as an aggressor."

"Taneem's not a typical K'da."

"I know that," Alison said. "And before you get all hot and bothered, I'm not accusing Draycos of lying to us. But it's possible there are sides to this that he doesn't know."

Jack chewed the inside of his cheek. And there *was* still the unanswered question of why the Valahgua would come all this way just to continue their war against the K'da and Shontine. "No," he said firmly. "There aren't any other sides. Draycos and his people are the victims—pure and simple."

"I just meant—"

"I saw what the Malison Ring did to Draycos's advance ships, Alison." Jack cut her off. "I know the sort of people Arthur Neverlin and the Chookoock family are. If the Valahgua are some poor, put-upon victims, they've picked themselves some *really* strange allies."

"Okay, fine," Alison said. "I'm sorry—I didn't mean to upset you."

"I'm not upset," Jack insisted. From behind a row of tall ferns to the right came a soft sound like a multiple cough. "And now if you'll excuse me, I have to go help one of my herd."

"Help him do what?" Alison asked, frowning as she looked around. "What's wrong?"

"It's nothing serious," Jack said, levering himself to his feet and brushing the leaves off the back of his jeans. "It's just Dumb Dog. That's the other big green Phooka—I call him Dumb Dog to distinguish him from Greenie. He has a habit of poking his head under roots to chase grubs and then not being able to get back out again."

"Oh," Alison said, looking rather taken aback. "I never heard about that."

"That's because you're just the leader," Jack said loftily. "*I'm* the herdsman."

"I guess so," she acknowledged, a slight frown on her face as she looked up at him. "You need any help?"

Jack shook his head. "No, I just have to tuck his ears back and hold them there while he pulls his head out. Anyway, you should probably give Hren a nudge and get everyone ready to move again."

"Okay," Alison said, standing up and picking up her machine gun.

Jack frowned as something about the weapon caught his eye. "What happened to the gun?" he asked, pointing to the spot where the front handgrip used to be.

"Oh, there was a second tracker in the front grip," Alison said matter-of-factly, holding out the weapon for closer inspection. "Like you said, Frost likes to keep things fresh. No big deal—I spotted it last night, right after we headed out again, and had Taneem slice it off."

"What did you do with it?"

"We put it on a big piece of bark and sent it sailing off on the next stream we passed," she said with a mischievous smile. "Taneem seemed fascinated by it all."

"Like you said, it's all new and exciting," Jack said. From behind the ferns came another series of coughs, this batch louder than the last. "I wish I could say the same about Dumb Dog," he added with a sigh. "Go get Hren, and let's get out of here."

Draycos had also been unaware that the Kapstan transport had returned the previous night. Rather to Jack's private annoyance, he seemed as unconcerned as Alison had been that the girl hadn't mentioned it to them earlier.

"Actually, I've been expecting it to return for the past two days," the K'da told him as they trudged along at the rear of the group. "To be honest, I am somewhat surprised Colonel Frost brought it in along such a vector that Alison was able to hear it at all. Had I been in command, I would have tried to avoid that."

"Maybe he doesn't care whether we know it's back or not," Jack said with a grimace. "Maybe he's got so much fire-power now that he thinks he can just charge in and roll over us. Means our best bet is to get to the river and whistle up Uncle Virge before they're ready to make their move."

For a minute Draycos was silent. "What will you do if Uncle Virge and the *Essenay* did not survive?" he asked at last.

"They did," Jack said firmly. Automatically. "He'll be there when we need him. I know he will."

"I hope you're right," Draycos said. "But a warrior must always make certain there are avenues for retreat. Perhaps we should watch for caves in which we could wait for Alison's friends."

Jack shook his head. "We'll never make it that far west," he said. "Especially not with Frost already expecting us to jump that direction. We have to do something completely different."

"You have an idea?"

"Yes, but I don't think you're going to like it," Jack said. "Do you remember what the terrain is like to the east of the forest?"

"As I recall, there were quite a few miles of plains and

grasslands," Draycos said. "A few groups of trees, but otherwise very little cover."

"Which should make it the last place Frost would expect us to go," Jack said. "I'm thinking we could borrow the trick you used to draw out that ambush line a couple of nights ago."

"Where we pretended you were floating down the stream breathing through a reed?"

"Right," Jack said. "Only this time we do it for real. Maybe stick the reeds up through hollow logs or something to help camouflage them. Then we just float away down the river, right under their collective nose. Hopefully, we'll be through the grasslands to whatever's past them before Frost figures it out."

"This would be you and Alison, I presume?" Draycos asked, his voice flat.

"Actually, I was thinking it would be just you and me," Jack said. "Alison and Taneem can stay behind with the Erassvas and Phookas. Maybe they can all head east, away from the caves, and hunker down until Alison's friends get here."

Even without looking he could feel Draycos's disapproving stare. "You believe they could survive alone for two weeks?"

"It should be possible," Jack said doggedly. "As long as the Erassvas are putting out that new, improved smell of theirs the local predators should leave them alone."

"And the mercenaries?"

"They won't care about them once they realize you and I are gone." Jack took a deep breath. "Which is why as soon as we've found some decent cover we'll give Frost a call."

Draycos peered up at Jack's face. "You'll *call* him?"

"I told you you wouldn't like it," Jack said. "I figure it'll take us a day or two to find ourselves some kind of defensible position. Once we're ready, we call Frost and declare open season on Dragonbacks."

"At which point he will turn his full force against us."

"But at least it'll just be against *us*," Jack said. "Not against Alison and the others."

Draycos was silent a moment. "My apologies, Jack," he said quietly. "I did not understand."

"That's all right," Jack assured him. "Actually, I'm as surprised as you are that I'm being all noble like this. If Uncle Virge were here he'd have a fit."

"Indeed," Draycos agreed. "Let us hope we will have the pleasure of hearing his reaction together once we are safely back aboard."

"Sounds like a plan," Jack said. Something pressed against his right hand, and he looked down to find one of the Phookas nuzzling against his side. "If not, I figure that if it's just you and me out there we can give Frost a pretty good run for his money," he added, making his hand into a fist and rubbing the knuckles behind the Phooka's ear.

"Perhaps," Draycos said, craning his neck to look around Jack. "What are you doing?"

"What, here?" Jack asked, switching to the Phooka's other ear. "Nothing. This is Snip. He likes to get his ears rubbed."

" 'Snip'?"

"It's short for Special Needs Phooka," Jack explained. "He seems to need a lot of reassurance that we haven't run off and left him."

"I see," Draycos murmured. "Curious."

"Curious how?" Jack asked, giving Snip a rub along his jawline. "As I recall, *you've* liked your ears rubbed on occasion, too."

"I was referring to you," Draycos said. "In a few days, apparently without even trying, you have learned the character and personality of each member of your herd. That requires an eye for details."

Jack grimaced. "Blame it on Uncle Virgil," he said. "Attention to detail is a big part of a con man's job."

"It also takes great heart," Draycos said. "And *that* is not something Uncle Virgil taught you."

"It's no big deal," Jack insisted, suddenly uncomfortable with this. "I've got a soft spot for K'da, that's all."

"As you had a soft spot for Alison and your other comrades in the Whinyard's Edge?" Draycos reminded him. "You risked your life to rescue them."

"At your rather insistent nudging," Jack reminded him.

"You could have refused," Draycos said. "And as you also had a soft spot for your fellow slaves on Brum-a-dum?"

And that one Draycos *hadn't* pushed him into doing, Jack remembered. In fact, the dragon had been rather surprised by his decision. "I guess your warriors' ethic is starting to rub off on me," he said.

"It is indeed," Draycos agreed. "And it shows how my faith in you has been justified."

"Maybe." Jack looked up at the trees arching over them. "Let's just hope that all that faith doesn't get to go out in a blaze of glory."

CHAPTER 24

They made it to evening still without having seen, heard, or smelled any sign of Frost's mercenaries. Alison found them some partial shelter at the base of a steep hill, and within an hour they were fed and watered and settled in for the night.

"Tomorrow's the day," she warned as she and Jack and the two K'da sat together on top of the hill finishing their ration bars. "I'm guessing we'll reach the river by midafternoon at the latest." She eyed Jack. "At which point, it's going to be up to you."

Jack nodded. "My main comm clip's still wandering the forest attached to one of the hornheads, but I've got a spare in my shoe heel. Once we're close, I'll try giving Uncle Virge a call. With luck, he'll have a floater antenna up and will be able to hear us."

"And if we're not that lucky?" Alison asked. "You have a Plan B ready?"

"We have that covered," Draycos assured her before Jack could answer. "But I do not intend to give up on Uncle Virge quite so quickly."

"I'm not giving up on him," Alison protested mildly. "I'll

be the first to cheer if we hit the riverbank and find the *Essenay* sitting there with its hatch open, ready to lift." She frowned. "*Essenay,*" she repeated thoughtfully.

"What is it?" Jack asked.

"I was just thinking," she said slowly. "*Essenay* is a really odd name for a ship. Is that its christening name?"

Jack shrugged. "It's the only name I've ever known it by. Why? Does it mean something?"

"Not to me," Alison said. "Though now that I think about it I suppose it *could* be initials—'S and A.' Did Virgil Morgan have two middle names?"

"As far as I know, he didn't have any," Jack said.

"What is this christening name you speak of?" Taneem asked.

"That's a ship's official name, the one registered in the Orion Trade Association files," Alison explained. "A lot of people then give their ships what are called private or personal names."

"Like a nickname," Jack added. "A ship might be listed as the *Rick's Café of Casablanca III,* but its owners just call it *Ricky.* There are an awful lot of ships flying around out there, and they all have to have unique christening names."

"And again, *Essenay* sounds like a private name," Alison said. "Have you ever looked it up on the official lists?"

Jack snorted. "This may come as a shock, but I've spent most of my life *avoiding* everything official that the Orion Arm has to offer. This doesn't strike me as a good time to change that policy, either."

"I understand that," Alison said patiently. "I was just wondering."

"Wondering is wonderful exercise as long as you don't overdo it." Jack looked back at Draycos. "You think we should wonder about scouting ahead a ways and see what Frost might have cooking?"

"I don't think that will be necessary," Draycos said. "I have not heard the floater or the Kapstan at all today."

"But he could have sent some troops in along the river by boat," Alison pointed out.

"True," Draycos agreed. "We shall have to be careful as we near the river itself."

"So we don't take a walk?" Jack asked.

"*I* take a walk," Draycos said, standing up and stretching, cat-style, with his forelegs thrust forward and his tail high in the air. "There is no need for you to go with me. But I will require your comm clip."

"Be careful," Jack warned, digging the comm clip from its hiding place in the sole of his left shoe and handing it over. "Out here in the middle of nowhere, Frost wouldn't have much trouble locating it."

"I understand," Draycos said, fastening the clip to his crest at the back of his neck. "Alison, can you adjust your comm clip frequency to match Jack's? We may need to use them together at some point."

She nodded. "No problem."

"Good." Draycos lifted his head and darted his tongue in and out a few times to taste the air. "I will be back as soon as I can." With a final look at Jack, he loped down the hill and disappeared into the forest.

"He should not go alone," Taneem murmured, her tail lashing restlessly as she gazed after him.

"Draycos knows what he's doing," Jack assured her, trying to hide his own quiet misgivings. "He can take care of himself."

"You mean up to now he's been lucky," Alison said bluntly. "We all have been, mainly because Frost has been trying to take us alive. But sooner or later, even the best warrior's luck runs out."

"Not tonight it doesn't," Jack said, glaring at her. "And you're not going to talk that way again. Understand?"

For a moment they locked gazes. Then, Alison's eyes flicked to Taneem, and her lip twitched. "You're right," she apologized. "I'm sorry."

"Yeah," Jack growled. "Give me the gun and go find someplace to lie down. I'll take the first watch."

"Sure." Alison handed over the machine gun. "Taneem, you feel up to doing a little night patrolling?"

"Yes, of course." Taneem stood up, her eyes still on the spot where Draycos had vanished. "What do you wish me to do?"

"Nothing fancy," Alison said. "Just take a few circles around the camp, watching for predators and soldiers. If you smell or hear anything that seems threatening or even strange, you come and get either Jack or me. Understand?"

Taneem ducked her head. "Yes."

"We just want to make sure nothing sneaks up on the Erassvas and your fellow K'da," Jack added.

"Phookas," Taneem corrected him, looking down at the group of dragons at the bottom of the hill. "They are not K'da."

She looked back at Jack, an oddly intense look in her silver eyes. "Not yet."

The river turned out to be considerably closer than Alison had guessed. Barely two hours after leaving camp, Draycos caught his first scent of the water. He spent the next half hour moving cautiously toward it, his senses stretched to their limit, watching for the ambush that must surely be waiting.

But there was nothing. No soldiers, no booby traps, no Kapstan, no floater, no boats, no hint of the enemy. It was as if the Malison Ring had given up.

He'd remembered from their earlier aerial view that the river was a wide one. But natural features always looked larger and more impressive at close range. For a minute he stood at the edge of the river, gazing outward at the water flowing slowly past, its edge rippling quietly against the bank. Even at night, it was a majestic sight.

But majestic or not, a river was a terrible barrier for a soldier to be trapped against. Perhaps that was why Frost's soldiers hadn't bothered to capture the riverfront. Perhaps their plan was to simply sweep in from the south, behind the fugitives, and pin them here with nowhere else to go.

Alison had said that the Erassvas and Phookas spent their lives circling the edge of the forest as they foraged for food. That meant they had to cross the river twice per circuit, which implied they either could swim or else knew how to construct boats.

But in this case neither method would do them any good. As soon as they were on the water and out from under the protection of the forest canopy, they would be easy targets for airborne gunners. That was undoubtedly what Jack had been thinking about when he'd suggested that he and Draycos slip away and try to draw Frost's attention.

The problem with Jack's plan was that it wouldn't work. There was simply nowhere in the eastern grasslands where the two of them could hide from the mercenaries. Certainly not for the ten or eleven days it might take for Alison's friends to arrive. If Jack was going to evade capture, he would have to stay with Alison and the others in the forest.

Which meant that if they were going to have any chance of drawing the Malison Ring away, Draycos would have to do it alone.

And of course, without Jack along, he would die in the process.

He gazed across the river, snatches of old epic poems and songs running through his mind. As a warrior of the K'da he'd had to face the possibility of death many times. But it was somehow always different each time it happened. And it wasn't something he'd ever became used to.

Especially when it would mean abandoning such a young and inexperienced host. Would Jack be able to manage alone?

More important, would he be able to learn the location of the refugee fleet's rendezvous point alone and be able to save the rest of the K'da and Shontine?

There was no way to know. But Draycos had no doubt that the boy would try his very best to do so. Jack had fully adopted the K'da warrior ethic of service to others. Even with Draycos gone he would continue the mission as long as life remained in him.

The K'da lashed his tail firmly. Yes, Jack would do his best. But Draycos had no intention of laying such a heavy burden on the boy's shoulders, not unless and until there was no other choice. Retrieving the comm clip from its place on his crest, Draycos gave the air one final sniff and clicked it on. "Uncle Virge?" he called softly.

There was no answer. "Uncle Virge, this is Draycos," he said again. "If you can hear, please respond."

Again, nothing. Draycos left the comm clip on another few heartbeats, then switched it off again. As Jack had pointed out, the device would stand out like a beacon in the wilderness, and there was no point in giving the Malison Ring the exact location where he and the others would be coming out.

Unless . . .

Attaching the comm clip to his crest again, he leaned out over the water and looked in both directions. Downstream, he decided. Backing up into better cover, he headed east, looking for a good spot.

He found it a hundred yards away and a few yards in from the river: a stand of the by-now familiar rubbery trees and their attached vine meshes. He hadn't brought any rope along, but the vines should be strong enough for what he had in mind.

Quickly, he cut a group of them from their trees and tied them together. When he had about sixty feet he tied one end to the base of one of the trees and began climbing the tree next to it, the other end of the vine rope in his mouth.

He'd already done this once, back when he and Jack had taken out the Malison Ring's double ambush line, and he had the technique down to a science. Within a few minutes he had the tree bent over and tied in place. Cutting one final length of vine, he walked over to the treetop, which was now sticking out sideways a few feet above the ground. The other time he'd done this, he remembered, his approach had flushed a group of birds from those upper branches.

Sure enough, another small flock erupted from the tree as he neared it, the branches swaying madly as the birds flapped away from the potential threat.

Perfect.

Tying his last piece of vine to the treetop, letting it hang loosely down, Draycos retraced his steps back to where he'd first emerged from the forest to the riverbank. There, he retrieved the comm clip from his crest and switched it on. "Uncle Virge, this is Draycos," he called again. "Please respond."

Again, there was no reply. Leaving the comm clip on, he backed away from the river into the concealment of the forest and silently counted out thirty seconds. Then, tucking the comm clip beneath his left foreleg, he broke abruptly into a loping run eastward toward his rigged tree. To anyone monitoring the comm clip's movements—and he had no doubt Frost's men were doing just that—it should look like he had just fastened the device to an animal and sent it scurrying away.

He and Jack had already used this trick once, of course.

Still, it was likely Frost would simply assume his opponents were running out of fresh ideas.

Draycos came within sight of the bent tree and slowed to a trot. The birds had returned to their meal in the upper branches in his absence, again taking off as he approached. Fastening the comm clip to the piece of vine he'd left hanging, he backed away to watch.

Sure enough, with the threat gone, the birds began to return to their meal. Each one that landed set the branches swaying, the movement translating down the vine to send the comm clip moving in small, unhurried circles.

Draycos smiled again. Frost might be suspicious, but he would have no choice but to conclude that the comm clip hadn't simply been dropped in the leaves in hopes of making him look in the wrong direction. Between the breeze and the birds, there should be enough movement to prove the comm clip was attached to *something,* and he would certainly conclude that that something wasn't Jack or Draycos.

And he would also know the area where such a diversion had been arranged would be the last place the fugitives would actually head for in the morning.

Which meant that when he set up his watchers above the riverfront in the morning, this would be the one spot on the entire river they would be most likely to ignore.

It was late when Draycos got back to the camp. Almost too late, and he could feel the uncomfortable tingling in his scales as he exchanged nods with Alison and slid up onto Jack's arm.

He had thought he'd been quiet enough not to disturb the boy's sleep. But even as he positioned himself on Jack's back the other stirred. "Draycos?" he murmured.

"Yes," Draycos confirmed, feeling strength flowing back into him. "All is well. Alison is on watch, and there are no enemies nearby. Go back to sleep."

"Okay," Jack said, clearly sliding back toward unconsciousness again. "You find Uncle Virge?"

Draycos grimaced. "We will find him in the morning," he promised. "Sleep now, and I will do likewise."

" 'Kay," Jack mumbled. "Pleasant dreams."

Under the circumstance, Draycos doubted that any of his dreams would be pleasant. But he would nevertheless make sure to get as much sleep as he could.

One way or another, this would end tomorrow.

CHAPTER 25

The next morning, as the Phookas performed their morning dance, Draycos told Jack, Alison, and Taneem the whole story.

They were, to put it mildly, unimpressed. "That's it?" Alison asked when he'd finished. "You've got us an exit point barely a hundred yards from where they're expecting us to come out anyway?"

"I did not have time to go farther," Draycos told her stiffly. "And it is not merely those hundred yards. If they believe we sent a decoy east, they will almost certainly conclude that we have gone west. They will therefore concentrate their forces on that part of the riverbank."

"He's right," Jack said, coming to his partner's defense. But it was clear the boy wasn't any happier than Alison was. "At least it gains us a little time."

"Only if the *Essenay* is hanging around somewhere nearby and happens to be listening when we need it to," Alison countered. "Otherwise we're no better off than we are right now."

"Fine," Jack said. "What do *you* suggest we do, then?"

"Only one thing *to* do," Alison said. "We pull back, dig ourselves in as best we can, and wait for my friends."

"Who could still be ten days away?" Jack shook his head. "Not a chance. Frost will nail us long before then."

"Unless there are more opponents to deal with than he expects," Taneem offered.

"What do you mean?" Draycos asked.

"You are a warrior of the K'da," she said. "Could you not train us to fight alongside you?"

Draycos looked at Jack, saw his same surprise reflected in the boy's face. That wasn't the kind of idea he would have expected Taneem to come up with, certainly not this quickly. "In theory, yes," he agreed, looking back at Taneem. "But it is not as simple as it sounds."

"On the other hand, I only had ten days of training in the Whinyard's Edge," Jack reminded him.

"And we see the kind of results *that* produced," Alison commented under her breath.

"My *point*," Jack continued, sending her a dark look, "is that any training he could give her would be worth something."

Alison shook her head. "It's a point, but it's a pointless point," she said. "Even if he could bring her completely up to speed, two K'da warriors aren't going to be enough to tip the balance here."

"Why must it be just two?" Taneem asked. "You woke me. Can you not wake the others?"

Alison sighed. "The problem, Taneem—"

"Wait a second," Jack cut her off, a cautious excitement in his voice. "That's not such a bad idea. Remember, they only need an hour on a host for every six hours off. That means that if we can shake them out of their sluggishness, you and I could handle ten to twelve K'da between us. Draycos?"

Draycos gazed out at the dancing Phookas, a whisper of cautious hope moving through him. If it were at all possible . . .

But it wasn't. It had taken Alison a full day to awaken Taneem, and both of them had been effectively helpless the whole time. It would take far too long to build up the kind of fighting force Taneem and Jack were talking about. "In principle, you are correct," Draycos said reluctantly. "But in actual practice, we simply do not have enough time."

"Unless we can find a way to get Frost off our backs for a while," Alison said.

Draycos looked sideways at her. The girl was watching him, a darkly suspicious look on her face. Had she guessed what he was planning? "Indeed," he said, forcing himself to meet her gaze. "We shall have to think about ways of doing that."

"Looks like they're done," Jack commented, nodding to the Phookas as he got to his feet. "Time to be off."

"Draycos will have to stay up front with me today—he's the only one who knows exactly where we're going," Alison reminded Jack. "Unless you'd like to take point this morning and let me handle the Phookas?"

"No, you go ahead," Jack said. "Their day's going to be strange enough without breaking the routine right out of the box."

"Okay," Alison said, standing up as well. "Taneem can stay with you and help with rear guard. You'd better take the machine gun, though."

"Fine by me," Jack said, scooping up his pack and the weapon. "Go get Greenie, and I'll tell Hren we're breaking camp. Come on, Taneem."

Jack headed off, the gray K'da trotting alongside him. "We will be going that way," Draycos told Alison, indicating the direction with a flick of his tongue. "I will await you."

"Just a second," Alison said as he turned to go. "I want to know what you and Jack are planning that you haven't seen fit to tell me about."

"Jack and I have no private plans," Draycos said, choosing his words carefully.

Alison snorted. "Fine; I'll rephrase. What are *you* planning that you haven't seen fit to tell me about?"

Draycos's first impulse was to again deflect the question. But if he was going to leave Jack in her care, she deserved to know the entire truth. "Unless we can make contact quickly with Uncle Virge, I intend to take the comm clip and head downriver," he told her quietly. "With luck, I will be able to draw the Malison Ring soldiers into pursuit before they realize that Jack is not with me."

"And then what?"

"And then, as you suggested, you and he must try to hide until your friends arrive."

"I meant what happens when your six hours are up."

Draycos turned to look at Jack, busily urging Hren to his feet. "I will die."

For a moment Alison was silent. "I gather Jack doesn't know anything about this," she said at last. "How were you planning to keep him from finding out?"

Draycos grimaced. "I expect the Malison Ring to be gathered in force by the time we reach the river," he said. "In the fury and confusion of combat, I should be able to slip away unnoticed."

"Leaving us to fight them alone?"

"I will make sure you have made it to safety before I leave," Draycos said. "At that point, it will be up to you to lead."

"Terrific," Alison growled. "My first military command. That'll look really impressive on my grave stone."

"Do not speak that way," Draycos said sternly. "You have had military training. I can see that. You can do it."

She exhaled noisily. "Let's just hope it doesn't come to that." She tapped her collar. "I presume you still want me to code my comm clip to the *Essenay*'s frequency?"

"With Jack's comm clip dangling from a tree, yours is now our only way to contact Uncle Virge," Draycos reminded her.

"I'll take that as a yes," Alison said dryly. "Easy enough to do while we're traveling—"

"Quiet." Draycos cut her off as the sound of distant lifters caught his ears. "They are in the air."

"Where?"

"To the west," Draycos said. "Moving . . . southeast, I believe."

"South*east*?" Alison echoed, frowning. "Like they're circling around behind us dropping troops?"

"That is the correct pattern," Draycos confirmed. "But they are not dropping soldiers. The transport is moving too quickly and too steadily for that."

"Which means Frost has something new planned," Alison

said, grabbing her pack and slipping it over her shoulders. "Great. Jack! Hustle it!"

Jack looked quizzically up at her; and as he did so, Draycos's straining ears caught a new sound. "Quiet," he warned Alison. "The floater is coming this way."

"Good morning, Jack," a booming voice came faintly from the direction of the floater. Frost's voice, amplified by a set of loudspeakers. "I hope you had a good night's sleep. My men tell me you're in this area somewhere, so I'm assuming you can hear me."

"Come on," Alison said, beckoning to Draycos.

"You've caused me a lot of trouble, Jack," Frost continued as they scrambled down the hill and came alongside Jack and Taneem. "Way more trouble than you should have. Almost more trouble than you're worth. But that trouble ends right now."

"Any idea what he's up to?" Jack murmured, peering up at the trees in the direction the voice was coming from.

"He's got the Kapstan circling around behind us," Alison said. "But Draycos says it's going too fast to be dropping troops."

"So here's the deal," Frost said. "You've got ten minutes to follow the sound of my voice and get to a big clearing right below the floater. If you surrender there, I promise your girlfriend and the Erassvas can go in peace."

Draycos frowned, flicking out his tongue. There was a new scent suddenly drifting toward them, an odor he couldn't quite place.

"Option two is that you keep going until you reach the

river," Frost went on. "Means more walking for you, but, hey, you're probably used to that by now. If you want to do that, fine. We don't mind waiting a little longer to pick you up."

"What is that smell?" Taneem asked, her tongue flicking out rapidly as she tasted the air.

"What smell?" Jack asked, sniffing.

"I don't know what it is," Draycos said. "But it seems familiar."

"And then there's option number three," Frost said, a sudden dark edge to his voice. "That's the one where you stay right where you are . . . and you and all your buddies get to burn to death."

Alison inhaled sharply. "No," she breathed. "He *wouldn't.*"

And suddenly the strange odor clicked. "He would, and he is," Draycos said tightly. "The transport is spraying a semicircle of aviation fuel across the trees behind us.

"He is going to set this part of the forest on fire."

CHAPTER 26

On their previous days the group had walked carefully and deliberately through the forest. Jack and Alison and Draycos had tried to watch all directions at once, watching for ambushes and traps.

Today, all that was forgotten.

They ran. All of them, even the Erassvas. They ran as fast as they could, dodging trees and bushes, stumbling over roots and small hollows hidden beneath the matting of dead leaves.

And as they ran, one by one the brightly colored Phookas faded to black.

The rest of the forest animals were on the move, too. Small animals scampered around them, and at least two herds of hornheads went lumbering past in the distance. Large and small predators alike were also on the move, ignoring potential prey as they fled from the fire chewing its unstoppable way toward them through the trees.

And it was gaining. At first Jack had dared to hope that Frost was bluffing. But after the first five minutes of their mad dash he was able to hear the distant crackling of the flames whenever the group paused for a minute's rest. Slowly but steadily the sound increased until he was able to hear it even over the rapid swishing of their feet and his own hoarse panting.

He could smell the smoke, too, as the wind generated by the fire blew it ahead of the flames themselves. He had no idea how fast a forest fire moved, but already he could tell that they would have little margin for error. Clenching his teeth, blinking his eyes against the tendrils of acrid smoke burning at them, he focused on his footing—

And nearly ran into Hren as the Erassva suddenly stopped in front of him. "What?" he gasped as he managed to brake to a halt. "What is it?"

"There," Hren said, panting even harder than Jack as he pointed ahead. "The river."

Jack stepped around him. It was there, all right, glimpses of blue water between the trees. At the front of the group he could see Alison and Draycos talking together in low voices. "Stay here," he told Hren. "Try to keep everyone together."

Jack maneuvered his way through the crowd, automatically patting and stroking the heads of the more frightened Phookas as he passed them. Off to the side, behind some bushes, he caught a glimpse of Draycos's diversion tree, still bent over with the comm clip dangling from it. "I hope you two have a plan," he said as he reached Draycos and Alison.

"We must first see how the enemy is positioned," Draycos said, keeping his voice low. His green eyes glittered unnaturally brightly against his black scales.

"Then let's do it," Jack said. "Alison, stay here and watch the others."

"Watch them what?" she retorted. "Panic? Hren and Taneem can watch them do that. Give me the machine gun—we're wasting time."

Jack glared at her. But she was right, and the distant crackling of the flames was getting louder. Unstrapping the gun from his shoulder, he handed it over. "Now be quiet," she warned. She started forward, Draycos moving into place beside her. Jack followed, hoping it wouldn't be as bad as he feared.

It was. In fact, it was worse. A hundred yards north, the Kapstan transport was hovering fifty feet above the river. Its stubby wings were discolored from the smoke of the fire it had started, its nose and weapons pointed vigilantly at the forest where Frost expected them to emerge. Behind and above it, moving up and down the river like a roving patrol, was the floater.

And that was it. There were no ground troops on the riverbank that Draycos could ambush, no air or ground vehicles nearby they might be able to grab, nothing at all within their reach. Frost and his men would simply sit high up out of harm's way until their quarry came to them.

Or else died in fiery agony.

Jack looked at Draycos, a hard lump in his throat. "I guess that's it, then," he said as calmly as he could.

"Cork it, Morgan," Alison said tartly. "We're not finished yet. Draycos, how high can you jump?"

"Not as high as the transport," Draycos said, his tail making thoughtful circles. "But if we can lure it here, I won't have to. I can use the bent tree as a launching platform."

"Oh, I can get it here," Alison promised, hefting the machine gun. "The question is, once you're up there will you be able to disable it?"

"Probably not the transport itself," Draycos conceded. "The lifters are on the underside, and the power and control mechanisms will not be easily reached." He arched his crest. "But I do not expect the pilot will be nearly so well protected."

"Wait a second," Jack cut in as he suddenly saw where they were going with this. "You kill the pilot and the ship's going to drop like a rock."

"As long as the transport remains at its current height, I will be all right," Draycos assured him. "Especially if it stays over the river."

"I thought hitting water was like hitting concrete."

"It can be, yes," Draycos agreed. "But I know how to enter the water so as to minimize the risk."

"What if they go higher before you crash them?" Jack persisted. "You could be killed."

"That is a possibility a warrior must always face," Draycos said quietly. "I am willing to take the risk. At any rate, we have no choice."

"Sure we do," Jack said. "I can surrender."

"And then what?" Alison demanded. "You really think Frost will let any of the rest of us live? Okay, Draycos, we've got a plan. Go get ready."

"It will not take long for me to get to the tree," Draycos said. "It will be a better lure if we give them a chance to see me."

"Fine," Alison said. "Just don't hang around long enough for them to also get the range and start firing. Jack, you'd better get back under cover."

Jack took a deep breath. "No thanks. I'll stay."

"Don't be an idiot," Alison growled. "Aside from everything else, you're standing right where *I'm* going to be running in a second. Now, *get back.*"

"Please, Jack," Draycos seconded.

Clenching his teeth, Jack turned to go.

And jerked as he found himself staring into a pair of silver eyes glowing from a black K'da face.

"Taneem," he breathed as his brain caught up with him. He hadn't realized she'd followed him up here. "Come on, move back. We need room."

For a second Taneem didn't move. Then, her eyes flicking to Draycos, she turned and padded back into the trees. With one final look at Alison, Jack did likewise. "Okay," he called.

Alison nodded. "Here goes nothing." Lifting the gun, she squinted along the barrel and squeezed the trigger.

For a couple of seconds the stutter of the machine gun drowned out even the crackling of the flames behind them. Alison paused, fired a second burst, then paused again. "Well?" Jack called.

"They see us," Alison called back. "Maybe trying to decide—here they come," she interrupted herself, lowering her gun and backing hurriedly away from the bank. "Make a hole, Jack."

Jack took another step backward, glancing over at the bent tree as Draycos slipped past him—

And caught his breath. Taneem was crouched on the treetop, gazing up at the incoming transport, the claws of her right forepaw poised over the vine rope.

Draycos spotted her the same time Jack did. "Taneem!" he barked. *"No!"*

Taneem twitched her tail. "You are needed," she said simply. "I am not."

And as Draycos leaped toward her, her claws sliced through the vine and she was catapulted upward toward the river.

"What's going on?" Alison demanded, crowding against Jack.

"Out of the way," Jack snapped, shoving past her and sprinting back to the river. Grabbing a branch for support, he leaned out over the water and looked up.

Taneem was there, all right, balanced on the Kapstan's portside wing. Her hind claws were dug into the metal for support, her forepaws slashing away at the side hatchway. Another minute, and she would be through.

"Have they attacked her?" Draycos asked anxiously from his side.

"They don't have to," Jack said, a sinking feeling in the pit of his stomach.

Because Frost had clearly anticipated this move. Even as Jack and Draycos watched helplessly, the transport began to rise straight up into the air.

Locked up safe and sound in his transport, Frost was simply going to go high enough to ensure that his attacker couldn't survive, then turn over and dump her off.

"They will pay for this," Draycos said, his voice crackling with anger and bitterness. "All of them. They will pay with their lives."

"That won't help Taneem," Jack snarled back. The Kapstan was a hundred feet up now and still rising. "*Think,* blast it. There must be something we can do."

"How about a net?" Alison suggested from Draycos's other side. "Cut one of these vine meshes and use it to catch her."

"No time," Jack said. "Besides, as long as he stays over the river there's no place for us to anchor it."

"Probably why he's still there," Alison growled. "Any chance she'll know how to hit the water safely?"

"At the height they are at there is no safe way," Draycos said grimly. "As Jack said, it will be like striking concrete."

"Yes," Jack said slowly as an idea suddenly came to him. "*If* she hits the water."

Alison frowned at him. "What—?"

"Rope," he snapped, shoving her halfway around and grabbing at her pack. Getting it open, he scooped out her coil of rope. "Come on, Draycos."

Jack sprinted upstream, his feet making huge splashes at the edge of the water as he ran. "What are you going to do?" Draycos demanded from behind him.

"You'll see," Jack said, dropping his own pack off his shoulders as he ran, craning his neck to look up. Frost was still over the same spot, and still rising. They had to be getting close to two hundred feet by now. Jack looked down at the water, trying to estimate the current—

"Here," he decided, splashing to a sudden halt and flicking his wrist to send the rope uncoiling into the trees. "Grab the other end and hold on," he told Draycos as he tied the other end around his waist. Taking a deep breath, wondering if this was as insane as it seemed, he threw himself into the river.

The water was icy cold, but he hardly noticed. Kicking

out, he sliced his arms hard into the surface, swimming for all he was worth.

"There!" he heard Draycos shout from behind him.

He paused and looked up. The K'da was right: Jack was now directly beneath the Kapstan. He turned around, treading water, putting his back to the low waves threatening to splash into his face.

And then, abruptly, the transport did a sudden midair roll around its long axis, dropping its portside wing to vertical. For a few seconds Taneem's claws held her to the wing. Then her grip gave way, and she tumbled off and dropped toward the water.

Jack swore under his breath, splashing himself into final position as he watched her fall. She had flattened out, he saw, turning her belly downward and stretching her legs out sideways in an instinctive skydiver's minimum-speed posture.

But it wouldn't slow her enough. Not from a fall of that distance. If this didn't work, she would be dead.

In fact, there was a fair chance she and Jack would both be dead.

But there was no time to think about that now. Pumping his legs to hold himself steady, Jack grabbed his left sleeve with his right hand and yanked it all the way back to his shoulder, leaving the arm bare. The more skin surface she had to aim for, the better. Lowering his right arm back into the water, paddling hard, he raised himself as far up as he could and stuck his left arm straight up. "Taneem!" he shouted. "Taneem!" She was dropping toward him like an avenging angel—

And then, suddenly, she shifted out of her flat posture, turning her body head downward. Her forelegs stretched out, pointing straight for Jack's face. The paws slammed into his arm like a falling boulder—

And as he was shoved violently down into the water, he felt her slide around his arm and down onto his back, the momentum of her fall driving him straight toward the bottom of the river.

For a long, terrifying minute he plummeted downward, the churning water battering against his face and body, his lungs fighting to keep in what air he had, the sudden increase in pressure stabbing pain into his ears. Something slammed up hard against his feet, knocking them out from under him and sending his back and head to hit only slightly less hard against sticky muck. His impact sent a surge of mud swirling around him, cutting off the faint light of the surface as the blow to his head sent stars flashing across his vision and scrambled his sense of direction.

But even as he fought against a rising surge of confusion and panic, the rope tightened around his waist, and he felt himself being pulled up and sideways against the current. The swirling mud was left behind; the glow from above returned and grew stronger—

And suddenly his head broke through the surface of the water.

"Jack!" Alison shouted.

Gasping in a lungful of air, Jack shook the water from his eyes. Alison was knee-deep in the river, she and Draycos together hauling him in by his rope. "Are you all right?" she called.

"Yeah," he managed, a fresh burst of adrenaline surging through him as he looked up. With all of them now out in the open like sitting ducks, all Frost had to do was drop back down to treetop height and open fire.

But the transport wasn't moving in for the kill. In fact, as Jack's eyes darted around the sky, he couldn't find either it or the floater anywhere.

He looked back at Alison and Draycos in confusion—

"There," Draycos said, nodding his head downstream.

Jack looked, to find the transport was indeed in that direction.

But it wasn't flying, and it was definitely not interested in shooting at anything. It was lying half-submerged in the water, spinning slowly around as the current dragged it eastward. The floater was there, too, hanging on to the transport's single visible wing, clearly trying to keep it from sinking the rest of the way.

He frowned back at the others . . . and then, slowly, his waterlogged brain understood.

He turned his head in the other direction. There, also half-submerged, was something that looked like a frozen bulge of water sitting in the middle of the river. Even as he watched, the bulge faded away, replaced by the familiar bulk of the *Essenay*, its lasers pointed watchfully toward the crippled Kapstan.

"What do you know," he heard himself say as Alison grabbed his right arm and started pulling him up onto the bank. "I guess the chameleon hull-wrap *does* work underwater."

And then she took hold of his left arm, and a sudden flash of pain arced through him, and everything went dark.

CHAPTER 27

"I hope you realize, Jack lad," Uncle Virge said sternly, "that by all rights you should have had your whole arm torn off at the shoulder."

"Okay, so it was a gamble," Jack admitted, wincing as the *Essenay*'s medic chair finished bandaging his left arm. Even through the painkillers the elbow and shoulder still ached. "But I figured that if Taneem could get around onto my back fast enough most of her momentum would spread itself over my whole body and just shove me down into the water instead of breaking my arm."

"Thereby offering you an excellent chance of drowning," Uncle Virge countered. "Wonderful set of options you gave yourself."

"Yeah, but it worked," Jack reminded him. "Better than just worked, too. If Taneem hadn't been up there distracting Frost's men, you might not have gotten away with that sucker shot that took them down."

"It was *not* a sucker shot," Uncle Virge said stiffly. "I'd been locked onto your comm clip signal for two hours, just waiting for you to give the order to go into action. Why didn't you?"

"For starters, we weren't sure you were still even with us, let alone hanging just offshore," Jack said. "Anyway, what are we arguing for? You crippled the Kapstan, and Frost and his buddies are miles away by now trying not to drown. Life is good."

"Anyone home?" Alison's voice called from out in the corridor.

"Like there's somewhere else I could go?" Jack called back.

She stepped through the doorway, Draycos and Taneem at her side. "Not really," she agreed. "What's the damage?"

"Just a sprain," Jack told her, lifting his bandaged arm for her inspection. "No bones broken, no ligaments or tendons torn. A week or so and I should be fine."

"I owe you my life," Taneem said, ducking her head shyly. "I do not know how to thank you for that."

"No thanks needed," Jack assured her. "K'da warriors' ethic says you do what's right no matter what the risks." He lifted his eyebrows at Draycos. "Right?"

"Correct," Draycos said.

Uncle Virge snorted again. "Courage and ethics are fine in their place, Jack lad," he said. "But there's a not-so-fine line between them and reckless stupidity."

"Actually, I have to agree with Uncle Virge on this one," Alison seconded. "That was a pretty boneheaded thing to try."

"There was nothing boneheaded about it," Jack insisted. "It was simple basic physics. The big danger with water landings is hitting the surface, right? I just arranged things so that I was already through the surface, and she never actually hit it."

"It was still a terrible risk," Taneem said. "I will dedicate my life to repaying my debt."

"Fine," Jack said. In his opinion, she was blowing this way out of proportion. But there would be time enough later for Draycos to talk some perspective into her. "I take it that means you've decided to stay with Alison?"

"You weren't really expecting her to go back to the Erass-vas, were you?" Alison asked.

"I just wanted to make it official," Jack said, trying very hard not to be irritated. Now that they were safe, Alison's knack for rubbing people the wrong way was coming out full bore again. "Besides, it's not just up to her. K'da don't impose on someone without the host's permission."

Alison looked down at Taneem. "Actually, this is pretty cool," she said, stroking the gray K'da's crest gently with her fingertips. "I'll let her stick around. At least until the rest of her people get here."

"Her *people* are out there," Uncle Virge muttered.

"Her *former* people," Jack told him firmly. "Speaking of which, did they all get across the river okay?"

"They swam it like fish," Alison assured him. "Large, lumpy fish, of course, but fish nonetheless."

"Hren said they would attempt to cross the forest and then circle back around the edge to rejoin the rest of their group," Draycos added.

Jack suppressed a grimace. Walking through the middle of a dangerous forest, only this time with no true K'da there to look after them.

"They'll be all right," Draycos assured him. "The Erassvas still have the altered odor that seems to ward off predators. And the Phookas, too, seem somewhat more alert than they were when we first met them."

"Spending a few days running for your life will do that, I suppose," Jack agreed reluctantly. "I just hope it lasts long enough to get them all the way to the other side of the forest." He raised his eyebrows at Alison. "What about you? You want to go back and wait for your friends to show?"

"With Frost still here?" Alison snorted. "No thanks. I'll give them a call and tell them I've made other arrangements. That is, if you don't mind me tagging along a little longer."

"Just like the baby sister I never had," Jack said dryly.

Alison's eyes narrowed a little. "Watch it, pal," she warned. "I'm at *least* five months older than you are."

"Can we hold off a comparison of birth records until we're clear of this place?" Uncle Virge asked impatiently. "I'd really rather not be around when Frost gets the Kapstan's lifters working again."

"Yes, we can go," Jack soothed him. "Actually, no—we have to find and get rid of that ECHO-transmitter gadget of his first."

"Done and done," Alison said.

"It was fastened to the hull in front of the aft ECHO pole," Uncle Virge added. "I had some time on my hands while drifting down the river, and was able to locate it."

"So it's off?" Jack said, his last unanswered question about Alison finally fading away. Something on the *Essenay*'s outer hull could have been planted there by anyone at any of the spaceports they'd passed through on their way here.

"I already had it neutralized, but Alison insisted on removing it as well," Uncle Virge said. "She seemed to think that it would bring a good price in the proper market."

"Oh, *did* she, now?"

"Would you rather hitchhike home?" Alison countered. "Gadgets like that can be a good way to keep the fuel tanks filled."

"Whatever," Jack said with a sigh. "Sure, let's get out of here. Oh, and make a pass over the Kapstan on your way out—I want to make sure Frost knows we've left."

"But don't make it *too* low a pass," Alison warned.

"I didn't mean we would," Jack said, fighting for patience. "So where exactly would you like us to drop you?"

The cockpit was dark as Alison came in, lit only by the various indicator lights on the control boards. "Good evening, Uncle Virge," she said. "How are things running?"

"Smoothly," the computerized personality said tartly. "What are you doing here?"

"I came to look over the nav maps," Alison said, sitting down in the pilot's seat. "Jack asked me where I wanted to be dropped off, remember?"

"We could have discussed that from the dayroom or your cabin," Uncle Virge said stiffly. "You shouldn't be in here without Jack or Draycos."

"Come on, give me a break," Alison growled back. "Jack's sleeping off his pain medication, Draycos is giving Taneem advanced English lessons in the dayroom, and I'm going stir-crazy in that cracker box you call a cabin. All I want is to look at some charts and figure out where I want to go. Okay?"

Uncle Virge sighed theatrically. "Fine. But I'm recording everything." One of the displays lit up with a map of the southern Orion Arm. "Jack's heading to Nikrapapo to try to get into the Malison Ring base there," he said. "Somewhere not too far off our vector would be handy."

"I understand," Alison said, bracing herself. If her guess about this ship was correct . . . "You've only got a couple of months left to locate the fleet's rendezvous point, don't you?"

"It's a few days more than that at the moment," Uncle Virge said. "But of course by the time we reach Nikrapapo—"

"Privacy lock code activate," Alison said.

The computer went silent. "Uncle Virge?" Alison called tentatively. "Uncle Virge? Computer?"

There was no response. "I'll be fraggled," Alison murmured to herself. But there was no time now to sift through all the possibilities this suddenly opened up. Swiveling her chair around, she activated the *Essenay*'s private and very expensive InterWorld transmitter.

It took only a minute to make the connection. "Smith," a voice replied.

"Kayna."

"About time you checked in, girl. Let's have it."

She gave her report in clipped military fashion, the way she'd been taught. "Interesting," Smith said when she'd finished. "I trust Morgan has no idea who you are?"

"Not a clue," Alison assured him. "Do you know if Frost got off Rho Scorvi all right?"

"Let me see . . . yes, he checked in with Neverlin from Im-mabwi. Probably not a very happy camper."

"As long as he made it out alive," Alison said. "We don't want to lose him. Not now."

"Agreed," Smith said. "Anything else?"

"Yes," Alison said, grimacing. A part of her didn't really want to do this. "The Phookas."

There was the faint sound of a sigh. "All of them, I suppose?"

"All of them," Alison said firmly. "They're wild cards. We can't let them stay on the playing field."

"You're mixing metaphors, of course," Smith pointed out. "But I take your point. All right, we'll deal with them. What about the Erassvas?"

Alison shook her head. "Doesn't matter. Whatever you want."

"We'll handle it," the other promised. "I gather you want to stay with Morgan for the moment?"

"For as long as I can," Alison confirmed. "He's the only inside source there is on this half of the game."

"Okay, but only until he makes you," Smith warned. "Be ready to bail the minute that happens."

"I will," Alison said. "I'll report again when I can."

"Right. Good luck."

Breaking the connection, Alison shut down the transmitter.

She gave it another minute, just to make sure there weren't any lingering effects in the system that the computer might spot and wonder about. Then, leaning back in the chair, she took a deep breath. "Privacy lock code release," she called.

"—it'll be almost exactly two months," Uncle Virge said. "So the less time we have to waste chauffeuring you around, the better."

"I understand," Alison said, getting up out of the chair. "Though come to think of it, let's make it easier on everyone. I'll just stay here with you and Jack for the moment."

"You sure?" Uncle Virge asked, sounding surprised.

"Yes." Alison smiled. "Very sure."

Timothy Zahn is the author of more than twenty-five original science fiction novels, including the very popular Cobra and Blackcollar series. His recent novels include *Night Train to Rigel, The Green and the Gray, Manta's Gift,* and *Angelmass.* His first novel of the Dragonback series, *Dragon and Thief,* was named a Best Book for Young Adults. Jack Morgan's adventures continued in *Dragon and Soldier* and *Dragon and Slave.* Zahn has had many short works published in the major SF magazines, including "Cascade Point," which won the Hugo Award for best novella in 1984. He is also author of the bestselling *Star Wars* novels, *Heir to the Empire* and the Hand of Thrawn duology, among other works. He currently resides in Oregon.